A Scone to Die for

OXFORD TEAROOM MYSTERIES
BOOK ONE

H.Y. HANNA

DEDICATION

For my high school English teacher,
Frank Devlin, who told me: "The road less travelled
is the one for you"—and gave me the courage to
follow my writing dreams.

CONTENTS

CHAPTER ONE

They say you have to make sacrifices to follow your dreams. I just didn't expect the sacrifice to involve an American tourist and a killer scone.

The week started normally enough, with the usual influx of tourists and visitors to our tiny Cotswolds' village of Meadowford-on-Smythe. Filled with winding cobbled lanes and pretty thatched cottages, Meadowford was like a picture-perfect postcard of rural England. But quaint and gorgeous as the village was, it would probably never have got much notice if it hadn't sat on the outskirts of the most famous university city in the world.

Over nine million tourists came to visit Oxford each year, and after they'd posed for photos in the college quadrangles and wandered reverently through the cloisters of the oldest university in the English-speaking world, they drifted out into the surrounding Cotswolds countryside. Here, they would coo over the quaint antique shops and village markets, and look forward to rounding everything off with some authentic English "afternoon tea".

That's where I came in. Or rather, my new business: the Little Stables Tearoom. Offering the best in traditional English refreshments, from warm buttery scones with jam and clotted cream, to home-made sticky toffee pudding and hot cross buns, all served with fragrant Earl Grey or English Breakfast tea—*proper* leaf tea—in delicate bone china... my little tearoom was a must-stop on any visitor's itinerary.

Well, okay, right now, my little tearoom was more of a "must go next time"—but we all have to start somewhere, right?

And so far, things were looking pretty promising. I'd opened three weeks ago, just at the beginning of October and the start of the Michaelmas Term (a fancy name for the first term in the school year; hey, this is Oxford) and I'd been lucky to catch the end-of-the-summer tourist trade, as well as the flood of new students arriving with their families. My tearoom had even got a write-up in the local student magazine as one of the "Top Places to Take Your Parents" and looked set on its way to becoming a success.

And I desperately needed it to succeed. I'd given

up a top executive job in Sydney—much to the horror of family and friends—on a crazy whim to come back home and follow this dream. I'd sunk every last penny of my savings into this place and I needed it to work. Besides, if my venture didn't become profitable soon, I'd never be able to afford a place of my own, and seriously, after being home for six weeks, I realised that moving back to live with your parents when you're twenty-nine is a fate worse than death.

But standing at the counter surveying my tearoom that Saturday morning, I was feeling happy and hopeful. It was still an hour till lunchtime but already the place was almost full. There was a warm cosy atmosphere, permeated by the cheerful hum of conversation, the dainty clink of china, and that gorgeous smell of fresh baking. People were poring over their menus, happily stuffing their faces, or pointing and looking around the room in admiration.

The tearoom was housed in a 15th-century Tudor building, with the distinctive dark half-timber framing and walls painted white. With its thatched roof and cross gables, it looked just like the quintessential English cottages featured on chocolate box tins. Inside, the period charm continued with flagstone floors and thick, exposed wood beams, matched by mullioned windows facing the street and an inglenook fireplace.

It hadn't looked like this when I took it over. The last owner had let things go badly, due to a combination of money troubles and personal lethargy (otherwise known as laziness), and it had taken a lot of effort and dedication—not to mention all my savings—to restore this place to its former glory. But looking around now, I felt as great a sense of achievement as I had done the day I graduated with a First from that world-famous university nearby.

I scanned the tables, noting that we were starting to get some "regulars" and feeling a rush of pleasure at the thought. Getting someone to try you once—especially when they were tired and hungry and just wanted somewhere to sit down—was one thing; getting them to add you to their weekly routine was a different honour altogether. Especially when that honour was handed out by the residents of Meadowford-on-Smythe who viewed all newcomers with deep suspicion.

Not that I was really a "newcomer"—I'd lived here as a little girl and, even after my family had moved to North Oxford in my teens, we'd always popped back to visit on school holidays and long weekends. But I'd been gone long enough to be considered an "outsider" now and I knew that I would have to work hard to earn back my place in the village.

Still, it looked like I was taking my first steps. Sitting at the heavy oak table by the window were four little old ladies with their heads together, like a group of finicky hens deciding which unfortunate worm to peck first. Fluffy white hair, woolly cardigans, and spectacles perched on the ends of their noses... they looked like the stereotype of sweet, old grannies. But don't be fooled. These four could have given MI5 a run for their money. They made it their business to know everybody's business (that was just the basic service—interfering in other people's business was extra). It was rumoured that even the Mayor of Oxford was in their power.

But the fact that they were sitting in my tearoom was a good sign, I told myself hopefully. It meant that there was a chance I was being accepted and approved of. Then my heart sank as I saw one of them frown and point to an item on the menu. The other three leaned closer and there were ominous nods all around.

Uh-oh. I grabbed an order pad and hurried over to their table.

"Good morning, ladies." I pinned a bright smile to my face. "What can I get you today?"

They turned their heads in unison and looked up at me, four pairs of bright beady eyes and pursed lips.

"You're looking a bit peaky, Gemma," said Mabel Cooke in her booming voice. "Are you sure you're getting enough fibre, dear? There's a wonderful new type of bran you can take in the mornings, you know, to help you get 'regular'. Dr Foster recommended it to me. Just a spoon on your cereal and you'll be in the loo, regular as clockwork. Works marvellously to clear you out." She leaned closer and added in a stage whisper, which was loud enough for the entire room to hear, "*So* much cheaper than that colon irritation thing they do, dear."

I saw the couple at the next table turn wide eyes on me and felt myself flushing. "Er... thank you, Mrs Cooke. Now, can I take—"

"I saw your mother in Oxford yesterday," Glenda Bailey spoke up from across the table. As usual, she was wearing bright pink lipstick, which clashed badly with the rouge on her cheeks, but somehow the overall effect was charming. Glenda was eighty going on eighteen, with a coquettish manner that went perfectly with her girlish looks. "Has she had her hair done recently?"

To be honest, I had no idea. I had only been back six weeks and I thought my mother looked pretty much the same. But I suppose her hair was in a different style to the last time I'd returned to England.

"Er... yes, I think so."

Glenda clucked her tongue and fluttered her eyelashes in distress. "Oh, it was shocking. So flat and shapeless. I suppose she went to one of those fancy new hairdressers in Oxford?"

"I... I think she did."

There were gasps from around the table.

"She should have come to Bridget here in the village," said Mabel disapprovingly. "Nobody can do a wash and blow dry like our Bridget. She even gave me a blue rinse for free the last time I was there." She patted her head with satisfaction, then turned back to me with a scowl. "Really, Gemma! Young hairdressers nowadays know nothing about lift and volume. I don't know why your mother is going to these fancy new hair salons."

Maybe because not everyone wants to walk around wearing a cotton wool helmet on their heads, I thought, but I bit back the retort.

"It's because they have no concept of 'staying power'," Florence Doyle spoke up. Her simple, placid face was unusually earnest. "They've never been through the war and have no idea of rationing. They don't know how to make things last as long as possible. People wash their hair so frequently these days." She gave a shudder.

"Well, a wash and set once a week was good enough for my mother and it's good enough for me," said Mabel with an emphatic nod. She eyed me suspiciously. "How often do you wash your hair, Gemma?"

"I... um... only when I need to," I stammered, thinking guiltily of my daily shower and shampoo. With a determined effort, I changed the subject. "What would you like to order for morning tea?"

"I'd like some of your delicious warm scones with jam and clotted cream—and a pot of English Breakfast, please," Ethel Webb spoke up.

The quietest of the group, Ethel was a kindly, absent-minded spinster who used to be the librarian at the local library until she retired several years ago.

I remembered her gentle face smiling at me as she stamped the return date on my books when I was a little girl.

She gave me that same gentle smile now. "And I think you've done a lovely job with the tearoom, Gemma. I'm really proud of you."

I looked at her in surprise, a sudden tightness coming to my throat. Since announcing my decision to ditch my high-flying corporate career for a village tearoom, the reactions I'd received had ranged from aghast disbelief to horrified disapproval. I hadn't realised until now how much a bit of support meant to me.

"Thank you..." I said, blinking rapidly. "Thank you, Miss Webb. I... I can't tell you how much I appreciate your words."

Her eyes twinkled at me. "Now that you're nearly thirty, Gemma, do you think you could call me Ethel, dear? I'm not behind the library desk anymore, you know."

I returned her smile. "I'll try, Miss... Ethel."

I managed to take the rest of the orders without further comment on my bowels, my mother's hair follicles or the young generation's lack of economy, and hurried back to the counter in relief. My best friend, Cassie, met me on the way. She had been looking after a large group of American tourists, which had just arrived by coach and was now settled in the tables along the far wall.

"Looks like you survived another encounter with

the Old Biddies," she said with a grin as we both rounded the counter.

I rolled my eyes. "If I have to hear one more thing about Mabel's 'regular' bowel habits, I think I'm going to take a running jump."

"You'll get no sympathy from me," said Cassie. "You've only had to put up with them for three weeks so far. I've been putting up with them for the past eight years while you've been gallivanting off Down Under."

Cassie and I had known each other from the time we both believed in Santa Claus. That moment when we'd first sat down next to each other in the classroom of our village school had been the start of an unexpected but wonderful friendship. Unexpected because you couldn't have found two people more un-alike than Cassie and me. She was one of five siblings in a large, rowdy family where everyone talked constantly—when they weren't singing, dancing, painting, or sculpting—and the house was in a constant state of cluttered chaos. Cassie's parents were "artists" in the true sense of the word and believed that the most important things in life were creative freedom and personal expression. It was no surprise that Cassie had done Fine Art at Oxford.

I, meanwhile, was the only child of an upper-middle-class household where nobody spoke at any volume above a well-modulated murmur and certainly never with excessive emotion. Our house had always been a perfectly ordered sanctuary of cream furniture and matching curtains. My parents were "British" in what they believed to be the true sense of the word: the most important things in life were a stiff upper lip and correct etiquette. You couldn't do "Ladylike Decorum" as a degree at Oxford so my mother had had to settle for me doing English Language and Literature.

Like most artists, Cassie worked a series of part-time jobs to help make ends meet. When she learned about my plans to return to Meadowford-on-Smythe and re-open the tearoom, it had taken very little to convince her to ditch her usual day job and come work with me. In fact, her past waitressing experience had been invaluable. Even now, I watched in admiration as she expertly balanced several plates laden with scones, cheesecake, and crumpets—as well as a pot of tea and two teacups—and started to make her way to the table of Japanese tourists by the door.

A strange snapping noise caught my attention and I turned towards the sound. It was coming from a large man who seemed to be part of the tour group that had just come in. He was sitting alone at a table at the edge of the group and had his left hand in the air, snapping it impatiently, like someone calling a disobedient dog. I frowned at his rudeness, but reminded myself that I was in the hospitality industry now. *Professional, friendly service no matter what.* I took a deep breath and went over to him.

"Can I help you, sir?"

"Yeah, I wanna glass of water."

He had a strong American accent and an aggressive manner, which put me instantly on edge, but I kept my smile in place.

"Certainly." I started to turn away but paused as he spoke again.

"Wait—is it tap? I only drink filtered water."

"I'm afraid we don't have a filter, sir. It's plain tap water. But it's very safe to drink tap water in the U.K. We do have bottled water on the menu, if you prefer."

He scowled. "What a rip-off. Water should be free."

I stifled a sigh. "You can certainly have water for free, but it'll be tap water. We have to pay for the bottled water so I have to charge you for that."

"All right, all right…" He waved a hand. "Get me a glass of tap water. And put some ice in it."

I turned to go but was stopped again by his voice.

"Hey, by the way, the service is terrible. I've been sitting here forever and no one's come to take my order!"

I stared at him, wondering if he was serious. Surely he realised that he had only just come in a few minutes ago? The rest of the group were still looking at their menus. One of the women in the group, sitting at the next table with her little boy, met my eyes and gave me a sympathetic smile. I took a deep breath and let it out through my nose.

"I'll just grab my order pad, sir."

"Yeah, well, be quick about it. I haven't got all

day."

Gritting my teeth, I headed back to the counter. My mood was not improved when I got there to find Cassie with an exasperated look on her face.

"The shop's empty again."

"Arrrrgghh!" I said under my breath. "Muesli, I'm going to kill you!"

No, I don't have an abnormal hatred of cereals. Muesli is a cat and, like all cats, she delights in doing the exact opposite of what you want. The Food Standards Agency inspector had been adamant: the only way I'd be allowed to have a cat on the premises was if it stayed out of the kitchen and dining areas. *Easy*, I'd thought. *I'll just keep Muesli in the extension where we had a little shop selling Oxford souvenirs and English tea paraphernalia.* The fact that I thought of the words "easy" and "cat" in the same sentence probably tells you that I don't know much about felines.

Okay, I'll be the first to admit—I've always been more of a dog person. I think cats are fascinating and beautiful and look great on greeting cards. But not on my lap leaving hairs everywhere and certainly not in my tearoom, getting under everyone's feet. So why, you wonder, is the tabby terror even here? Well, she came as a packaged deal with my chef. And Fletcher Wilson is a *magician* with a mixer and a spatula. Trust me, once you've tasted his sticky toffee pudding, you'd be ready to give him your first born child. So agreeing to let him have his cat with him at work seemed like a small price to pay in exchange for his culinary expertise.

The problem was, I hadn't counted on the cat being quite so sociable. Or such a great escape artist. Muesli had quickly decided that there was no way she was going to remain in the shop area when all the real fun was going on here in the dining room and she made it her life's mission to escape at any opportunity. I couldn't really blame her. In fact, I felt guilty every time I saw that little tabby face—with her pink nose pressed up to the glass—peering wistfully through the door that separated the shop from the dining room. But food hygiene laws were one thing I couldn't ignore if I didn't want to lose my licence.

"One of the Japanese tourists must have gone in the shop to check out some of the stuff and she slipped out when they opened the door," commented Cassie.

I sighed and scanned the room, looking for a little tabby shape between the tables. I couldn't see her. I crouched down to get a better view. All I could see was a forest of legs... I bit my lip. *Where was that cat?* I had to find her before any of the customers noticed her loose in here. The last thing I needed was for Mabel and her cronies to discover my Food Standards violation; the news would be halfway across Oxfordshire before the day ended.

"Hey! Can I get some service around here?" came an irate American voice.

I straightened up hurriedly. *Oh God, I'd forgotten*

about Mr Charming. I gave Cassie a harassed look. "Keep looking for her, will you?"

I grabbed the order pad—then, on an impulse, also picked up a plate of fresh blackberry cheesecake, which had just come through the hatch from the kitchen. *Well, they did say the way to a man's heart was through his stomach.* I added a knife and fork, and a dollop of cream, then walked over and set it down in front of him.

"Sorry for the wait, sir. Compliments of the house. This is one of our specialties."

"Huh." He looked surprised. He picked up the fork and cut the corner off the soft, creamy cake, putting it cautiously into his mouth. His eyes glazed over slightly and his face softened. "Say... this is not bad."

I suppressed the urge to roll my eyes. Coming from him, that was probably considered high praise. Still, trying to be charitable, I told myself that maybe he was just one of those people who got really grouchy when hungry. I observed him surreptitiously as I took his order. He was a large, thickset man, with a blocky, almost square-shaped head, fleshy cheeks and prominent ears. His mouth drooped slightly on one side as he talked—the result of a stroke?—and I put him in his early forties, though he looked older. He seemed slightly incongruous sitting there with the other tourists. He was certainly dressed like a tourist in chinos, a loud shirt, and sports jacket, and he had a sort of knapsack on the chair next to him, but somehow he didn't quite fit in.

"...and I gotta have the bread soft, d'you hear? I don't want any hard crusts on the sandwiches."

"All our tea sandwiches are made the traditional way with untoasted bread and the crusts cut off, so they're all very soft to eat," I assured him. I noticed the tourist map of Oxford spread out on the table in front of him and gave him a polite smile. "Visiting Oxford, sir?"

"What?" He glanced down at the map. "Oh... oh, yeah." He gave me a sheepish grin. "Yeah, first-time visitor here; never been to Oxford before. Gotta figure out how to get around. Say, you know how long it takes to walk from the Bodleian Library to Magdalen College?"

"No more than ten or fifteen minutes, I should think. You can take the shortcut through Catte Street onto High Street, and then just turn left and walk straight down to the bridge."

"Catte Street... that comes out opposite the bank, doesn't it?"

I frowned. "You mean, the Old Bank Hotel?"

He blinked and a look of confusion flashed across his face, to be replaced quickly by a bland smile. "Sure, yeah, that's what I mean." He folded up the map. "Well, thanks for that. You gotta restroom here?"

I directed him to the door beside the shop, then hurried back to the counter to put his order through. I could hear raised voices in the kitchen and winced. I wondered if Cassie was telling Fletcher about his missing cat. I hoped it wouldn't upset him too much. Fletcher was... "sensitive", for want of a better word. He was painfully shy and didn't relate to people like most of us did—in fact, he found it difficult to even make eye contact when he spoke to you. Animals seemed to be the only thing that helped him come out of his shell and I knew that having Muesli here played a big role in calming his nerves and helping him cope with things.

Remembering the request for water, I hurriedly poured a glass and added a few ice-cubes, then took it back to the American man's table. As I was putting it down, the little boy at the next table jumped up with a yell and jostled my elbow. Water sloshed out of the glass and onto the man's knapsack.

"Blast!" I muttered.

"Oh, I'm so sorry!" said the woman at the next table. "Hunter, apologise to the lady."

I gave the little boy a distracted smile. "That's okay. It was an accident."

I set the glass down and picked up the knapsack, trying to shake the water off. It was unzipped and a lot of water had spilled onto a folder inside. I hesitated a second, then pulled the folder out and grabbed a napkin from the holder on the table to mop up the moisture. My heart sank as I saw that water had seeped into the folder and wet the sheaf of papers inside. I could just imagine the American's reaction when he came out and saw what had happened.

Hastily, I pulled out the sheets and dabbed at them with more napkins. The water had soaked through the first page. I hoped it wasn't anything important. It had the look of an official letter, with the *University of Oxford* letterhead at the top, but what I was more worried about was the bottom where the signature—obviously done in fountain pen—had smeared across the page. I dabbed at it, thinking to myself frantically: most signatures were illegible anyway, weren't they? This one, for instance, you could hardly make out what the name was. It looked like a "G" and then "Hayes" or "Hughes", but in any case—

"WHAT THE HELL DO YOU THINK YOU'RE DOING?"

I gasped as a hand grabbed my wrist and yanked me back from the table. Conversation at the next table ceased and the whole room went silent as everyone turned to stare. The American towered over me, one hand clamped on my wrist, the other holding something that gleamed dully. My eyes widened as I realised that it was a knife.

CHAPTER TWO

"N-n-nothing…" I said, stammering in surprise. I tried to pull my hand out of his grip. "I spilled some water on your papers and I was just trying to mop up the mess."

By now, the American had become aware of the whole room staring at him. He released my wrist, laid the knife back down on the cheesecake dish, and made an attempt at a smile.

"Oh… oh yeah. Sorry… can't be too careful these days, you know, especially when you're travelling. All this identity theft stuff…"

I rubbed my wrist. "Well, I can assure you, sir, I wasn't attempting to steal your identity. I was just trying to mop up the water as quickly as possible."

He gave an awkward wave. "It's no big deal anyway. Just some tourist brochures and stuff." He shuffled the papers back into the folder and closed it firmly.

I took the half empty glass and promised to return with another one, then retreated. But my interest was piqued. Why was he lying? It was obvious the papers were not just some tourist brochures. Bloody hell, he'd acted like they were state secrets or something! Still, I reminded myself that it was none of my business. One thing I'd learnt since opening this tearoom was that you met all sorts of people in the hospitality industry and it was best to turn a blind eye to their eccentricities. All I cared about was that they ordered my food and paid their bills.

Besides, I had bigger problems than some cranky American. I looked at Cassie hopefully as I returned to the counter but she shook her head.

"Still can't find her—though I can't look under the tables properly unless I get on my knees and crawl around." She nodded over my shoulder. "What's with American Psycho?"

I shrugged. "Heaven knows. Got out of the wrong side of the Atlantic this morning. Anyway, forget him... I'm more worried about the cat."

"I had to tell Fletcher," said Cassie uneasily. "I went into the kitchen to see if Muesli might have slipped in there and he asked me what I was up to."

"How did he take it?"

"Not good." Cassie made a face. "He was all ready to come out and look for her himself, but I assured him that we had it covered. He's in the middle of plating up the orders for the tables by the window, and then he's got to do that big tour group and we can't have them delayed. Their coach will be leaving for Oxford in forty-five minutes."

I sighed and turned to scan the room again. Suddenly, I froze.

"Cassie!" I hissed. "What's that over there?"

Cassie's eyes widened. I knew she'd seen what I'd seen: a little grey tail flicking behind Mabel Cooke's chair, by the wall.

"Nooo..." Cassie groaned. "Of all the tables in the place, the little minx had to choose that one? What are you going to do?"

Luckily, at that moment, the order for the Old Biddies came through the hatch. I loaded it onto a tray and hurried across the room.

"Here you are..." I said as I rested the tray on the table. I leaned to the side slightly and tried to look behind Mabel's chair. The tail twitched back and forth, then flicked out of sight underneath the table.

"Are you all right, dear?" said Glenda. "You look a bit odd."

"Oh, no, I'm fine," I said hastily. I unloaded their order from the tray, then shifted my weight from foot to foot, wondering how I could find an excuse to reach under the table and grab the cat. The four old ladies looked at me expectantly.

"So... um... Is there anything else I can get you?"

They shook their heads.

"No, dear. You run along; we can see you have lots of customers to look after."

"Um... Yes... it's lovely and busy today, isn't it? It's great to be so busy—although I suppose it's only to be expected, since it's Saturday and that's always the busiest time of the week," I babbled. "Not that you want to be *too* busy, of course, but it's good to be a *bit* busy and find a balance..."

They stared at me, obviously wondering if I had lost my wits. In desperation, I grabbed the edge of the table and gave it a little jiggle.

"Oh, it looks like your table isn't very steady. I think one of the legs might need a bit of propping."

Mabel Cook gave the sturdy oak table a good shove. "It feels all right to me," she said doubtfully

"Really? Because it seems really shaky to me," I said. "In fact, I think I'll just slip a wad of paper under one of the legs. Excuse me while I do that..." I grabbed a napkin, then dropped to my knees and crawled under the table before they could react. The table was positioned with its short end against the wall, jutting out with two chairs on either side. Muesli sat at the other end, with her back to the wall, looking at me with bright green eyes.

"Muesli!" I hissed under my breath. "Come here!"

She blinked at me innocently.

"Come here, you blasted cat!"

She gave me a disdainful look, lifted a paw and languidly began to wash it.

Grrrr. I debated what to do. I could try to reach out and grab her by the collar, but that would mean sticking my hand through the row of legs in front of me, and even if I caught her, I would have to pull her through the legs. If the Old Biddies felt the cat's furry body brush against them, they would probably all erupt in screams.

"Gemma, dear, are you all right?"

"Oh! Uh... Yes, of course... Just a moment longer..."

"Would you like some help?"

"No, no," I said desperately. "I'm fine, thank you."

I turned my attention back to the cat. I decided to try a different tactic. Making a monumental effort, I forced my voice into a gentle whisper. "Muesli... here kitty, kitty, kitty..."

The cat paused in her washing and regarded me curiously. *"Meorrw?"*

"Gemma, dear, did you say '*meow*'?"

"Uh... no! No, I said '*no-ow*'. I said I'm almost done *now*."

"Well, you're obviously having trouble. Let me come and help you," came Mabel's booming voice. I saw her chair being pushed back.

"No! No!" I yelped, jerking up in alarm. I smacked my head on the underside of the table. "Ow!"

The loud bang startled the cat; she shot out from under the table and scampered across the room towards the tour group. I crawled out backwards and stood up, rubbing my sore head.

"Gemma, dear... Are you *sure* you're all right?"

I met four pairs of sceptical eyes. "Yes, fine... sorry, so clumsy of me. Right, I'll leave you to have your tea in peace now!"

I beat a hasty retreat across the room, heading for the tour group. I stopped short. I could see a little tabby face peeking from between two of the chairs. I swear, the cat stuck her tongue out at me.

Little minx. I scowled. Strolling over as nonchalantly as I could, I bent down slowly as I approached the cat. She looked up at me with her big green eyes, her tail wrapped around her front paws, but just as I reached out to grab her, she darted under the table.

"Blast!" I muttered under my breath.

"Is there a problem?"

I looked up to see a woman turning around on the chair that Muesli had been sitting next to. It was the mother with the little boy, Hunter—the one who had given me the sympathetic smile earlier.

"No, no problem," I said hastily. "Has anyone taken your order yet?"

"Yes, that other nice young woman came and did it a moment ago." She smiled at me, then her face clouded and she glanced sideways at the American man at the next table. She lowered her voice. "I hope you don't think all Americans are like *him.*"

I returned her smile. "As long as you don't think all English men are like Mr Bean."

She laughed but whatever she was about to say was cut off as her son suddenly sprang up in his chair and pointed an excited finger.

"Hey, Mom, look! There's a cat!"

I groaned.

Half the tour group stood up to look and the sudden scraping of so many chairs scared Muesli out from underneath the table. I made a lunge for her but she darted nimbly past.

"I'll catch it!" cried the boy, jumping after her.

Muesli easily evaded his grasping hands. She dived between his legs, around his chair, and across to the next table where the American man was sitting. He had glanced up at the commotion and was now rising from his chair.

"What the..." he growled.

I ran over to him. "I'm so sorry, sir! Just give me a moment and I'll catch her—"

"Say, why is that animal in here? What kind of place is this?"

"Sorry! Sorry!" I panted, diving around him to try and grab a furry tail. "There's been a bit of a... um... accident. The cat isn't normally in here."

Muesli scooted sideways around the table, then made an attempt to rush past the American. He screwed his face up in disgust and kicked at the cat as she ran past him.

"Mangy animal!"

There was a loud gasp. I jerked around to find Fletcher standing in the kitchen doorway. His eyes bulged as he stared at the American.

"Fletcher..." I put up a placating hand. "Fletcher, I'm sure Mr... um... didn't mean to hurt Muesli..."

I glanced at the American, half expecting him to

jump in with his own apologies and excuses but, to my surprise, what I saw was not a look of remorse but a smile of satisfaction. I felt a wave of dislike for him. It was obvious that he was enjoying the distress he was causing. The man was a bully and, like all bullies, he got pleasure from watching others squirm.

"That was uncalled for, sir," I said sharply. "I realise that the cat should not have been in here but that doesn't give you the right to kick her."

He swung back to me. "Oh yeah? Well, why don't you tell that to the Health Department," he sneered "I can report you and get this place shut down tomorrow."

"I—"

I bit off the words. He was right. At the end of the day, food and hygiene laws would trump the RSPCA. I swallowed and took a deep breath, forcing an apologetic look to my face. "I'm very sorry sir. I... I can offer you your meal free of charge, to make up for the inconvenience."

"Yeah, that's more like it." He grinned, then with a last glance at Fletcher—who was being hustled back into the kitchen by Cassie—he sat back down at the table.

I was relieved to see that the ruckus had scared Muesli enough that she had run back into the shop of her own accord. At least there was one silver lining to this fiasco. Slowly, peace returned to the tearoom and I hoped fervently that this was the end of dramas for the day.

CHAPTER THREE

The next half hour was a race to serve the tour group before their coach departed. I was looking forward to the American man leaving with them—his rude demands and obnoxious behaviour had continued, and it was all I could do to hold on to my temper. To my surprise, however, he got up before the rest of the group had finished and made his way over to the counter.

"Your meal is complimentary, sir," I reminded him. "But the rest of your group haven't finished yet."

"Huh?" He glanced towards the tour group, then turned back to me. "Nah, it's all right. I'm going to head off first. Hey, I hear that you're famous for your scones. Can I get some to take out?"

"Sure—how many?"

"Give me half a dozen."

Cassie joined us and began preparing the takeaway order of scones. I saw the American make a great show of eyeing her up and down. She was wearing a simple black T-shirt and faded jeans, with a frilly pale pink apron over the top. I had an identical apron but in pale blue. I had found them at a local market and decided they did pretty well as a sort of unofficial uniform. Hopefully when I had a bit more money, I could get some aprons custom-made with the tearoom's name and logo embroidered on the edge. But for now, these would have to do.

The American winked at Cassie and said, "I like your outfit... sorta like a kinky French maid, huh?"

"No," Cassie snapped. "Not unless you have a dirty min—"

"Ahhh... what she means is that isn't quite the look we had in mind," I interrupted hastily, giving my friend a quelling look.

He guffawed. "You English chicks are so uptight. What you need is a good..." He trailed off, waggling his eyebrows suggestively.

I recoiled in distaste. Cassie gave him an icy glare, then turned and bent over to retrieve a paper bag for his scones from the cupboard behind us. Suddenly, he reached over the counter and grabbed her bum, giving it a squeeze.

She yelped and whirled around. "What the hell are you doing?" she snapped.

"Aw, don't be such a prude. I was just admiring

your butt in those tight jeans and couldn't help myself." He smirked.

"You creep! I have half a mind to report you for sexual harassment!" Cassie seethed. She caught my horrified look and took a deep breath, then said with cold dignity, "But I wouldn't want to waste time on a rotter like you." She shoved the bag of scones at him, obviously just wanting him to be gone.

I gave the American an icy look. "I'd appreciate you keeping your hands to yourself, sir."

He laughed uproariously. "Maybe if you get to know me better, you'd change your mind." He leaned across the counter towards Cassie. "Listen, why don't you come over to my room tonight? I'm staying at the Cotswolds Manor Hotel on the outskirts of the village. I could have a great time with a feisty girl like you…"

Cassie's hand twitched and I grabbed it before she could slap his face.

"Thanks for the offer, but I think I'll pass," she said through gritted teeth.

He shrugged. "Your loss, hon. Anyway… I'll see you tomorrow. I think I'll come back for some breakfast." He winked at her. "But you know where to find me tonight if you change your mind." He included me in his parting smirk, then picked up the bag of scones and strolled out of the tearoom.

Cassie let out a growl of frustration. "I hope he bloody chokes on those scones!"

I realised that the entire dining room was silent

and looked up to see everyone staring at us. I felt my cheeks redden, but forced a smile to my face and said as breezily as I could, "Show's over, folks!"

A few people laughed awkwardly and the moment passed. I gave Cassie a sympathetic pat on the shoulder as she went off into the kitchen to fetch the next order. Then I turned to deal with the next customers at the counter. It was the Old Biddies, coming to settle their bill as they were hurrying off to catch a matinee show at the cinema in Oxford.

Glenda held out a half-finished plate of scones. "Can you put these in a bag for me, dear? I couldn't quite finish them, but I know my great-nephew would love to have some."

I wrapped up the scones, put their bills through, and watched them leave with some relief. The rest of the lunch hour passed in a blur as Cassie and I raced to take orders and serve the tables. I was pleased that the place was so busy—it was a great sign. Still, I was glad when the lunchtime rush was over and I could sit down and catch my breath. My stomach growled and I glanced at the clock on the wall. It was nearly three o'clock. I hadn't eaten since early that morning. I threw a quick look around the room. There were only two tables occupied at present: an elderly couple by the windows and a lone young man poring over a map of the Cotswolds in the corner. They had both been served and would not need attention for a while. In any case, there was a little hand-held bell on the counter for them to call for service.

Rising wearily, I made my way into the kitchen, hoping that I might be able to scrounge some sandwiches. I pushed open the swinging door to the kitchen and was instantly enveloped by the wonderful smell of baking—sweet cinnamon and rich chocolate and that delicious fragrance that comes from fresh bread and warm, buttery pastries. Cassie and Fletcher were sitting at the large wooden table in the centre, the former stuffing her face with toasted teacakes and the latter putting the finishing touches to a batch of traditional English shortbread.

I went over to join them and helped myself to a teacake from Cassie's plate. I slathered some butter on it before biting into the soft, chewy bun. Like a lot of British desserts, teacakes had a slightly misleading name. They weren't cakes at all but a type of lightly spiced sweet bun, often filled with juicy raisins, currants, and sultanas. You cut them in half and popped them under a grill (or over an open fire if you were of a romantic bent), so that they became soft and puffy, with crisp golden edges. Topped with oozing melted butter and accompanied by a hot cup of tea, they were one of the ultimate comfort foods. I sat back with a contented sigh as I enjoyed my teacake and sipped the hot mug of tea that Cassie had placed in front of me.

"Hey… Fletcher, sorry about what happened earlier," I said.

He nodded. "I saw Muesli. She's okay."

"Yeah, I just looked in on her again and she's

curled up in her little bed, sleeping. I don't think that guy actually touched her with his foot when he tried to kick her."

"Rotten swine," Cassie muttered.

"Let's hope that's the last we see of him," I said with a sigh.

"Didn't he say he was coming back tomorrow morning?" Cassie made a face.

"I'll serve him," I promised. "You don't have to go anywhere near him." I looked around the kitchen, noting the trays of freshly baked scones and butter crumpets. "Things are probably going to be quiet now for the rest of the afternoon and I can see that we've got lots of supplies." I turned to Fletcher. "Why don't you take Muesli and go home early today?"

He thought a moment, then nodded and stood up, shuffling to the back of the room to collect his things and the cat carrier. I'd been meaning to speak to him about the feasibility of continuing to bring Muesli to work every day—especially after the disaster this morning— so I followed him as he went to get her.

Muesli woke up as we entered the shop area and arched her back in a perfect cat stretch, then yawned widely, showing sharp white fangs in a little pink mouth. She looked none the worse for wear after her adventures that morning. She came trotting up to me with her tail in the air and rubbed herself against my legs. I wanted to be mad at her—if it hadn't been for her, none of the fiasco would have happened—but looking down at that cheeky little face, with her bright green eyes and tiny, heart-shaped nose, I felt myself soften. Almost involuntarily, I crouched down and reached out to stroke her. Her fur was silky soft, a pale dove grey patterned with a series of darker grey stripes across her body, broken only by the white on her chest and paws. She climbed onto my lap, kneading with her front paws and purring like an engine.

"She likes you," said Fletcher.

"Yeah, I like her too," I said automatically. Then I realised to my surprise that I was actually speaking the truth. I *did* like the mischievous little cat. Friends had warned me that felines could worm their way into your heart, but I hadn't believed them. How could you like anything as infuriating and contrary as a cat? And yet I had to admit that even in my short acquaintance with Muesli, her saucy impudence had won me over. It was ridiculous, but there was something very appealing about the way cats walked around, acting as if they owned the place.

I lifted Muesli off my lap and deposited her gently into the carrier. She didn't resist—used to the routine by now—and simply pressed her little face against the bars as we shut the door and latched it securely. Then Fletcher lifted the carrier and stood up.

"I will see you tomorrow," he said solemnly.

I started to say something about Muesli, then changed my mind. *Maybe I'll talk to him about it tomorrow.* I knew I was just being a chicken. The truth was, I was so grateful I'd found him—I didn't want to do anything to rock the boat. Fletcher was the baking godmother to my tearoom Cinderella and, without him, my little business would never have had a chance. Cassie had been the one who had suggested him when I was looking for a chef for the tearoom. She taught occasional classes at the dance studio in the village—another of her many jobs—and she'd met Fletcher when he came in to fix the broken ceiling fan. He was sort of an unofficial handyman in Meadowford—helping the local residents with odd jobs—but he was also known for being a brilliant baker. Cassie had insisted that I consider hiring him for the tearoom.

I'd been doubtful at first: after all, Fletcher wasn't a trained chef and I'd been thinking of getting someone with a proper qualification. But when I'd tasted one of his scones, I hired him on the spot. Cassie was right, his baking was divine. And funnily enough, giving Fletcher the job had won me brownie points with the villagers, who had been bracing themselves for some snooty chef from London.

The arrival of a group of Chinese tourists put a stop to my reminiscing and I hurried to seat them and hand out menus.

***

"Whew!" said Cassie, sinking down into one of the chairs at the tables. "I'm knackered."

I gave her a grateful look. "Thanks so much for helping out today, Cassie. It's been really full on, I know."

She waved my thanks away. "It's what you want! And tomorrow should hopefully be even busier because loads of local tourists come to the Cotswolds for the weekend, so we'll have them on top of the internationals..."

"As long as there aren't any more visitors like that American today," I said with a dark look.

"Yeah, he was an obnoxious plonker, wasn't he? Still, he made a good subject."

"You sketched him?"

She shrugged. "You know I like to do quick sketches of interesting faces if I have a moment free. I've actually had a couple of customers ask me if they can buy theirs—maybe I should start a sideline business in portraits." She grinned.

"I'm surprised you want to remember his face," I said.

"Yeah, he's got an ugly mug, all right, but quite interesting from an artistic point of view. I did one of him from memory this afternoon—look..." She got up and went to the counter, returning in a moment with a piece of paper.

I took it and looked down at the sketch. Cassie was really talented. She had managed to capture the American's likeness with a few swift strokes, from his block-like head to his jutting ears and fleshy cheeks. There was something hard and cruel about his eyes.

I shuddered and pushed the sketch away. "He gives me a bad vibe."

"You mean, aside from being a lecherous old git?"

I nodded. "There was something that just didn't add up... I mean, he was trying really hard to put on this image of a hale and hearty American tourist but he seemed fake somehow."

Cassie laughed. "Fake tourist? Why would anyone want to fake being a tourist?"

"That's just it—I don't know! It seems such a stupid thing to do, doesn't it? And yet, I'm sure he was lying. For example, he asked me directions to Magdalen College."

"So?"

"Well, he called it 'Maud-lin'! Not 'Mag-da-len', which is how most tourists—especially American tourists—say it. Only locals and students who've been to Oxford know that it should be pronounced 'Maud-lin'. It's one of the first things that flags you as a foreign tourist—when you can't say the college names correctly."

Cassie shrugged. "Maybe he read about the pronunciation in a guidebook somewhere. It's hardly a state secret."

"I suppose so..." I said. "But it wasn't just that. When we were talking about directions to Magdalen, he also mentioned Catte Street being opposite the bank."

Cassie looked at me blankly.

"He meant an actual bank," I explained. "Not the

Old Bank Hotel, which is what's there now. He tried to cover it up but I could tell that that was what he meant."

Cassie frowned. "So? Gemma, I really don't see what you're getting at..."

I leaned forwards. "My point is, he wouldn't have known that the Old Bank Hotel used to be a bank, unless he was actually here in Oxford when it *was* a bank—*before* they turned it into a hotel."

Cassie shook her head in exasperation. "Well, he could have read about that as well! I mean, there's a reason it's called the Old *Bank* Hotel, isn't there? It would be logical to assume that there used to be a bank there."

"But it's not the way you'd talk if you were a tourist and read the information on Wikipedia or Trip Advisor," I said stubbornly. "You would have just said Old Bank Hotel, not 'the bank'. That suggests someone who used to see it as a bank. It's that kind of casual assumption you use when you've walked past a place loads of times. And we know that the hotel used to be a branch of Barclays. My parents bank with Barclays and my father had his account there before it shut down. I remember going in with him as a little girl to see the tellers in that old Georgian building."

"I think you're splitting hairs," said Cassie impatiently. "Or letting your imagination run away with you."

"Well, I wasn't imagining his crazy psycho

behaviour when he jumped on me with that knife!" I said. "That was totally over the top. And he wasn't just being careful about identity theft, in spite of what he said. I think he got upset because he thought I was looking at his papers."

"So? A lot of people would get upset if you looked at their private papers."

"Yeah, but they wouldn't jump on you and threaten you with a knife!"

"Well, maybe he over-reacted. Or maybe it was a kind of reflex thing. You know, like he just grabbed anything within reach on the table."

"It was still an extreme reaction," I insisted. "And besides, I did get a glimpse of one of the papers in the folder."

"And?"

"And it looked like an official letter from someone at Oxford University."

Cassie gave another impatient sigh. "So?"

"So he said that he had never been to Oxford before, right? He specifically told me that he was a first-time tourist and acted like he knew nothing about the place... so why did he have an official letter from the University?"

"Are you sure the letter was for him?"

"No, I'm not," I admitted. "But if it wasn't his, why was he so sensitive about it?"

"I don't know!" Cassie threw her hands up in exasperation. "Honestly, Gemma, I think you're letting the whole thing blow up into a huge deal in your head." She got up and shoved her chair back under the table. "Come on, let's get out of here. You coming to the pub for a drink?"

"I don't know... I'm supposed to have dinner with my parents," I said

Cassie threw a glance at the clock on the wall. "It's only six. You've got time for a quick drink before heading back. Besides, after a day like today—you need a drink."

She was right. Quickly, I helped to tidy up the room, then switched off all the lights and shut up the tearoom.

CHAPTER FOUR

We left by the back door which led out into the side courtyard. The building in which my tearoom was housed used to be a Tudor inn, with accompanying stabling for the guests' horses. A long, narrow courtyard ran along the side of the building, paved with cobblestones and bounded by white-washed walls. It was probably where they used to saddle up and mount the horses, but now it made a valuable addition to the tearoom premises. Especially in the warm summer months, I could see lots of customers enjoying the open air and having their tea and food at the tables out here. I planned to dress the place up with some big wooden tubs of pansies, hanging flower baskets in the corners, and generally make it look so pretty and inviting that no tourist could resist if they walked past and looked in the courtyard entrance.

For now, though, with the chilly autumn weather, the courtyard was mostly empty and un-used. I kept the wrought iron gates open, though, so that anyone could use the tables and chairs if they just wanted somewhere to rest their weary feet or a quiet place to eat their packed lunch. I knew that the local dog owners appreciated having somewhere they could sit down together with their hounds, after a walk, and I made sure to always leave a bowl of fresh water by the back door of the tearoom.

There was a real nip in the air that night—a good reminder that winter was just around the corner—and I pulled the collar of my duffel coat up around my neck as I followed Cassie down the high street to the local village pub. Once the sun set, the Blue Boar was the place to be—it was the heart of the village and the place where all the locals congregated for a pint and a gossip.

I pulled the door open and stepped into the warmth, looking around me with appreciation. Like my tearoom, the pub was housed in a 15th-century Tudor house, although with lower ceilings, giving the place an almost cellar-like feel. And instead of a large open space, the interior was filled with cosy nooks and crannies—behind the pillars and around the fireplace—and dominated by a hand-carved, dark mahogany bar in the centre.

The place was heaving. With the typical English

habit of heading straight to the pub after work and in the evening on the weekends, this was the busiest time of the evening—and the numbers were swelled by the visiting tourists. Many of them would be staying at the various B&Bs and hotels on the outskirts of the village and probably came here for an authentic English pub experience.

"Seth said he might meet us here, if he could get away in time..." Cassie scanned the room. "Ah, there he is! And he's got a couple of seats for us by the window—good on him," she said with satisfaction.

"I'll get the drinks," I said. "You go and join him first."

Cassie nodded and headed across the room. I elbowed my way through the crowd to the front of the bar. Brian, the landlord, was busy at the beer tap, his sleeves rolled up to show his beefy arms as he pulled on a lever and filled a glass with foaming amber liquid.

He glanced up and gave me a smile. "Gemma! What can I get ya?"

"Half a cider for Cassie, please, and a shandy for me."

"Still a lightweight, eh? I would have thought that living in Australia would've cured you of that. On the other hand, Aussie beer..." He made a face. "Maybe I'm not surprised that you're opting for soft drinks."

I laughed. "Hey, the Aussies are pretty proud of their beers."

"I stand by my opinion. A beer's not a beer unless

it's a proper pint of English ale."

I smiled, refusing to be drawn into that age-old debate. "Busy here tonight," I commented, looking around the place.

He nodded, casting an experienced eye over the crowd. "Aye, a good bunch. A lot of tourists, but."

I noticed his eyes were fixed on a particular figure on the other side of the bar and as I followed his gaze, my heart sank as I realised suddenly who it was: the American from that morning. He was standing at the bar with a pint of ale in his hand, arguing with another man. From the expression on their faces, it wasn't a friendly debate. I could see the look of concern in Brian's eyes. He had been a publican for thirty years and he could recognise trouble brewing.

"Some of these tourists ought to know when to keep their mouths shut," he muttered as he pulled the lever and filled Cassie's half pint, tilting the glass with expert skill so that the foam stopped just short of spilling over the edge. "And some of the locals should learn not to let others wind them up so easily."

I looked over at the arguing men again and belatedly recognised the other punter. It was Mike Bailey, one of the local "troublemakers". He was a belligerent young man in his early twenties, with a tendency to get violent when drunk—which was often. Long acquaintance and respect for his family, who had lived in the area for centuries, had led most of the villagers to ignore Mike's sullen outbursts and put up with his behaviour. But when his surliness took a physical turn, Brian was quick to kick him off the premises. Cassie had told me that there had been a couple of incidents which had ended in assault charges, but so far, Mike Bailey had managed to stay out of Oxford Prison.

As I watched, he squared up to the American, jutting his chin out and jabbing a finger in the other man's chest. A third man was standing between them, smiling weakly and attempting to calm the situation.

"I'm not sure you can blame Mike this time," I said to Brian. "I had a run-in with that chap myself earlier today and I have to say, he's pretty obnoxious."

Brian grunted. "Obnoxious or not, he's a customer. Mike had better watch himself. If they've got a problem, they can take it outside. I'm not having a fight in my pub."

As we watched, the third man tried again, this time inserting himself bodily between the two arguing men. They seemed to calm down slightly and both stopped to take a drink from their glasses. I breathed a small sigh of relief. I didn't think I could handle any more drama today.

Brian set my drinks in front of me, took the money I offered, and handed me a packet of pork scratchings. He gave me a wink. "On the house."

I smiled my thanks, then tucked the packet under my arm, picked up the drinks, and, balancing them carefully, made my way over to join Cassie and Seth.

"I've just been telling Seth all about our day and our American Psycho," said Cassie as I sat down. Her eyes flicked across the room. "And then I look up and he's there! And as charming as ever, I see."

I groaned. "I know; it's like some kind of curse—I can't get away from the man! When he said he was going into Oxford earlier, I was hoping that he wouldn't be coming back any time soon."

"Well, the coach probably brought the whole tour group back to the hotel this afternoon," said Cassie. "Anyway, forget him." She turned to Seth, sitting next to her. "So how's life in the 'dreaming spires' these days?"

Seth cleared his throat and pushed his thick-framed glasses up his nose. It was a gesture I could remember from the day I met him when I first arrived as a Fresher in college. He had come up to read Chemistry, whilst I'd opted for the more genteel degree of English Literature. He had a room on my staircase in college and he had found me on that first day in Noughth Week, struggling with my suitcase at the bottom of the four-flight staircase. He had gallantly insisted on carrying my case up for me, in spite of nearly keeling over under the weight of it, and we had been firm friends ever since.

Seth was sweet and shy, although his earnest sharing of information could occasionally make him come across as pompous. Maybe because of this, he had opted to remain in the insular safety of academia and had gone straight from his undergraduate degree to a DPhil (PhD to the rest of the world), then a Junior Research Fellowship, and finally a Senior Research Fellow. I didn't think it would be long before he was made Professor. I suspected that Seth harboured a secret crush on Cassie all these years, but was simply too shy to tell her.

He was blushing slightly now as he recounted a story about his adventures at High Table. All the Oxford colleges had stately halls where a communal dinner was served and the dons and "fellows"—the academic staff—normally sat at High Table, usually at the very top of the room. Politics at High Table could be treacherous, especially for a younger member of the Senior Common Room—as Seth was finding out. With his naturally diffident manner, he was an easy target for the more domineering members of the SCR.

"You should have just told him where to stuff it," said Cassie heatedly as he finished his story. "I would have—"

"THAT'S A LOAD O' BOLLOCKS!"

We all jerked our heads around. Mike Bailey was thrusting himself aggressively at the American, his face mottled with anger.

"Hey, don't get mad at me just because you don't like to hear the truth," said the American loudly. "Your country is a sad relic of the last century, stuck in your stupid traditions and elitist attitudes, with crap food and miserable, stuck-up people. Come to the U.S. and see what real progress is!"

"I've had enough o' you bloody Americans coming here, throwing your money around an' thinking you know everything! I'm telling you—"

"Whoa, gentlemen..." Brian came hurriedly out from behind the bar, his hands raised in a placating manner. "Why don't we step outside and talk this out—"

"I don't need to step outside," Mike snarled. "I know what I need to do right here!"

And he lunged forwards and punched the American in the face. Cries of alarm erupted around the room and several people sprang up from their seats. I noticed, though, that the men standing around Mike had expressions of satisfaction on their faces. Guess the American hadn't been making himself too popular. No one stepped in to help him either as he slowly picked himself up off the floor.

Rubbing his jaw, he glared at Mike and said, "Is that your best shot, you drunk loser?"

"Why you—!" Mike went for him, his hands around the American's throat. This time, some of the other men jumped in to try and separate them.

"Hey! Enough of that!" cried Brian, shoving his way between them and forcing them apart. The American said something with a sneer—too low for me to catch from the other side of the room—but it caused Mike to make another lunge for him.

"You bastard! I'll make you pay for that!" he yelled, as several of his friends tried to restrain him.

Brian turned to the American. "Sir, you seem to

be deliberately provoking him. I must ask you to leave."

The American gave a shrug. "Sure, no skin off my nose. Don't know what the big deal is about this place anyway." He gave the room a contemptuous look as he adjusted the collar on his shirt. "Bet I'll find better drinks for cheaper in Oxford."

The door slammed shut behind him and there was an audible sigh of relief in the room.

"Good riddance," said Cassie in disgust. "What a pillock."

Brian was now talking to Mike Bailey and also asking him to leave. The latter was indignant.

"I can't believe you're taking that bloody American's side in this!"

"I'm not taking anyone's side," said Brian wearily. "But I can't have different rules for locals and tourists in my pub. You've caused trouble so I'm going to have to ask you to leave just like him."

Mike swore viciously, then he turned and banged out of the pub. I hoped that the American was already a good distance away otherwise there was likely to be another brawl out on the street. Several of Mike's friends must have shared the same thoughts because they hastily followed him out. The sudden clearing of the pub made the whole place seem a lot quieter and reminded me of my dinner appointment.

"Yikes!" I glanced at my watch and sprang to my feet. "I'd better get going. I'm going to be late for dinner!"

"It's only your parents. I'm sure they won't mind if you're a few minutes late," said Cassie.

"Are you kidding?" I gave her a look. "You know what my mother's like. Punctuality is one of the Ten Commandments in her household." I bent down and gave them both a peck on the cheek, then added to Cassie, "See you tomorrow."

"Don't forget Daylight Savings ends tonight," Seth spoke up. "So remember to turn your clocks back, otherwise you'll be getting up an hour early for nothing."

Cassie groaned. "Oh my God, that's what I did one year—and I got up and had showered and dressed for work before I realised it was still practically the middle of the night!"

I laughed. "I nearly did something similar in Sydney. Anyway, it's great to know that I'll get an extra hour of sleep tonight. See you!"

I gave them a smile and a cheery wave, and made my way out of the pub.

CHAPTER FIVE

I made it back to my parents' house with a minute to spare but by the time I'd hung up my cycle helmet and dashed into the downstairs toilet to wash my hands, I was definitely late when I arrived at the table.

My parents were already seated—my father, Professor Philip Rose, at his customary place at the head of the table, with a full dinnerware place setting laid out in front of him and a linen napkin at his elbow. My mother, Evelyn Rose, had just served the first course: split pea soup with croutons and a drizzle of sour cream, in elegant porcelain bowls. No chipped crockery in my parents' house or any stained mugs either. I don't know how my mother did it but she kept all her china looking as pristine as the day she bought them from the Royal Doulton section in the local department store.

"Sorry I'm late!" I gasped as I dropped into my seat. "I was—"

"Darling, *volume...*" My mother frowned at me.

I sighed and made an effort to lower my voice. "Sorry, Mother—I was having a drink with Cassie and Seth at the Blue Boar."

"Oh, how is Seth? Such a nice boy."

"He's not really a boy anymore, Mother. But yes, he's fine. He's having some teething troubles settling into his new college, but otherwise he seems on good form."

"Which college has he transferred to?" My father spoke up for the first time. My father was an Oxford professor and the stereotype of the absent-minded academic, spending more time with his nose buried in his books than in the real world. Even though he was now semi-retired, he still kept an active interest in all things to do with the University.

"Gloucester College," I informed him.

He nodded. "Good cricket team." He lapsed into silence again, concentrating on his soup.

"Yes, well, I was thinking, dear..." my mother continued smoothly. "Perhaps you could ask Seth to help you."

I looked at her in puzzlement. "Help me with what?"

"Why, find a job, of course!"

I gave her an exasperated look. "Mother, I have a

job. I run a tearoom."

She made a clucking sound with her tongue. "Yes, that's nice, dear—but surely that's not what you intend to do long term? I mean, you didn't go to Oxford just to become a... a tea lady!"

I sighed. We'd already had this conversation a thousand times. While I shall always be grateful that I attended one of the best universities in the world, it did come with a lot of baggage—the main one being a nagging sense of failure if you didn't win a Nobel Prize, become a multi-billionaire top CEO, or run for Prime Minister once you'd left Oxford. Somehow you were always dogged by the constant question of: "What have you achieved that's worthy of your brilliant education? You've been to Oxford! Why aren't you living up to your potential?"

I'd lived with that guilt for years—it was what had driven me to climb the corporate ladder, even though my heart wasn't in it, and to remain in a career which had left me feeling empty and miserable—just so I could hold my head up and have an impressive title to whip out when people asked me what I had done since graduating from Oxford.

But three months ago—when I turned twenty-nine and realised that the big 3-0 was rushing towards me—I had one of those "Oh my God, what have I done with my life?" moments. Maybe it was an early mid-life crisis. Suddenly I was sick of doing what was expected of me; I wanted to rebel, to do something crazy, to be *that person* that family and friends whispered about—with horror and disapproval and yet also admiration and envy—for having the *guts* to just do what the hell they wanted to and not care what other people think.

The next day, I'd walked into my office in Sydney and handed in my resignation. A week later, I heard about the tearoom in Meadowford-on-Smythe while on an internet chat with Cassie: the owners were selling out and moving to the Costa del Sol, and the beautiful 15th-century institution was under threat. I didn't know the first thing about running a food business—and I couldn't bake to save my life—but I fancied a challenge... and I missed England.

So I made probably the first impulsive decision in my life: I sold my swanky penthouse apartment in Sydney, bought the Little Stables Tearoom, packed my things, and came home. Of course, once I'd tasted a couple of weeks of British weather and maternal smothering, the romance did begin to fade a bit... but still, I didn't regret it.

I pulled myself out of my thoughts and back to the conversation at the dining table. "Why can't I just run a tearoom if it makes me happy?"

My mother looked at me as if I had grown two heads, then she continued as if I hadn't spoken.

"Dorothy Clarke told me that her daughter works for the University in their Alumni Office. She was having her highlights done at the hair salon when I was there last month and she told me all about Suzanne's job. It sounds very glamorous and

Suzanne gets to travel sometimes on University business. Wouldn't you like a job like that, dear?"

"No," I said firmly. "I *had* a job like that in Sydney, Mother. Don't you remember? And I hated it."

My mother tutted. "You didn't *hate* it. How could you have done it for eight years if you hated it?"

"Trust me, Mother. I'm much happier now. I'm proud of my little tearoom and I want to make a success of it. I don't need another job."

My mother was silent as we finished the rest of our soup and I thought that she might have finally accepted my position on the subject. It was too much to hope for. As we began our main course (roast lamb with spiced parsnips, carrots, and crispy roast potatoes, accompanied by home-made mint sauce— ah, I'd missed a good traditional British roast) she launched a new attack from a different angle.

"Has Cassie got a boyfriend yet?"

I shook my head.

"Why is she never with a nice young man?"

I shrugged. "Cassie is just... a free spirit, I guess. Besides, you know her first love is her paintbrush."

"Well, it's about time she thought about settling down, you know..." She gave me a meaningful look. "I mean, Cassie isn't as young as she used to be and everyone knows that once a woman passes thirty, everything starts to go downhill."

I had a sneaking suspicion that she was not talking about my best friend, but I could be as obtuse as my mother when I chose to be.

"Oh, I wouldn't worry about Cassie—I think everything is still very uphill with her," I said cheerfully

My mother pursed her lips. "Yes, but it is so strange, dear. Such a pretty girl too. I would have thought that the men would be flocking around her."

"They do flock around her," I said. "The problem is that she's not very interested in what they have to offer."

My mother gave a gasp and put a hand up to her throat. "Do you mean Cassie is a lesbos?"

"Lesbian, Mother. The word is lesbian. Lesbos is an island in Greece. And no, Cassie is not lesbian. Not that there's anything wrong with that anyway." I glowered at her.

"No, of course not, dear. I'm sure lesbians are lovely people."

Argh. Argh. Argh. I resisted the urge to face plant on the table.

"Anyway, I was thinking..." my mother continued airily. "Perhaps you're right, after all. Career isn't everything. There are *other* things a woman can do that are very worthwhile—perhaps even more worthwhile. Such as making a home and starting a family..."

"You could be right," I said dryly. "But she usually needs someone to make a home and start a family with."

My mother pounced on me. "I'm so glad you say that, darling, because I've been thinking the very same thing! You'll never meet anyone stuck out there in Meadowford-on-Smythe all day. Why, most of the men in the village are old enough to be your grandfather! So I was thinking, perhaps I can help you become acquainted with some of the young men in Oxford."

I gave her a wary look. "Mother, I don't need you to set up blind dates for me."

"Who said anything about blind dates?" She gave a shudder. "What a horrible, common word. No, no, you see... I was chatting with Helen Green the other day and she mentioned that Lincoln is back in Oxford now. He's got a consultant position at the John Radcliffe, in their ICU Department. And I thought: what a wonderful coincidence! You're both back again after a long time away—perhaps it would be a good idea for you to get together and swap notes—"

"Mother!" I said, forgetting the rule about restrained, ladylike volume. "I do not need you to set up a date for me with Lincoln Green!"

"Oh, but it's not a *date*, really. It's just sort of... socialising. He's ever so nice—and Helen tells me that he's one of the top Intensive Care specialists in the U.K., you know. He's bought a townhouse here in North Oxford—a beautiful Victorian maisonette." She looked around distractedly. "Helen gave me his number and if I can just get into my iPad, I could find it for you... I don't know why, darling, but my password isn't working..."

"Did you capitalise the first letter? You know that the first letter is always a capital in your Apple ID password."

"Oh… is it, dear? Well, you'll have to show me after dinner."

That would be the sixth time I'd showed her this week. I sighed. I don't know what had possessed me to suggest that my mother should get an iPad.

My mother was continuing, "Helen sent me a recent photo of Lincoln and my, he's grown up into such a handsome young man! It seems like only yesterday that he was that adorable little boy going off to Eton and now he's a dashing young doctor." She sighed dreamily.

I rolled my eyes. It wasn't that I didn't believe her. I was sure Lincoln Green was a lovely chap. In fact, I'd sort of known him since childhood. Helen Green was my mother's closest friend and Lincoln and his younger sister, Vanessa, had been frequent visitors to our house when we were growing up. I remembered a tall, serious-looking boy with impeccable manners. I was sure he had grown up into a very nice young man but I had no particular desire to renew the acquaintance. Nevertheless, from the look my mother was giving me, I could see that I was not going to avoid this acquaintance easily. I wondered if it might be easier just to have the date with him and get it over with.

My mother was saying something which brought me back to the present. Something about a book club and her turn to host the meeting this coming Monday.

"I'm sure you'd like to join the club, now that you're back," she said.

I groaned. "Mother, I'm not really into book clubs. I like to read what I fancy, when I fancy—the minute I get told I *must* read something, it totally puts me off the book."

"Well, I think you should get involved with *some* local community activities," said my mother severely. "It is the best way to make connections and meet the right sort of people. We're very exclusive in our book club and only admit a certain class of member."

I shuddered. The last thing I wanted to do was sit around for a couple of hours making small talk with my mother's snooty middle-class friends.

"Well, I don't want to sit around with a bunch of strangers, arguing over whether the author meant the blue curtains to signify depression or hope— when it probably didn't have any special meaning at all and he just liked the colour."

"Oh, but they're not all strangers. You *do* know some of them—like Dorothy Clarke and Eliza Whitfield... oh, and Mabel Cooke has just joined too."

There was no way I was going to join this book club now!

"Monday mornings I'm busy," I said quickly. "I've got the tearoom, remember? I've got a full time job now."

My mother frowned. "Really, Gemma... This

ludicrous business with the tearoom…"

I sighed and tuned her out as I focused on finishing the rest of my dinner. For dessert, we had a spotted dick—that wonderful British classic made with delicious sponge cake filled with juicy currants, steamed to perfection, and served with a dollop of custard. In spite of my irritation with my mother, I had to admit that her culinary skills were exemplary. Shame that the domestic gene seemed to have skipped a generation. Considering how bad I was at baking anything, it was probably a joke that I wanted to run a tearoom. Still, I enjoyed *eating* the items, which I considered half the qualification for the job.

I put the last spoonful in my mouth and licked my lips appreciatively, wondering if I should ask my mother for the recipe. Perhaps Fletcher had one of his own already. I would have to check with him tomorrow…

***

The next morning, I discovered a flat tyre on my bike and had to swap my usual routine of cycling to the tearoom for a bus ride into Meadowford-on-Smythe. As I alighted from the bus, I took a deep breath of the fresh morning air, a smile coming to my face. Much as I hated early starts, I had to admit that there *was* something nice about being awake at this time, when the streets were still empty, the air was quiet except for the chirping of birds, and everywhere was that hushed feeling of waiting for the day to begin.

I crossed the village high street and walked the few hundred yards down to the Little Stables Tearoom, feeling the same rush of pride as I did every morning when I saw the sign hanging above the front door. I was looking forward to another busy day. And it seemed that customers were arriving already. As I approached the entrance of the tearoom courtyard, I saw someone sitting at one of the outdoor tables, facing away from me. *Blimey, they're early.* The tearoom didn't officially open until nine o'clock—nearly another thirty minutes—but I decided I didn't mind starting a bit earlier to keep a customer happy.

"Be with you in a minute!" I called.

I glanced at the figure again as I walked past and my heart sank as I recognised those heavy-set shoulders and square-shaped head with the large, prominent ears. It was the American from yesterday. I had been hoping that he would have changed his mind about coming back here for breakfast. Still, a customer was a customer.

I hurried into the tearoom and bustled about, putting on my apron, pulling back the curtains, re-arranging some tables and chairs. Fletcher wasn't in yet, which was a bit odd. Normally, he would be here already to get an early start on the day's baking. Never mind, I could offer the American some coffee while he was waiting. Grabbing a menu, I let myself out the back door and into the courtyard.

"You can come and sit inside the tearoom now, if you like, sir. It's a bit chilly out here...."

I trailed off as I walked around his chair and turned to face him.

The American was leaning back, his eyes staring and his face a strange mottled colour. There was something wedged in his mouth—a scone, I realised—and his face was contorted painfully around it, with crumbs littering the front of his shirt.

My first thought was: "Oh my God, he's choking!" and I sprang forward to help him, even as my brain finally made sense of what I was seeing. My fingers brushed the clammy skin of his neck and I jerked back.

He wasn't choking.

He was dead.

CHAPTER SIX

I don't remember much of what happened afterwards. It was as if I was moving in a blur. Somehow I had stumbled back into the tearoom and picked up the phone to dial 999, then I sank down at one of the tables and sat quietly, staring at my hands. They were shaking.

I tried not to think of the man sitting out there in my courtyard. He had still been slightly warm when I touched him. I shuddered. It seemed like an eternity before the police arrived, though it was probably no more than ten minutes. I heard cars pulling up outside, the brief wail of sirens, but when I got up to open the door it was Cassie who rushed in, her eyes wide with surprise.

"Gemma! What on earth is going on? Why are the

police here?"

Before I could answer, two police constables bustled into the room. I led them wordlessly out into the courtyard and stood there numbly, watching as they looked at the body and talked in low tones. One of them hurried off—presumably to radio for reinforcements—but the other one stayed on the scene, carefully examining the table at which the American had been sitting but not touching anything. The knapsack I remembered from yesterday was on the chair next to him and a familiar paper bag half filled with scones was on the table.

"Is this how you found him?"

I nodded.

"Touch anything?"

I shook my head. Then I remembered. "Well, I did touch him briefly... You know, to make sure that he was..." I broke off, swallowing back a sudden wave of nausea.

He nodded understandingly. "You can go back in to wait inside if you like, ma'am. We've contacted Oxfordshire CID and the detectives should be here any moment."

I nodded but, instead of going in through the back door, I walked out of the courtyard and onto the street, going the long way so that I would re-enter the tearoom from the front. I wanted a bit of time to recover my composure and a little longer in the fresh air. As I approached the front door, I bumped into a tall figure hurrying up. It was Fletcher, looking harried and flustered.

"Oh, Gemma! I am sorry! I missed my alarm and I overslept! And then I was looking for Muesli and I—"

"It's all right, Fletcher," I said. In fact, I was thinking that it was a blessing he had overslept. If he had come early and been the one to find the body...

"Listen, Fletcher..." I said cautiously. "The police are here—"

"The police? Why?"

"Um... Well, you remember the American tourist who was here yesterday?"

His face darkened. I could see that he still hadn't forgiven the man for kicking Muesli.

"He's... He's had a bit of an accident and... well, he's dead. The police are with him now."

Fletcher stared at me. "Dead?" he said. "Why?"

I shrugged. "I don't know. It looks like he might have choked on a scone—or rather, someone tried to force a scone down his throat and he choked... Anyway, don't worry—the police are here now and I'm sure they'll catch who did it."

I propelled him towards the kitchen and we found Cassie sitting at the big wooden table inside. She had been sketching something on her drawing pad but she looked up as we came in.

"Gemma, why are the police he—?" she broke off as her eyes narrowed on Fletcher. "Hey Fletcher—is something wrong?"

"It's Muesli," he said miserably. "She's gone!"

I looked around, suddenly realising that he didn't

have the cat carrier with him. In all the excitement with the police, I hadn't even noticed.

"What do you mean 'gone'?"

"She's gone. Run away." Fletcher's lips quivered.

"What happened? Did something go wrong when you were putting her in the carrier this morning?"

He shook his head. "She ran off last night. Didn't come when I called. I went out and I called and called… but she never came back. I couldn't sleep. I tried to search again this morning but I couldn't find her."

I reached out to pat his hand. "Don't worry, Fletcher. I'm sure Muesli will come back. She's probably just decided to have an adventure in the woods behind your house. Cats often go off for days, don't they?"

He shook his head again. "Not Muesli. She always comes back. For bedtime. I give her a treat, see? It's shaped like a fish. I put it in her bed. Every night."

I looked helplessly at Cassie, then gave him another reassuring pat. "Well… maybe she's just being a bit naughty. I'm sure when you get home today, you'll find her waiting on the front doorstep for you."

My confidence seemed to reassure him. Putting on his apron, he went over to the giant industrial fridge and began taking out the ingredients for making a Victoria sponge cake. Cassie dragged me back out to the dining room.

"Gemma, what on earth is going on? The

constable told me not to go outside."

Quickly I told her what had happened—how I'd found the American when I arrived. Cassie stared at me disbelievingly.

"Dead? Do you think he choked on the scone?"

"I... I don't know what to think... He had the whole thing in his mouth. That's a weird way for somebody to eat a scone. I mean, you'd normally take a bite, not cram the whole thing in your mouth, wouldn't you? No, it looked as if someone had forced it down his throat and held it there until he..." I shuddered.

"Bloody hell." Cassie looked stunned.

The sound of a car pulling up outside distracted us. I drifted over to the window to see who had arrived. There were two cars, actually—one produced a middle-aged man in white overalls, whom I guessed to be the forensic pathologist. The other was an unmarked car but something told me that this was Oxfordshire CID. A sandy-haired young man climbed out of the driver's seat. I guessed him to be the junior officer—maybe the detective sergeant. No one who had been in that job for a while could look so cocky and smug. Then another man got out of the front passenger seat and I caught my breath.

"No..." I whispered.

There was no way he could have heard me through the glass, but he looked up, straight at me. My heart gave a kick in my chest as I met that steely blue gaze. Time seemed to shift. Suddenly I was back at Oxford again... eleven years ago... a wide-eyed

Fresher... falling in love for the first time in my life.

He held my gaze for moment longer, then he turned and followed his sergeant and the pathologist around the corner into the courtyard. I struggled to take a breath. It felt as if there was suddenly a lot less air in the room.

What was he doing here? Surely he couldn't be a CID detective?

I paced the room, questions whirling in my head. Cassie looked at me curiously, but for once I didn't feel that I could confide in my best friend. In any case, she got her answer soon enough when the front door opened fifteen minutes later and a tall man stepped into the room. The years fell away as he approached me. I remembered the very first time he had walked across the college quadrangle towards me. His hair had been long then, swept back in a dark, leonine mane, which hung down to his shoulders. It was cut short now, although that lock of hair still hung down rakishly over one eye. The chiselled cheekbones were the same too, as well as the hard, sensual mouth, but most of all, there was no mistaking that intense blue gaze.

He introduced himself and took out his warrant. Even as my eyes read the words: "Detective Inspector Devlin O'Connor, Oxfordshire CID", my brain still refused to process it. For one thing, he didn't *look* like a detective. Okay, so I don't know much about the usual detective inspector's working wardrobe but I had a feeling that it didn't include classic grey suits from Saville Row, Italian silk ties, and stylish leather brogues. He looked more like a model for *GQ Magazine* than a member of Oxfordshire's Criminal Investigation Department.

"Miss Gemma Rose?" he said.

You know my name, I wanted to shout at him. Instead I nodded and said, "Yes. I'm Gemma Rose."

"I understand that this is your establishment? And that you found the body?"

I nodded again.

"I'd like to ask you a few questions."

His manner was cold and distant, with no hint of the passion that had once flared between us. It was like a slap across the face and it helped me pull myself together. I raised my chin and gave a cool look to match his.

"Certainly," I said in my best BBC voice. My mother would have been proud of me. I waved a hand around the room. "Any table you like."

He gave me a sardonic look, then led me to a corner table whilst his sergeant escorted Cassie back into the kitchen. We sat down and he began firing rapid questions at me:

When had I arrived at the tearoom? Had everything looked the same as normal? Had I seen anyone loitering in the area? When did I notice the body in the courtyard? Did I know the deceased? When was the last time I had seen him alive? Had I recognised the item in his mouth?

"Of course I recognised it," I said impatiently. "It

was a scone!"

"One of yours?" Devlin said.

"I don't know. It's not like they come with a logo on them, is it?" I snapped.

He raised an eyebrow at my tone but didn't comment.

I felt slightly ashamed and added grudgingly, "He did buy a bag of scones to take away when he left yesterday. It looks like the bag that's on the table with him."

"We'll take one of your scones for analysis and comparison. Now, you say you arrived slightly later than normal—any reason for that?"

"Because I had to get the bus. I don't normally—I usually cycle—but I had a flat tyre this morning. Besides, I thought it would be nice to have a break from routine."

Devlin didn't say anything, but again he raised that mocking eyebrow. I bristled. His implication was obvious—that he didn't think I could break from routine. I remembered all our arguments of old; him accusing me of never being able to be spontaneous or do anything without meticulous planning and total control of the situation. Looking back now, I wondered how we could have ever been together. We were such opposites in every way.

Devlin's eyes met mine briefly and I had an uncomfortable feeling that he knew exactly what I was thinking. To cover my discomfort, I launched into a rambling account of the American's rude behaviour in the tearoom yesterday but, to my irritation, he cut me off, asking me instead to tell him about the incident last night at the Blue Boar again.

"But I don't think Mike Bailey did it," I said when I had repeated the story. "I think this is something to do with the University. I think you need to check the American's—"

"Thank you, Miss Rose, I know how to do my job. I don't need you to think about what I need to do—I just need you to answer my questions."

Devlin O'Connor had never spoken to me in that tone of voice before. I stopped and stared at him. For the first time, I realised that this was not the boy I used to know—this was a cold, hard man who was a stranger to me. I hadn't had a chance yet to tell him about the American's unusual knowledge of Oxford or his abnormally aggressive reaction yesterday, but now faced with Devlin's curt attitude, I decided that I wouldn't bother. If Devlin wanted any more information from me, he could bloody well ask for it! I wasn't going to volunteer anything else!

"Can I go now?"

He nodded. "I may have some other questions, but for now... yes."

I stood up stiffly and went into the kitchen, where I could hear raised voices. I opened the door to see the young sergeant sitting on the wooden table, leaning menacingly over Fletcher, in his best imitation of a hard-boiled detective from one of the American TV crime dramas. My poor chef looked like a nervous wreck as he stammered to answer the questions being fired at him. Cassie was sitting on the other side of the table, flushed and angry as she watched helplessly.

"You say you normally arrive at the tearoom a couple of hours before it opens—so why were you so late this morning?" The sergeant's voice was harsh and accusatory.

Fletcher seemed to shrink into himself. "B-b-because I was sleeping. The alarm w-went off but I didn't hear it."

"And why were you so flustered? I see that you're sweating—you look like you've been running. Care to explain why?"

Fletcher looked at him in bewilderment. "B-b-because I was late! I'm supposed to start making the scones really early, otherwise they won't be ready."

The sergeant leaned into his face. "So where were you running from?"

"Oh for God's sake!" Cassie burst out. "Are you stupid? He overslept and was late, so he was running from his house, which is on the other side of the village!"

Fletcher looked at Cassie in distress. "Don't say 'stupid'. It's not nice to call someone that," he said, wringing his hands.

The sergeant gave Cassie a cold stare. "I'd thank you to let me question the suspect in peace, or I may have you for police obstruction, miss."

Cassie sprang to her feet, her face red. "You—!"

"Whoa!" I said quickly, stepping into the kitchen.

Fletcher looked up gratefully. "You tell him, Gemma! You saw me come! I was late because I didn't hear my alarm!"

I glared at the sergeant, feeling a wave of dislike for him. I knew that he was probably just doing his job but he was a bit too cocky for his own good.

I raised my chin and said levelly, "Fletcher's right—I met him as he came in, just before 9 a.m. He lives on the other side of the village, about a fifteen-minute walk from here... or ten, I suppose, if you are running."

"Any neighbours who can verify his whereabouts?"

"His house backs onto the woods on one side and Miss Ethel Webb lives on the other. She used to be the village librarian before she retired."

"We'll need to speak to her and check his alibi," the sergeant said importantly. Then he turned back to Fletcher, who flinched under his gaze. "Now, about yesterday, I want to know—"

"I don't think Fletcher can help you," Cassie cut him off. "He was in the kitchen most of yesterday."

"Yes," I agreed. Then I added, glancing sideways at Fletcher and lowering my voice, "And he's not really the type to talk much to people. It's a waste of time asking—"

"Gemma."

I whirled around. Devlin was standing in the kitchen doorway. I wondered if he realised that he

71

had called me by my first name.

He said in an impatient tone, like someone speaking to an annoying child, "We have to question everyone. We can't make exceptions. It will all be over quicker if you let us do our job."

"Yes, but you don't understand." I hurried across to him and said in an undertone, "Fletcher is... different. He... he doesn't interact with others like most—"

"I'll keep that in mind," Devlin said, his voice making it clear that this was the end of the discussion. "I'd like to speak to Mr Wilson myself now. If you and Miss Jenkins could wait outside please?"

There was a pause, then Cassie got up and stalked out. I hesitated, then gave Fletcher an encouraging smile and walked to the kitchen door. As I got there, however, I looked back. Devlin was standing with his head bent, reading the notes the sergeant had scribbled on a pad. The light from the kitchen windows caught the glint of his dark hair and highlighted his aquiline profile. It brought to mind those paintings of Celtic warriors... I shook my head sharply. I had to stop thinking of Devlin O'Connor like that. He was no longer the romantic hero of my youthful dreams—he was now the detective in a murder investigation.

CHAPTER SEVEN

As it was, Devlin didn't keep either Cassie or Fletcher long; their interviews were even shorter than mine and they were soon released. I was glad to see that Fletcher looked slightly less distressed as he came out of the kitchen and felt grateful that Devlin had obviously acted with sensitivity. However, my goodwill towards him vanished when he came back in, after a hasty conference with the pathologist, and told me that I would have to shut the tearoom for the next two days.

"What? You can't be serious!"

There was no sign of humour on his face. "I'm perfectly serious. This is now a crime scene and until the SOCO unit can go over the place, we can't have a dozen tourists trampling around destroying evidence."

"But... he was found outside in the courtyard! Can't you just fence off that area and leave the rest of the tearoom as normal?"

He shook his head.

"But... but weekends are our busiest times! I can't shut the tearoom!" I glanced out the windows. Already, I could see a crowd of curious bystanders forming outside. If anything, it looked like I would have even *more* business than usual.

"I'm sorry. I'm afraid you have no choice."

I opened my mouth to argue, caught the look in his steely blue eyes, and thought better of it. Instead, I asked: "So you're sure that this is murder?"

"We think there's been foul play, yes. The pathologist is certain that it was not death by natural causes. He'll know more after the post-mortem."

"Did... did someone force a scone down his throat and choke him to death?"

Devlin's expression was guarded. "That's one theory. It's certainly what it looks like."

To my frustration, he refused to divulge anything further, and five minutes later I found myself being hustled out into the street by the cocky young sergeant. Devlin followed us out and was immediately accosted by Mabel Cooke, with Florence Doyle and Glenda Bailey right behind her. I noticed that Ethel was missing.

"Now, young man, what's going on here?" demanded Mabel, arms akimbo as she stared up at him.

To his credit, Devlin didn't flinch under that ferocious gaze. Perhaps it was easier to face bossy little old ladies when you were six foot one and all lean muscle. I expected him to deliver more of that curt detective attitude but, to my surprise, he put on a pleasant expression and addressed the crowd. He gave them a brief account of the situation—simply saying that an American tourist had been found dead—and appealed to anyone who might have information. He was as smooth and charming as a politician working the polls and I could see the crowd instantly responding to him.

This was a side of him I had never seen before— the Devlin I'd known would have barged into the crowd with hot-tempered impatience, but this Devlin was cool and quietly authoritative. He was also incredibly good-looking, I thought sourly. I could see several of the women in the crowd eyeing him with open appreciation. Glenda Bailey actually fluttered her eyelashes at him and giggled when he asked her to answer some questions. To my disgust, in less time than it takes to describe it, Devlin had a line of people eagerly queuing up to be questioned by him and his sergeant.

I turned to go. There was no point in me hanging around. As I made my way to the back of the crowd, I bumped into Nicky Wilcox, a pretty young mother who was one of the locals and a new regular at my tearoom. She had her baby with her in a stroller and she gave me a sympathetic smile.

"My goodness, Gemma... what a nightmare for you." She gave a little shiver. "Is it the American who was in the tearoom yesterday?"

I nodded.

Nicky lowered her voice. "I suppose I shouldn't really say this—not speaking ill of the dead and all that—but I have to say, I'm not really surprised. He was so... well... he seemed like the type who would provoke people..."

"And how!" I agreed fervently. "I kept telling myself yesterday that all sorts of tourists pass through the Cotswolds every day and I just had to grit my teeth until he moved on to the next place in his itinerary."

"Well, I hope things get back to normal for you soon. I'm dying to bring my sister in to show her the tearoom. I'm sure she'd love it—and she loves scones."

"Does she live locally too?"

"Yes, but she doesn't go out much. She suffers from chronic fatigue syndrome," Nicky said with a sad smile.

"Oh, I'm sorry."

"Her doctor's just started her on a different medication and we're hoping that she responds well."

"Well, tell her there's a plate of scones waiting in the tearoom with her name on it," I said with a smile.

"I will," Nicky promised, returning the smile.

I left her and hurried across the street. Cassie and Fletcher had both already left. I had no plans of my own and had nothing more exciting to look forward to than recounting the morning's events to my mother. The bus for Oxford was pulling up outside the school and I made a run for it. I managed to get in just before the doors shut and collapsed onto the first seat.

"What's going on at the tearoom?" asked the bus driver, turning around to peer out of his window.

I followed his gaze, seeing the police cars parked haphazardly outside the tearoom and the crowd of people milling in the street. There were constables circling the building, putting up crime scene tape, and already I could see what looked like a reporter with a cameraman arriving on the scene. It looked like something out of a TV show, not a corner of a quiet Cotswolds village. The news would probably be all over Oxfordshire by evening so I doubted I'd be giving anything away. Quickly, I told the driver what had happened.

"Blimey!" he said as he eased the bus away from the curb and started on the road to Oxford. "I can't believe it—he was only on my bus yesterday!"

"Really? Did you take him into the city?"

The driver nodded. "Aye, just after lunch, it were. He asked me to drop him somewhere near the K.A."

My ears perked up. "The K.A.? Did he ask specifically for the K.A.? He didn't say the King's Arms?"

The driver shook his head. "No, he asked for the K.A. Got out at the bottom of Broad Street. That was as close as I could get him."

I was silent, thinking hard. The King's Arms was one of the most popular pubs in Oxford, but its nickname—the K.A.—was used mainly by students. The fact that the American had referred to it as such confirmed my suspicions that he had once been at Oxford as a student himself.

As the Victorian townhouses of North Oxford came into view, I made a sudden decision. Leaning forwards, I said to the driver, "I've changed my mind. I think I'll pop down into the city—get some shopping done."

He nodded and bypassed the stop near my parents' house, continuing down the road to the heart of the city.

CHAPTER EIGHT

I alighted at the same place on Broad Street that the American had and wandered around aimlessly for a bit. This was the heart of the University—as close to a "campus" as most foreign tourists could hope for—and where most of the famous landmarks of Oxford were collected. There was Hertford College with its distinctive bridge—often called the Bridge of Sighs, after the bridge in Venice, which it was supposed to resemble; the Radcliffe Camera (known affectionately as the "Rad Cam")—the Bodleian Library's iconic reading room and perhaps the most photographed building in Oxford; the fantastic Gothic towers of All Souls College, which made up much of the "dreaming spires"; and the 17th-century Roman-inspired Sheldonian Theatre, with its thirteen busts of emperors' heads standing vigil on posts around its boundary.

I stopped outside the theatre and looked up at its circular façade, with the distinctive green-roofed cupola at the top. I thought of the many times I had been in that building—for matriculation and graduation ceremonies and numerous classical concerts in between. It was strange to be back in Oxford again, to see how the buildings, which had once been so much a part of my daily life, now seemed so alien to me. It was a bittersweet experience.

Finally I drifted down to the Kings Arm's, on the corner of Holywell Street and Parks Road, and stood looking at the pub thoughtfully. Although the King's Arms was used by all students of the University, it was probably most frequented by those at the colleges nearby, such as Hertford, Wadham, Gloucester, Trinity, and New College. What were the chances that the American had been at one of those colleges? It was a long shot, but it was a place to start.

I didn't stop to ask myself why I was even doing this. Why was it so important to find out if my suspicions about the American had been right? Was it Cassie's sceptical attitude? Or Devlin's offhand manner with me that morning? Maybe it was just my own nosiness, I thought with a wry smile. My curiosity had been piqued ever since I'd realised that the American was lying yesterday. I don't know what I wanted to prove or who I wanted to prove it to but... well, the tearoom was closed for the rest of the day, I had no wish to return to my parents, and I might as well do something with my time.

I headed towards Gloucester College. There was no particular reason for my choice, other than the fact that it was the closest and one I was particularly familiar with—it was where Seth had transferred to. I glanced at my watch. He was probably giving tutorials now. Perhaps I might bump into him in one of the college quads.

As I approached the huge iron-studded doors that guarded the college gate, I was glad that some perverse impulse had caused me to take out my old University card and slip it into my wallet when I first arrived back in England. Most Oxford colleges only allowed tourists and the general public to enter at certain times. As a member of the alumni, however, I could get in –just as I had as a student—by flashing my old University card. I showed this now to the porter at the gate. He gave it a cursory glance, then nodded and waved me past.

I paused inside the main quad and considered my next move. To be honest, I had no idea how I was going to find out if the American had been a student here. Then my eyes alighted on a couple of students in a corner of the quad taking a selfie with their phone. That gave me an idea.

Matriculation photos.

One of the things that set Oxford apart from many other universities was the Matriculation ceremony when you arrived as a new student. It was your first chance to parade around in the formal academic dress of *sub fusc* (and do your part for the Oxford tourist trade) as you walked with your fellow Freshers to the Sheldonian Theatre to be given official membership of the University.

It was custom that after your Matriculation ceremony, you'd return to your college for the official photo: the entire year of new Freshers lined up on a multi-tiered stage—what the Americans called "bleachers"—solemn and proud in their black gowns and mortarboards, all captured by Gillman & Soame, who had been the University's official photographers for over 150 years. Actually, I had looked at my own Matriculation photo recently, when I first got back home and was sorting through the things left in my old bedroom: my eighteen-year-old face had looked ingenuously at the camera from the top row, where the shortest people were placed. Poring over Matriculation photos and giggling over the way you once looked was a time-honoured tradition for Oxford grads.

Perhaps if I could look through Gloucester College's old Matriculation photos, I might be able to find our friend, the American. Again, it was a long shot. I didn't even know if I would be able to recognise him—judging by his age, he could have matriculated over twenty years ago, and people changed a lot in that time. But I thought it was worth a try. After all, what did I have to lose—an hour of my time?

On an impulse, I texted Cassie and asked her to send me a picture of her sketch of the American. My phone beeped a minute later and I opened the photo, zooming in and looking at it with satisfaction. The sketch was spare and highlighted his main features, including the sticking-out ears, squarish head, and fleshy cheeks. Even if he had changed a lot since youth, those dominant features were likely to remain the same.

I walked to the college library and made my way up to the upper gallery. I remembered Seth telling me that this was where the college archives were kept. A middle-aged lady sat at a desk near the front of the room. She looked up expectantly as I came in.

"Can I help you, dear?"

"Um…" I hadn't prepared a story and was caught off guard. "I was hoping to take a look at the college Matriculation photos."

"The archive is not usually open to the public, although access is possible for research or private reasons, if you are a member of the college."

"I *am* a member of the University," I said, flashing my old University card again. "But… uh… not of this college. It was… er… my uncle who was a member here. He… um… he passed away recently—"

"Oh, I'm sorry for your loss," the woman said, her eyes softening in compassion.

I winced. I didn't feel particularly good about lying and playing on the woman's sympathies. Suddenly I remembered one of the continual arguments Devlin and I used to have as students: he had always been a firm believer in the ends justifying the means, whereas I had always insisted on idealistic ethics. Now, as I thought of how glibly I had lied, I wondered if age and experience had changed me. Maybe I agreed with Devlin after all.

"Thank you," I said quickly. "We couldn't find his Matriculation photo amongst his things and I'd love to see what he looked like as a student. I was hoping I could find him in one of the photos here."

"You can order a replacement from Gillman & Soame, you know," she said. "They keep a wonderful archive."

"Er... yes... we'll probably do that. But I thought— since I was in the neighbourhood—I'd just pop in and see if I could find him here in the college archives...?" I trailed off hopefully.

The woman nodded. "Oh, yes, certainly. We keep a record of almost everything. The archive holds all the minutes of the college meetings and college clubs and societies, as well as documents related to the college finances and building projects. There are also copies of the college publications and photographs of events in the college history. And of course, we also have a copy of the Matriculation photos from each year, dating back to 1954." She looked at me enquiringly. "If you give me the year your uncle matriculated, I can help you find it."

"Um..."

Flip! How was I going to get out of this one? The

minute she started asking for details like my uncle's name and year of matriculation, she'd know I was fibbing. To my relief, the phone on her desk rang at that moment and she picked it up. From the sound of the conversation which ensued, there was a problem in the bursar's office—something to do with missing records.

"I'm so sorry," she said as she put the phone back in its cradle. "I have to go and sort this out." She gave a sigh of exasperation. "This is the fourth time this week they've had this issue and I think if I don't go myself, they will never resolve the problem."

"That's all right." I gave her my most winning smile. "Maybe I could just take a peek at the photos myself?" I gestured to the other side of the gallery. "Is that them hanging along the walls?"

"Well..." She looked behind herself doubtfully. "I'm not really supposed to let anyone have access to the gallery unsupervised." Then she smiled. "But I'm sure it'll be fine with you. Yes, most of the photos are hanging on the walls, although some of the older ones may be in that cabinet in the far corner. Just please make sure you're very careful about not rearranging anything—they've been painstakingly categorised and ordered."

I promised to take great care and, as soon as her footsteps had faded down the stairs, I whisked across the gallery. The photos covered most of the length of the long wall and were hung in chronological order. I paused in front of the first one and hesitated. Where should I start? I had no idea when the American had matriculated. If he had been here as an undergraduate, that would have been about twenty to twenty-five years ago, but if he had come to Oxford to do a graduate degree, he could have been older and been here much more recently.

I decided to start my search first at the photos from twenty-five years ago. I walked along the wall, studying them carefully. There was no face remotely like his. I moved on, trying the later years, going through them systematically.

Bingo.

I paused at the Matriculation photo from fifteen years ago and stared at a young man sitting in the front row. He had been much thinner then, his jowls less fleshy, but it was unmistakably him. He was sitting between a serious-looking young man with a receding hairline and a gangly young man squinting at the camera.

I threw a glance over my shoulder, then reached into my pocket and pulled out my phone. I held it up at arm's length and snapped a replica of the Matriculation photo with my phone's camera. I checked the shot, making sure that every face was clear. Then I remembered something else. All Matriculation photos were usually accompanied by a sheet of paper, listing all the names of the students in order. Carefully, I turned the framed photo over. It was there, glued to the back of the mounting board. I snapped another shot with my phone, then returned the photo to its original position on the wall.

I dashed back across the room, scribbled a quick note of thanks to the archive librarian, then hurried down the staircase, hoping that I wouldn't encounter her on the way up. I didn't. I got out of the library undetected and returned to the main quad with a sigh of relief.

Mission accomplished.

Except... what had I really accomplished? All I knew now was that the American had been at Gloucester College as a graduate student. *And I also have his name,* I thought. I pulled my phone back out of my pocket and checked the list of names, matching it against the photo. I found him, seventh along the front row from the left: "B. Washington". I wondered what the "B" stood for. The police would know, of course. My little bit of detective work wasn't really worth much when I knew that Devlin could have easily found out the victim's name by going through the man's personal items at the hotel.

But I didn't have police access to things and I had found out this information myself. I felt absurdly proud of that. And the police might not necessarily know of Washington's connection with Gloucester College and the University. Unless they found that folder I saw on Saturday...

Deep in thought, I didn't notice the young man coming towards me until I almost bumped into him just outside the Porter's Lodge.

"Seth!"

"Hey Gemma... what are you doing here?"

"I was... um... doing some research."

Seth's gaze sharpened. "Is this about the murder?"

"How did you know?"

"Cassie rang and told me what happened this morning. And I have no doubt that it will be on the six o'clock news tonight. But I thought the police were investigating—?"

"They are. I'm just doing a bit of my own investigating."

Seth raised his eyebrows. Then he glanced at his watch. "I've got to head out to the lab to check the results of an experiment now, but listen, would you like to come to High Table tonight? I haven't taken a guest yet." He grinned. "If I take you, I'd gain some brownie points for bringing the prettiest guest to Formal Hall."

"Flattery doesn't work on me, Seth Browning," I said dryly. I was about to refuse, then I paused. Perhaps visiting High Table wouldn't be such a bad idea. I might get a chance to speak to some of the older dons who might remember Washington. Another long shot but worth playing. I gave Seth a smile.

"All right, you're on. I'll have to dash back and change, though," I said, looking down at my jeans.

It was part of the custom at Oxford that many of the colleges held two sittings for dinner: an earlier "Informal Hall", which was a more casual meal, and a later "Formal Hall", which was a more ceremonial event. And one of the rules of etiquette for Formal Hall was changing for dinner: men had to wear a smart jacket and tie, and women something suitably dressy, together with their black gowns. "Formal Hall" was a unique experience, from the pre-dinner reception drinks in the ante-chamber and the solemn saying of Grace in Latin before the meal, to the leisurely three-course dinner, served by uniformed college staff, accompanied by wine and port. It was something that I had taken for granted during my years as a student and it was strange to think of experiencing it again.

"Will I have to dig out my old gown?"

"Well, you know they like it if you're a member— even an ex-member of the University—but you could always pretend you're not one of us." Seth grinned.

I rolled my eyes. "Okay, I'll see you back here at seven."

"Great! Got to dash now. See you later!"

I watched him hurry off across the quad. Suddenly I was looking forward to dinner very much...

CHAPTER NINE

I surveyed myself critically in the mirror. I was out of practice at this. Eight years of living in Australia had made me lazy about dressing up. The Aussies championed the more casual way of life—even the wealthiest billionaires and high-society figures often hung out at the local cafés dressed in faded jeans and flip-flops. The easy-going, relaxed nature of Down Under had suited me to a comfy old T-shirt but my mother—who is of the pearls and twinset brigade—had despaired every single time she had seen me when I had come back to visit, horrified at my lack of ladylike presentation.

Well, tonight she would have been pleasantly surprised. In my fine crêpe wool dress, sheer black tights, and stiletto heels, my short pixie crop brushed to gleaming, complemented by soft plum lipstick and classic black eyeliner, I looked the picture of stylish elegance.

I picked up my favourite pale pink pashmina and then, on an impulse, turned and went back to my wardrobe. From the deepest recesses, I dragged out a large black robe with voluminous sleeves and a gathered, stiffened yoke at the back. This was my Oxford scholar's gown. It had once been part of my life almost every day when I had been at Oxford, especially part of the ritual of attending dinner in Formal Hall. I stared at it for a long moment, then slipped it on and looked at myself once more in the mirror.

Strange how putting on something can instantly change the way you feel. Suddenly, I felt part of the University again —as if I was reclaiming a lost identity. I knew that I didn't have to wear it, but I decided to keep it on. I smiled at my reflection, picked up the pashmina again, and turned and left my room.

***

"More wine, Miss Rose?"

I turned to the elderly don next to me, who had introduced himself as Professor Edmund Wilkins, and gave him a smile. "Thank you."

I watched as he refilled my glass. So far, the experience was slightly surreal. It would have been strange anyway coming back to Formal Hall after all this time... but sitting at High Table just made it weirder. As an undergraduate, I had never been to High Table; in fact, I had never really paid it that much attention. It was simply the place where the members of the Senior Common Room sat during dinner; a table separated from the rest, on a raised platform at one end of the hall. Now that I was up here, it felt strangely "wrong". I looked down across the hall. I knew that this wasn't my own college and this wasn't the dining hall I had been used to, but still, there was a sense of not being where I should be. I felt like I ought to be down there, sitting at the long tables, eating with the other students...

The old don set the wine bottle down and glanced sideways at my gown. "So are you a member of the University, my dear? I don't seem to remember Seth bringing you before."

"Yes, though this isn't my college." I gestured to the students below us. "I was just thinking to myself that I feel like I ought to be down there. I can't believe that it's been over eight years since I was last at Formal Hall. In a way, it feels like I never left."

"Yes..." Professor Wilkins turned his eyes to the rest of the dining hall. "I've been at Gloucester College for nearly forty-seven years now—came here as an undergraduate and never left." He gave a dry chuckle. "I've seen so many students come and go, I feel like I'm beginning to see the same faces again."

"You must have a good memory then," I said,

smiling.

"One tries. Of course, some students stand out more than others." He looked at me curiously. "So are you back at Oxford doing further studies?"

Seth laughed from across the table. "She's back at Oxford serving tea," he said. "Gemma's taken over a tearoom in one of the Cotswolds villages."

"Running a tearoom?" said one of the female dons from farther down the table with an incredulous laugh. "Are you serious?"

I felt myself flushing and raised my chin. "Yes," I said.

"What did you read at Oxford?" she asked insolently.

"English."

"I suppose you're putting your education to great use at the tearoom," she said with a snide smile.

I felt my jaw clenching and deliberately tried to relax it. Seth looked from me to the female don and back again, and said hastily:

"Well, I think Gemma's doing a fantastic job with the tearoom. And she's got the most smashing scones." He turned back to Professor Wilkins. "Edmund, you must go and try them, if you haven't yet."

The old don nodded amiably. "What is the name, my dear?" he asked me.

"The Little Stables Tearoom," I said.

"You're the owner of the Little Stables Tearoom?" came a sharp voice from farther down the table.

I turned to see a thin man, with a balding head and wired-framed glasses, looking intently at me. Although Seth had made a round of introductions in the Senior Common Room earlier, I hadn't spoken to this particular don. He had kept to himself, nursing a glass of dry sherry and not making eye contact with anyone. This was the first time he had attempted to speak to me all evening.

"Prof Hughes, now *you* ought to get some scones into you, old boy," said Professor Wilkins jovially. "You're always such a sack of skin and bones. You need a bit of fattening up!"

Hughes? I thought of that signature on the American's letter and I looked at the man with new interest. I noticed that his face seemed strangely swollen and the skin around his eyes was puffy and red.

"Wasn't the Little Stables Tearoom on the news this evening?" another female fellow said suddenly. "A suspicious death?"

I coloured slightly as I saw everyone on High Table turn to look at me. "Yes," I admitted. "There was an unfortunate incident this morning. Um... One of the customers—an American tourist—was found dead in the courtyard."

There was a series of gasps, coupled with looks of sordid curiosity.

"Were you the one who found him?" asked the female fellow.

"Yes... unfortunately."

She gave a delicate shudder. "How frightful!"

"Do the police think it's murder?"

"Do they know what happened?"

"Have they got any suspects?"

I was very conscious of Hughes's eyes boring into me. I decided to be less than honest.

"I'm not really sure. The police have started an investigation, of course. Did they say anything on the news?" I glanced back at Hughes.

"No, they merely said that it was being treated as a suspicious death," he said shortly.

"Well, this is rather exciting!" cried another of the dons. "It's like one of those murder mysteries on the telly! Our very own Inspector Morse or Midsomer Murder!"

The others at the table joined in eagerly with the speculation.

"I'd bet on them finding that it was a jealous ex-mistress."

"Or a blackmailer! It's always a blackmailer "

"No, I think it was industrial espionage. He was American, right? He was probably selling trade secrets to some company in the U.K. and got silenced."

"It was very likely something much more prosaic," said Professor Wilkins with another dry chuckle. "Like a—what do the young people call it? A 'mugging gone wrong'. Or a homeless drunk, perhaps, cracking him on the head with a wine bottle..."

I noticed that Hughes had remained silent

through all this wild conjecture. I caught his eye and said, "Do *you* have any theories, Professor Hughes?"

His eyes slid away from mine. "Me? No, why should I? I don't even know the man."

Liar, I thought. I didn't have any proof but I was willing to bet that "Hughes" was the signature on that letter I had seen in the American's folder. He would be about the same age as Washington—they had probably been at Oxford around the same time. What were the chances that Hughes was the person Washington had come back to his old college to see?

"I'm sure it was something like industrial espionage," said one of the younger fellows again. He nodded eagerly. "He probably got involved with some organised crime syndicate and thought that he could handle things—but then found himself sinking deeper and deeper—"

Seth burst out laughing. "I think you've been reading too many spy thrillers, Gordon!"

The young fellow looked indignant. "It happens in real life too! Maybe he thought he could stay aloof, but it backfired. You know what they say—once you get your hands dirty, you can't ever wash them clean again."

"Sounds like something your favourite philosopher would say," said Professor Wilkins with a nod to Hughes. "What's that line again? About the abyss."

Hughes hesitated, then quoted, *"And if you gaze for long into an abyss, the abyss gazes also into you."*

"Nietzsche," I said, recognising the quote.

Hughes looked at me with new interest. "I thought you said you read English, not Philosophy?"

"Yes, but I always liked Nietzsche—from a language point of view, if nothing else—he had a real way with words." I paused and added, "My favourite quote of his is: *'And those who were seen dancing were thought to be insane by those who could not hear the music'.*"

The old don turned to me with a chuckle, "My goodness, you and Prof Hughes ought to put your heads together sometime. He is obsessed with Nietzsche—"

"I'm not obsessed," said Hughes sharply. "I just happen to admire him and agree with a lot of what he says."

"And have his quotes all over your office, on your answering machine, in your research articles, and in the signature at the end of your emails?" scoffed the young fellow. "I'd say that you're obsessed, Hughes! You should have made Philosophy your subject, and become an expert on Nietzsche, instead of going into Pharmacology."

"Don't encourage him even more," said another fellow, rolling his eyes.

Hughes looked slightly embarrassed. "I'm quite happy in my field," he said stiffly.

"So the police didn't tell you anything?" said the female fellow to me, bringing the conversation back to the murder mystery.

"Not really."

"Do they know anything about the victim?" asked Hughes. "Do they know where he was from or what he was doing in Oxford?"

I shrugged. "I don't know. You'll have to ask the police that. They weren't exactly forthcoming with me." That, at least, wasn't a lie. I paused, then looked at Hughes straight in the eye. "I'm sure they'll be looking into his background and movements, to see who might have had a motive—and opportunity—to kill him."

Hughes dropped his eyes from mine and busied himself cutting up some roast potatoes. The conversation on the table shifted to the rise of crime in Oxford and I could see that Hughes looked relieved. He contributed little more to the conversation and excused himself as soon as dessert was served.

I watched him leave the hall. He knew something about the American's murder—I was sure of it. As soon as politeness allowed, I made my own excuses to Seth and the other fellows and left the hall. As I was walking towards the college gate, I pulled my phone out of my handbag and flicked to the photo gallery, looking at the picture I had taken of the Matriculation photo again. I zoomed in and focused on the young man next to Washington. Yes, it was definitely Geoffrey Hughes—with a lot more hair— but with the same serious expression.

A surge of excitement gripped me. I thought of

Devlin. I knew I ought to tell him about this. It could have been a valuable lead. Then I remembered his cold, brusque attitude and his off-hand manner towards me. It was like a dash of cold water. And I recalled my vow not to volunteer any more information to him.

Let Devlin figure out the connections himself, I thought mutinously. He's not going to get help from me in this investigation!

CHAPTER TEN

"Gemma? Gemma, are you up yet? They'll be here any minute."

"Hmm?" I opened one eye and squinted in the sunshine coming in through a gap in the curtains. There was muffled knocking at my bedroom door, then my mother's voice came again. "Gemma, darling... It's nearly ten o'clock."

"WHAT?" I sat upright in bed. *Ten o'clock! How could I have slept so late?*

I rubbed my eyes. The recent weeks—since the opening of the tearoom—must have been more exhausting than I'd thought. With weekends being the busiest days in the tourist trade, I hadn't had a lie-in since I arrived back in England and the only reason I didn't have the alarm set for this morning was because I'd got a message from Devlin last night saying that the police wouldn't be done with the tearoom until lunchtime. So no business again today and no need to get up at my usual time. Still, I hadn't intended to sleep this late!

My bedroom door opened and my mother stuck her head in. She raised her eyebrows slightly at my dishevelled state. "If you hurry, dear, you'll still have time to shower before they arrive."

"Before who arrives?" I asked, yawning.

"The book club, dear! Remember I told you about it at dinner on Saturday night? I'm hosting the meeting this month. How lucky that you had to close the tearoom today—it means you can attend the meeting!"

She shut the door behind her. I flopped backwards on the bed with a groan. *Argh!* I'd forgotten all about the book club meeting. Now there was no way of escaping—not without upsetting my mother. I sat up again and got out of bed with a sigh. I might as well make the best of it. It wasn't as if I had anywhere else to be this morning.

I showered, dressed, and got down to the living room just as the first members were arriving. My smile faltered slightly when I saw Mabel Cooke march through the front door. I could see from the gleam in her eye that she wanted to grill me about the murder but I managed to forestall her by hastily telling my mother that I would take care of the refreshments. Ten minutes of skulking in the kitchen, however, was as much as I could stretch it to. Thankfully, by the time I returned to the living room with the tea tray, everyone had sat down and Mabel was too busily engaged in gossiping with another lady to notice me quietly join the group.

In general, there are two kinds of book clubs: those whose members are "serious" readers and spend their time ferociously dissecting the text for hidden nuggets of meaning that the author probably never intended, and those of the more social kind, where members simply want an excuse to meet and exclaim over each other's hairstyles and gossip about their kids and neighbours. I quickly realised that my mother's group was of the latter variety when twenty minutes had elapsed and we still hadn't even mentioned the title being read.

Most of the members were from my mother's social circle, dressed in scarily similar Marks & Spencer cashmere twinsets, court pumps, and pearls, but one woman stood out like a black swan in a flock of white ones. She was a lot younger than the others—closer to my own age—and decidedly glamorous, in a sensual sort of way. She arrived in a cloud of designer perfume, dressed in a silk sheath dress which highlighted every one of her ample curves and complemented her creamy white skin. Her eyes were green and expertly accentuated with mascara, and her hair fell to her shoulders in glossy red waves. Real red—not something out of a bottle. I found it difficult not to stare. It was rare to see such a glamorous, attractive creature outside the pages of a fashion magazine.

My mother introduced her as Justine Smith—a recent new member of the club—and as she greeted everyone in a pleasant drawl, I realised that she was American. I was pleased when I managed to find a seat next to her.

"So you are new to Oxford?" I said.

"Oh no," she said. "I've been living here for years. I have a house around the corner, actually."

"I think I've seen you," said my mother as she paused beside us to offer a plate of shortbread biscuits. "The large Regency townhouse in the crescent? You were unloading shopping from a big, black car at the front." My mother shook her head in admiration. "How on earth did you manage to get such a fantastic parking bay? Right in front of your house too! I was just speaking to Dorothy and she's been telling me what a nightmare it is to apply for an extra permit for on-street parking."

Justine gave a coy smile. "I guess I just got lucky."

My mother shook her head again and moved on to the ladies at the next sofa. I looked back at Justine. Somehow I had a hard time fitting her in my mother's social circle. I wondered what had prompted her to join the book club. Something of my thoughts must have shown in my expression. She gave me a smile and said, "I thought it was time I became a bit more cultured."

She laughed. She had a deep, throaty laugh, and

a graceful, self-assured manner. I felt suddenly gauche and unattractive next to her expensive sophistication.

"I'm not sure how much literature you're going to get," I said ruefully, glancing at the others who were busily chattering.

My mother and two friends were discussing the best way to store smoked salmon, Mabel was instructing another elderly lady on the best type of bran to have for breakfast, and three other ladies were aggressively comparing pictures of their grandchildren.

"What book is the club reading anyway?" I asked.

"*Persuasion* by Jane Austen."

"Oh—my favourite Austen book!" I said in delight.

She gave me a lazy smile. "Really? I thought most people's favourite was *Pride and Prejudice*."

"Oh, I like Darcy... which girl doesn't? But you can't beat Captain Wentworth for the most romantic letter of all time. Besides..." I hesitated. "I think there's something so poignant and beautiful about Anne Elliot's story—the story of second chances and starting again."

She looked at me in amusement. "Yeah, it's nice in a book. Shame it doesn't happen like that in real life."

"You're very cynical."

"Let's just say, I believe in the saying about a leopard not changing its spots."

"People aren't leopards."

"Oh, they're not that different." She gave a derisive smile. "You are who you are—and you don't change."

"I don't believe that. People change all the time!" I said hotly. "They start again, re-invent themselves..."

I trailed off as I saw her looking at me curiously. I realised that I was probably over-reacting. I took a deep breath. Maybe Justine had hit a nerve. The tearoom was my "second chance"—my chance to start all over again, now that I was older and wiser. I wanted to believe— *needed* to believe—that I could be completely different to the "old me" and still find success and happiness.

We were interrupted at that moment by my mother calling to me from across the room. She had her iPad in her lap and was frowning at it.

"Gemma, darling, what is my Apple ID password again? I thought it was 'gemmarose' but it's not letting me in."

"Did you capitalise the 'G'?" I asked. "Remember, your Apple ID password needs the first letter to be a capital." *And well done for broadcasting your password to everyone in the room,* I thought.

"Ah..." My mother tapped haphazardly at her iPad. "Oh, yes! Got it! Here, look..." She turned to Dorothy Clarke, seated next to her. "See, you can get *The Times* newspaper now in the iPad. Isn't that clever? So you don't have to have a paper delivered every day..."

Dorothy leaned over to look. "Oh, marvellous, Evelyn. Technology is amazing, isn't it? Maybe I ought to get an iPad. My daughter keeps telling me to join this Face-thing where you can see your friends' pictures on the computer."

"Oh, yes, I know all about Facebook. Helen helped me do that last week. I've got six friends on it, you know," my mother said proudly. "And they're so lovely. They like everything I say. This morning I posted a message about the shocking murder at Gemma's tearoom and I had ten people liking it within an hour! Though I'm not sure why I had ten 'Likes' when I only have six friends but—"

"Mother!" I looked at her in disbelief. "You shouldn't be telling random people on Facebook about the murder!"

Dorothy gave an exclamation and looked at me. "Why, Gemma! I had no idea that it was *your* tearoom when I saw the six o'clock news last night! A murdered American tourist! How ghastly!"

I felt Justine stiffen next to me.

"Yes," I said. "It's the reason I'm here today. I would normally be working, but we had to close the tearoom because the police are still working the crime scene."

Dorothy leaned forwards, lowering her voice to a dramatic whisper. "Were you the one who found the body?"

I sighed. I was beginning to feel like I ought to walk around carrying an FAQ with answers such as "Yes, I found the body", "No, I don't know who the police suspect", "Yes, he was found with a scone in his mouth", "No, I'm afraid we're fully booked this week but I can take reservations for next week" (okay, the last one was wishful thinking).

"I heard on the news that the police have a suspect in custody already," said one of the other ladies.

"Rubbish," said Mabel tartly. "They don't have anybody in custody. They just have a few outlandish theories—which is hardly surprising when you consider that useless excuse for a sergeant that I met. Really! That boy couldn't find his own willy if it wasn't zipped up in his trousers! The police have no idea what they're doing."

"I'm sure I heard that they had a suspect," said the other lady stubbornly. "Somebody who had attacked the American in a pub or something..."

Mabel sniffed. "Yes, they're trying to pin it on Glenda Bailey's great-nephew."

"The police suspect Mike Bailey?" I said.

"Yes, and all because they found some scones at his place that were from the tearoom!" Mabel shook her head in exasperation. "Glenda had to call and explain that she was the one who had given them to him."

I frowned. "But surely that wouldn't be enough for them to suspect him? I mean, several people bought scones from me on Saturday."

"It's because of that fight in the pub," one of the other ladies spoke up. "My son was there with his friends and he told me that Mike Bailey punched the

American in the face!"

Mabel waved a hand dismissively. "Mike has a temper on him—but he's not a murderer. I've known him since he was a child. He needs a good telling-off and his mouth washed out with soap—but he's not the type to kill anyone."

Maybe not on purpose, I thought to myself. *But I wouldn't put it past Mike to inadvertently hurt someone badly in a fit of temper.* It wouldn't be the first time someone got killed by mistake when people lost their tempers and things got out of hand. Besides, who was to know what anyone was really capable of?

I remembered Cassie telling me how Mike had become increasingly bitter in recent months, ever since he had lost his job at the car factory due to an American takeover of the company. He was the type who always needed to blame someone for his misfortunes, and in this case, a rich American conglomerate would have been the perfect scapegoat. It would have given him even more reason to feel wronged and victimised: the small man fighting an unfair battle against the powerful corporate giant.

Yes, Mike Bailey could easily have been nursing a grievance. And with the way Washington was taunting him on Saturday night, it would have hardly been surprising if Mike decided to get vengeance on a personal level, against one smug American.

"Well, *I* heard that the American choked on a scone," said another lady. "Fancy that!"

"Yes, it must have happened sometime between seven-forty-five and eight-forty when Gemma discovered him," Mabel said.

"How on earth could you know that?" I blurted out. "I doubt the police have even had the post-mortem report yet."

"Because he called the hotel reception at seven forty-five asking for his bathroom lightbulb to be changed. Frances Moore's niece works at the Cotswold's Manor Hotel. She told Jane Addison—who told Judith Powell—who told me at the post office this morning."

I could see Justine looking at Mabel with a mixture of astonishment and wonderment. Personally, I wasn't surprised. In fact, I was more surprised that Mabel hadn't found out what brand toothpaste Washington used and what size shoes he wore. On second thoughts, she probably had.

"I hear that the detective on the case is very good," Dorothy spoke up. "Detective Inspector Devlin O'Connor. I recognised his name when they mentioned him on the news last night. There was a piece about him in the papers earlier this year; it was to do with a murder up North... Leeds, I think it was... and no one had been able to solve it for seventeen years. Well, he cracked it."

My mother gave me a sharp look. "Devlin O'Connor? Is that—?"

"Yes," I said evenly.

She seemed about to say something else, then

glanced around and thought better of it. I saw Mabel watching us shrewdly

One of the other ladies spoke up. "You know, I remember reading that article too. And I seem to remember some scandal associated with that case—wasn't there a rumour that he'd got involved with one of the suspects or something? A very attractive young lady. And they were questioning his impartiality in the investigation—although he did solve the case in the end and bring the murderer to justice…"

"If it's the Devlin O'Connor I'm thinking of, I'm not surprised," said my mother, compressing her lips.

I felt a flare of annoyance, although I didn't know why. It wasn't like I felt any loyalty to Devlin.

"Well, a good-looking lad like him—I shouldn't wonder if he has a weakness for a pretty face," Dorothy tittered.

"Is there any man who doesn't?" said another lady and everyone laughed politely.

Mabel folded her arms. "Inspector O'Connor may be good but there will be things he doesn't see because he's not a real local. We know Oxfordshire, we live here, we're involved in the village communities, we know who to talk to… I think we have an advantage that the police will never have."

I looked at her in puzzlement. "Who's 'we'?"

"Florence and Glenda and Ethel and me," said Mabel, as if it should have been obvious. "We've decided we are going to conduct our own investigation."

I gaped at her. "Your own investigation?"

"Yes! We're not going to let the police arrest Glenda's great-nephew when he's innocent. This isn't a simple murder—there's a mystery behind this and we're going to find out what it is. After all, if Agatha could do it, so can we."

"Who's Agatha?" I said, really lost now.

Mabel looked at me impatiently. "Why, Agatha Christie, of course!"

"Er... But Mabel, you *do* realise that those are all just fictional stories? I mean, she made them up, so of course she knew who the killer was and how the murder was committed. She didn't actually solve any real-life murders."

Mabel waved this away as if it was a minor detail. "I'm sure the principles are the same, dear. When I get back to Meadowford-on-Smythe later, I'm going to speak to Inspector O'Connor myself."

Heaven help Devlin, I thought with a flicker of malicious amusement. It was a bit of retribution for his brusque manner towards me. He was going to suffer at the hands of the Old Biddies... and I was going to enjoy watching it.

"Ooh, Mabel—you must tell us what you find out from the police."

"Yes, and don't forget to mention that Mr Thomas's gnomes have been going missing from his garden—that might be significant."

"What about the sewage leak last month? I thought that was very suspicious."

"Yes, yes, the smell was awful."

"Do you think maybe it was a ritual killing? I mean, you hear about people getting involved in all sorts of dreadful cults—"

"Aren't we all rather jumping at conclusions?" my mother spoke up. "I mean, it sounds like the police have a strong suspect in Mike Bailey already and there's no need for much further investigation."

Mabel frowned. "But there *is* a need! I'm telling you, Mike is innocent. If they arrest him, the real murderer will get away."

"Does Mike have an alibi for Sunday morning?" I asked.

"No," Mabel admitted. "Not really. The poor boy was hungover and was in bed until nearly noon. But he lives alone so there was no one to confirm that. Glenda did speak to him around eleven o'clock when she rang to tell him what had happened at the tearoom."

"That's hardly an alibi," I said gently. "After all, the murder happened around eight-thirty in the morning."

"Well, he told her that he never saw the American again after leaving the pub—he and his friends went to have a curry and then he went home to bed." Mabel nodded emphatically. "And that's what he told the police when they questioned him last night."

"I wonder if the police spoke to anyone else last night," said Dorothy.

"Yes, they did," Justine spoke up for the first time.

"They questioned me."

All eyes turned on her.

"You?" Mabel said, "Why would the police question you?"

"Because..." Justine took a deep breath. "Because Smith is my maiden name. My married name is Washington. The murdered man was called Brad Washington and I was his wife."

CHAPTER ELEVEN

I was still pondering Justine's bombshell as I cycled slowly to Meadowford-on-Smythe a few hours later. *Brad Washington's wife?* I couldn't believe it. But there had been no doubting her cool certainty. She was married to the American—though they were separated and he lived in the U.S. while she lived in Oxford. As his spouse, she was automatically one of the first suspects the police would consider, but she had an alibi for Sunday morning: she had been at a yoga class, which had started at eight and didn't end until nine.

"In any case, why would I want to kill him?" she said with laugh. "Brad and I were separated, but it was an amicable separation. We kept in touch occasionally via email but we hardly saw each other.

I didn't even know he was in Oxford until the police showed up on my doorstep."

Something in the way she said "police" made me wonder if Devlin had been the one who had questioned her. The thought bothered me in a way I couldn't explain.

The book club meeting had deteriorated completely after that, with no one making any attempt to even pretend that they were interested in discussing books. Mabel and the others were practically falling over themselves in their eagerness to pump Justine for information. She dealt with them all expertly—smoothly answering their questions, talking a lot without actually saying much of anything. I'd watched her with admiration. It took some skill to evade Mabel's prying but Justine was a pro.

A woman skilled at hiding the truth, I thought. Or at least, spinning a version of what she wanted the truth to appear to be.

The meeting had finally concluded with the others none the wiser about the details of Justine's marriage, financial affairs, family, or background. Mabel's face had been flushed with frustration as she left my parents' place, although she was no doubt heading straight for Meadowford to share what little she had managed to glean.

I arrived at the Little Stables Tearoom to find that the police had left and Cassie was already there. She was clearing out the fridge, dividing the food into that which could still be used and that which had to either be eaten today or thrown away. I winced to see the amount of food that would go to waste. Because we had been closed for business for nearly two days now, we hadn't gone through our usual supplies, and since I prided myself on the tearoom only serving items which were freshly made, I couldn't save these to be served in the new week. Sighing, I rolled up my sleeves and joined Cassie. As we worked, I told her about the book club meeting and Justine Washington.

"Bloody hell... small world, eh?" She shook her head. "Do you think she's involved?"

"I don't know. She's an interesting woman... I was surprised that she volunteered all that information. But maybe it was actually quite clever of her. She must realise that in a place like Oxford—especially with Mabel Cooke around—the news about her identity would get out soon enough. By being really open and honest about everything, it makes her look less guilty than if she had kept quiet and then it had come out later that the police were questioning her. They obviously have her as one of their suspects for the murder."

"Yeah, and I know a few other suspects the police are considering," said Cassie wryly. "Me and Fletcher."

I stared at her. "You're not serious!"

She made a face. "I am. I had that cocky sergeant chasing me down last night, wanting me to account for my movements on Sunday morning. And he had the gall to say that with my short fuse, I was just the type to murder someone."

I grinned at Cassie. "He's not wrong, you know."

She scowled at me. "The prat just didn't like the way I answered back to him when he was questioning Fletcher yesterday morning." She shrugged. "Anyway, lucky for me, I was over at my parents' place on Saturday night and staying there this whole weekend. Half my brothers and sisters were there too. I wish the sergeant luck interviewing them all to verify my alibi..." She gave an evil chuckle.

"What about Fletcher?"

Her face sobered. "The sergeant's still got it in for him—keeps going on about wanting Fletcher to account for the fact that he turned up at work late. He can't get hold of Ethel to verify Fletcher's alibi: she's gone to visit her nephew in Bath and won't be back for a few days. So until then, I think Fletcher is being treated as a suspect." She sighed. "And Fletcher doesn't help. You know what he's like— having a strange policeman invade his home is bad enough without being bombarded by questions. He ends up acting all nervous, which makes the police think he's guilty... plus he's still upset about Muesli—"

"Has she not turned up yet?" I asked in sudden concern.

Cassie shook her head. I winced and felt slightly guilty for hanging around at home this morning. I should have come to the village early and gone to check on Fletcher.

"Why would they even consider you and Fletcher as suspects? You never met the man before Saturday."

"Well, they seem to be fixated on the scone as the murder weapon, so I suppose they're just going through everyone who could have had access to the scones from the tearoom."

"But that could be half of Oxfordshire, considering all the tourists who pass through here!"

Cassie gave me a curious look. "So the sergeant hasn't been to question you? Interesting. Maybe Devlin has decided to give you special treatment..." She raised an eyebrow suggestively.

"Of course he hasn't," I said, more sharply than I intended. "Why should he? There's nothing between us anymore."

"Did I say there was?" said Cassie with a smile.

I knew that look. "Cass... don't start. You know it's been over eight years since I last saw him."

"Yeah, and I also saw how you looked at each other yesterday when he walked in here. *Phwoar...* I could have lit a bonfire from the sparks in the room. Anyway, there's no expiry date on love."

"Who said anything about love? It was just a stupid college crush."

"College crush? Come off it, Gemma! You may fool everyone else but you can't fool me. Devlin O'Connor was the first man you really loved! You used to talk my ear off about him! You said he was your soulmate, your—"

"That was a long time ago and I was very young," I said quickly. "And okay, maybe he was the first man I had serious feelings for, but—"

"Everyone knows that first love burns the brightest."

"Maybe in books, but not in real life." I changed the subject. "Anyway, Mabel Cooke thinks that the police are making a mess of the investigation and I'm beginning to think that she's right."

"What do you mean?"

"Oh, she thinks they're focusing wrongly on Mike Bailey and letting the real murderer get away."

"Well, she *is* Glenda's friend—and Mike is Glenda's great-nephew—you don't think she might be a little... uh... biased?"

"Maybe. But I still think she's right. The police are missing a lot of connections."

"Like what?"

"Well, like Washington's weird behaviour when he was here on Saturday and those things he said which suggested a past connection with Oxford University—"

Cassie groaned. "Gemma, not that again!"

"I'm telling you, it was not my imagination! I'm sure it's relevant to the murder. Besides, even if I'm wrong about Washington's past, there was that folder with the letter."

"But the police must have found that folder when

they searched Washington's room. There's been no mention of it, has there? Which suggests that maybe it wasn't as significant as you think."

I paused. Cassie was right. If a folder had been discovered with a connection to Oxford University, you can bet that Mabel would have known about it. But she hadn't mentioned it that morning.

I frowned. "That *is* strange. Maybe I should contact Devlin—just to make sure that the police found the folder."

"Are you sure you're not just looking for an excuse to speak to him again?" asked Cassie with a sly smile.

"Cassandra Jenkins! You take that look off your face!"

She laughed. "What look? You're getting awfully defensive—in fact, you're blushing!"

"I am not," I said, as I fought the rising tide of colour in my face. This was ridiculous. I had nothing to be embarrassed about—and I certainly wasn't looking for an excuse to speak to Devlin again. In fact, I had been determined yesterday not to help him at all and not even tell him about Gloucester College and Geoffrey Hughes. But I had to admit—after a good night's sleep—I had calmed down a bit and felt slightly ashamed of my attitude. It seemed spiteful and childish. Whatever my personal feelings were about Devlin, I ought to share relevant information with the police.

"Well, it's probably a good idea to double-check

with the police about the folder. You would just be doing your civic duty," said Cassie kindly. Then she added with an impish smile, "Of course, it's always easier to do your civic duty when it involves speaking to a dashing, sexy, blue-eyed hunk of a detective."

I made a face at her and changed the subject. Cassie left soon after and I finished off on my own. Then, on an impulse, I took out my phone, dialled the number for police headquarters, and asked to be put through to Inspector Devlin O'Connor of Oxfordshire CID. I was informed that he was unavailable, but that they would give him my message. I hung up, resigned to not speaking to him until tomorrow morning, but to my surprise, my phone rang a few minutes later. It was a withheld number. My heart gave a little jolt as I heard Devlin's deep voice on the line.

"Gemma? They said you wanted to speak to me."

He had caught me off guard and I said the first thing that came into my head. "Oh.., I... um... well, I was just... um... I think it's ridiculous the way your sergeant is hounding Fletcher. I told you yesterday that he's sensitive about things and now I hear that your sergeant's been barging into his house, upsetting him with questions and—"

"Gemma."

He didn't raise his voice but I faltered into silence.

Devlin sounded amused. "Did you call me just to give me a lecture about police abuse?"

"No, I... um... there was something else but I do

think that Fletcher—"

He sighed. "My sergeant can be a bit... over-enthusiastic in his approach. I'll have a word with him. Now, you said there was something else?"

"Yes, I... I had some information which might be useful. About the American who was murdered."

There was a pause, then Devlin said, "Where are you at the moment?"

"At the tearoom."

"Okay, shall we meet?"

"Meet?"

"Yes, it's easier sometimes to speak face-to-face. Besides, I haven't had a chance to ask you properly about your movements on Sunday morning yet."

"Oh yes," I said coldly. "So you're adding me to the list of suspects too?"

He gave an impatient sigh. "It's standard police procedure. You know we have to question everyone about their alibis and eliminate all possible suspects."

I was contrite. "Yes, you're right. Sorry."

"Listen, I'm out working on another case at the moment but I should be finished by six. Why don't you come over to my place around then?"

"Your place?"

"Yes—I live just outside Meadowford, actually."

Somehow I had imagined the impersonal neutrality of a police interview room. Going to see Devlin in his own place was a different proposition entirely.

"Gemma?"

"Um… are you sure it's appropriate? I mean, me coming over to your place…"

He sounded amused again. "I promise not to abuse my police powers. Look, I just thought it might be more comfortable than the interview room down at the station. But we can meet there if you wish."

"No, your place is fine," I said. "I'll… I'll see you there at six."

He gave me directions and I hung up. I stood staring at the phone in my hand. A part of me wanted to ring Devlin back and tell him I'd changed my mind—that I would prefer to meet him at the station. Then I squared my shoulders. Why should seeing him alone at his place be a problem? After all, like I'd told Cassie, what Devlin O'Connor and I had was past history. It was over between us.

CHAPTER TWELVE

"Drink?"

Devlin looked at me from across the marble-top bar.

"Thanks—a cup of tea would be nice."

I tried not to watch him as he prowled around the kitchen, his movements lithe and precise. He had always had a beautiful economy of movement, a dynamic grace, and he had retained that, though there seemed to be more control now of that fire and nervous energy which used to emanate from him. Rather than burning at full force, as it had when we were students, it was as if the flames were banked down now and smouldering.

He also kept his emotions much more hidden now and it was hard to tell what he was thinking. For instance, I had no idea how he felt about being alone with me, whereas I wondered if my nervousness and unease were obvious for him to see.

I swivelled away on the bar stool and looked around, to give myself something to do. Devlin's place had been a surprise. He lived in a converted barn, renovated in an expensive but understated style. A soaring hammer beam roof arched overhead. On one side of the large interior space was the gleaming modern kitchen, and on the other side, a spacious living room surrounded by French windows. They were closed and covered by curtains at the moment but I imagined that in the daytime they would give onto sweeping views of the Oxfordshire countryside. An open staircase—the wide gaps between the treads adding to the feeling of light and airiness in the room—led up to the mezzanine level, which no doubt acted as the "bedroom".

It was very much a bachelor pad and I was embarrassed to admit that I was pleased. A part of me had been on tenterhooks as I approached his address, wondering if I would turn up on the doorstep of a three-bedroom semi in some suburban development and find Devlin opening the door with a wife behind him and a toddler hanging onto his leg.

Not that I didn't imagine there wouldn't be women in Devlin's life. Looking back at him surreptitiously, I could see that the years had simply made him more attractive.

"Milk and sugar?"

I started, pulled out of my thoughts. I looked up to meet Devlin's eyes and had the uncanny feeling that he knew what I had been thinking. "Just sugar please. One."

"I see you still take your tea the same way," he said, a smile at the corners of his mouth.

I looked at him in surprise. "You remember?"

"I remember lots of things about you," he said lightly.

I cleared my throat and said quickly, "Um... This is a nice place. How did you find it?"

"The usual way. I looked at some real estate websites and saw that it was for sale. I liked it—so I bought it."

"You bought it?" I was unable to conceal my surprise and I saw him give me a sardonic look.

Knowing the price of properties in the Cotswolds area, this place must have cost a fortune. Where had Devlin got money like that? I didn't know much about police salaries but I doubted that detective inspectors earned enough to afford this kind of property. And Devlin didn't come from money. In fact, his working-class background had been one of the biggest black marks against him from my mother's point of view when we had been together.

I dropped my eyes to the mug, busying myself taking a sip. Inside, however, I was reflecting on how much could change over time. Eight years ago, when things had ended between us, Devlin had been the one struggling to make his way in the world, whilst I revelled in my privileged background. Now, here I was, living back with my parents whilst Devlin swanned around in this luxury country penthouse. If he was the type to crave revenge, how he must have been enjoying the irony of it!

But when I looked back up, I didn't see any gloating in his eyes. Instead, there was some unfathomable expression in them.

He said gently, "You know, Gemma—I think it's really admirable what you've done, giving up your job in Sydney to come back and follow your dream."

I stared at him, my mouth open in surprise. I had been touched by the praise from Ethel but his words really moved me and I felt a sudden lump come to my throat. Embarrassed, I turned away and slid off the stool, walking over to the living room windows. I pushed the curtains aside and stared out into the darkness.

I cleared my throat. "Uh... The view from here must be fantastic."

He didn't answer for a moment, then he took his cue from me and said, "Yes, it's especially beautiful first thing in the morning. You should see what it's like in the early morning light."

For a mad moment, I thought he might ask me to come back and see the view in daylight—and I wondered wildly what my answer would be. Then, as the silence stretched between us, I chided myself for my fanciful thoughts. I was here on business, I reminded myself.

Following that thought, I cleared my throat again and said, "So... you wanted to check my alibi?"

He nodded, his manner changing instantly back to the professional detective. He took me quickly through a series of questions establishing my whereabouts for Sunday morning.

"But you know, this is stupid," I said as we finished. "I mean, Washington was a heavy man and the murderer had to be pretty strong to force that scone down his throat, and hold it down long enough for him to choke. That narrows the search down to big, strong men, doesn't it?"

"Not necessarily," said Devlin. "The forensic pathologist did the post-mortem this morning and I got the report an hour ago. It seems that there is evidence Washington had a stroke sometime in the past which left him with some nerve damage and impaired brain stem function. In particular, it looks like he may have suffered from a condition called dysphagia. It means he had difficulty swallowing and that he was more likely to choke."

"Oh... you know, I remember now... He made a fuss about his sandwiches, insisting that they had to be soft."

Devlin nodded. "Yeah, someone with dysphagia would probably prefer softer foods which are easier to swallow."

"So... you're saying that anyone could have been the murderer?"

"Well, I doubt a child could have done it, but yes, it's very possible that someone smaller and weaker could have been the murderer. They wouldn't even have had to hold him down very long for him to choke and asphyxiate." He looked at me thoughtfully. "In fact, even a determined woman could have done it..."

"You mean, like Justine Washington?"

He stiffened slightly and his expression became guarded. "What do you know about Justine Washington?"

"I know that the spouse is usually one of the first suspects when there's a murder."

Devlin inclined his head. "Yes," he said. "But she has an alibi."

Something in his tone told me that he had met Justine. He must have been the one to question her last night. I felt a prickle of something that was uncomfortably like... jealousy? I pushed the thought away. Don't be stupid. What was there to be jealous of? Devlin wasn't anything to me anymore. I didn't care who he associated with. If he found Justine Washington attractive, that was his business.

"I questioned her last night, right after speaking to Mike Bailey," Devlin continued. "She had no idea that Washington was back in Oxford and she had an alibi for Sunday morning. She was in a yoga class, at the dance studio in Meadowford-on-Smythe."

"I suppose you'll double check that."

Devlin raised an eyebrow, and I flushed.

"My sergeant is doing that tomorrow," he said.

"Just like he will be checking your, Cassie's, and Fletcher's alibis. And before you get on your high horse again, for what it's worth, I don't seriously consider *you* a suspect."

I noticed he didn't include Cassie or Fletcher in that comment.

Devlin leaned forwards. "Now... you said you had some other information for me?"

I told him about Washington's odd comments on Saturday at the tearoom, his aggressive reaction to my handling of the folder, and my suspicion of his past involvement with the University. I half expected Devlin to react with Cassie's scepticism, but to my surprise, he nodded and his eyes gleamed with satisfaction.

"Yes, I'd suspected a connection with the University."

"So you found the folder?"

He frowned. "No, there was no folder on him like you describe. We found his wallet and various cards—credit cards, driver's licence—confirming his name, Brad Washington, and his status as an American citizen."

"The killer must have taken the folder!" I said excitedly. "Which means that there must have been something incriminating in it, something that could point to the identity of the murderer."

"We know Washington arrived in the country via Heathrow last Thursday—the day before he came to your tearoom."

"What about the rest of the tour group? Don't they know anything about him?"

"He wasn't with the tour group. Maybe he gave you that impression on purpose, but he was actually travelling by himself. He just happened to be staying at the same hotel and he happened to come into your tearoom at the same time as the group."

I thought back. Devlin was right. Washington had never specifically said that he was part of that group—it was my own assumption, because they had been American too.

"If you know his name, surely you can find out his background?"

Devlin nodded. "We're doing that now. I've put in a request through Interpol and they're doing a complete background check, but these things can take a bit of time. The preliminary search seems to indicate that Washington was a businessman—he was head of some kind of pharmaceutical company in the States."

"And do you think he was really just here on holiday?"

"I think he wanted people to think so. But I think you're right and he was here on some other business—something connected with Oxford University." He rubbed his jaw thoughtfully. "The question is finding out what."

"Haven't you found out what he was doing when he went into Oxford on Saturday afternoon?"

"No. We managed to trace him as far as the city—

my sergeant spoke to the bus driver who drove him in—but we don't know yet where he went after that."

"I think I do," I said.

Quickly, I told him about my visit to Gloucester College and finding Washington amongst the matriculation photos. Then I told him about my dinner at High Table and Geoffrey Hughes's odd reaction to the news of the murder, as well as finding him in the Matriculation photo next to Washington.

"The letter that was in the folder—I got a glimpse of the signature and I'm sure now that the name was 'Hughes'. They were at Oxford together as graduate students. I think Washington came back to see Hughes."

"That's some pretty good detective work, Gemma," said Devlin. "I'm impressed."

I smiled, feeling absurdly pleased at his praise.

"Right now, I would say that Mike Bailey is our top suspect. He hasn't got an alibi for Sunday morning, he's got a history of violent behaviour, and he was seen assaulting the victim the night before. But I'll check on Hughes tomorrow and find out what he was doing on Sunday morning."

"I just can't believe Mike did it," I said, unconsciously echoing Mabel Cooke. "It seems out of character. I mean, I can see him beating up Washington the night after the pub, but to wait until the next morning and sneak up on the American while he's sitting in my courtyard—and to use a scone... It just doesn't fit!"

"People can surprise you sometimes," said Devlin. "In this job, I've learnt not to make any assumptions about human nature."

There seemed to be nothing more to say and I stood up, conscious of not wanting to appear like I was trying to prolong our meeting. "Um... I'd better get going. My parents will be expecting me to dinner."

He walked me out and watched as I mounted my bicycle. I flashed back suddenly to all those times when Devlin and I had ridden down the cobbled streets of Oxford together, side by side on our bikes. It was hard to stop the constant flood of memories whenever I was around him. *But I have to remember that it's all in the past now,* I told myself fiercely.

I bade him a cool goodbye and cycled away, conscious of his gaze on me the entire time but refusing to let myself look back.

CHAPTER THIRTEEN

I had been concerned that the murder might have affected business but I needn't have worried. If anything, the next morning was the busiest Tuesday we had ever had, probably because—in addition to the tourists—many of the locals had heard the news and come to the tearoom out of vulgar curiosity.

And they weren't the only ones. The press were already out in force, surrounding the tearoom like vultures. One reporter even had the cheek to pretend to be a customer and take a table inside, all in an attempt to get an interview with me or Cassie.

"No comment," I said in response to his questions, as I stood next to the table with an order pad.

"But you must have something to say," he said persuasively. He was a young man in his early twenties, with a lean, hungry look on his face. And I don't mean for food. "We're just interested in your reactions, that's all. No need for facts about the investigation or anything. You were the one who found the body, weren't you? What was it like? Was it a terrible shock?" He leaned forwards and lowered his voice to a dramatic whisper. "Was there a lot of blood?"

I stepped back and regarded him with distaste. "As I said, no comment. Now, unless you're going to order something from the menu, I'm going to have to ask you to leave—"

"Aw, don't be like that—I just wanted a few words!"

"You want a few words, young man? I'll give you a few words." Mabel stood up from the next table where she and the other Old Biddies had obviously been listening.

The reporter turned to her eagerly. "Yes? Were you a witness as well?"

"Oh yes, and I even met the victim the day before." Mabel nodded emphatically.

"Really? What was he like?" The reporter's tongue was practically hanging out.

"Flatulent."

"Er... fla...flatulent?" He looked bewildered.

Mabel nodded. "Yes, I didn't actually hear him break wind, you understand, but I could tell just by the tone of his skin. Not enough fibre in his diet. I'm sure of it. Now, all he really needed was to take a spoon of bran every morning—just like Mr Cooke does. My doctor recommended this marvellous stuff for my Henry. Particularly if you're constipated or if your haemorrhoids are acting up. No need for laxatives to hurry things along." She looked at the reporter intently. "Do you go regularly, young man?"

"I... er..." He leaned away from her. "Actually, you know, I've just remembered that I've got an appointment..." He began to rise from his seat.

"Wait..." said Mabel. "I haven't finished my story. You haven't heard the part about my day at the colonoscopy department—"

"That's... that's okay," gasped the reporter as he scrambled to collect his things. "I've got more than enough here. Thank you!"

And he bolted out of the tearoom. I didn't know whether to laugh or cry. Maybe I should have hired Mabel and her friends as a special team of geriatric bouncers to guard the tearoom!

However, the Old Biddies weren't able to protect me from all the malicious media interest and, as the morning wore on, I was a bit disturbed to look through the windows and see several people being interviewed outside. They were mostly residents from the local area who may have been in the tearoom once or twice—and obviously felt that that qualified them to comment on the murder investigation. They were pointing eagerly at the tearoom as they talked and, from the rapt expression on the reporters' faces, I had a bad feeling that the stories being told were based more on sensationalism than truth. The fact was, people loved their fifteen minutes of fame and if they got it by repeating juicy gossip—no matter how far-fetched—they didn't care. It made me uneasy, though, wondering what was being said about me and my tearoom...

Devlin appeared just before lunch and the reporters and camera crew swarmed around him as he walked up to the front door. He fended them off with practised ease and strolled in, his tall figure instantly dominating the room. I tried to ignore the little jolt my heart gave when I saw him. I noticed that many of the female customers watched him with interest as he walked across to me at the counter.

"I thought you'd like to know: we've checked your alibis—yours and Cassie's—and you're clear."

I wondered why Devlin had come in person—he could simply have rung—but I was too pleased to care. Then I remembered something. "What about Fletcher?"

He frowned. "We haven't managed to get hold of Ethel Webb yet—she's still in Bath, it seems. We've left messages for her. Until she can verify his alibi, Fletcher is still under suspicion. No one else saw him in the village that morning so no one can verify that he left the house at the time he said he did."

"But... that's ridiculous!" I cried angrily. "You can't seriously suspect Fletcher! He wouldn't hurt a lamb—"

Devlin compressed his lips. "Gemma... we've been

through this before. I can't afford to treat anybody differently. And he did behave out of character on the morning of the murder."

"Oh, for God's sake—he was late because he overslept! Hundreds of people all over the country do that every day! He'd had a bad night because his cat was missing and he probably didn't get to bed until very late."

"We still have to verify his alibi," said Devlin, unmoved.

I heaved a sigh. "Fine. But you're just wasting time on this when you should be chasing other leads."

"Real detective work is about checking every detail—not just rushing off after 'exciting' leads," Devlin said mildly. Then he glanced around the room and changed the subject. "I see that business hasn't been affected..."

"Not yet, anyway." I shot a worried look at the press camped outside the windows. "Yes, so far, it's actually helped business, I think. I never realised people had so much appetite for ghoulish entertainment! Locals who had never bothered to pop in before were suddenly here this morning, asking me for a table near where the murder had happened. They all seemed to be really disappointed when I told them that it was out in the courtyard."

Devlin grinned. "Shame the body couldn't have been found in here. Then you could have had a chalk outline on the floor and arranged tables around it so that people could have their afternoon tea with a side of murder scene."

I shook my head at him. "How can you make jokes about something like this?"

Devlin shrugged. "In my line of work, you have to make jokes sometimes. It's a coping mechanism, in a way. Otherwise you could never deal with all the darkness and pain that we see. Doctors do it too— it's called gallows humour."

I suppose he was right. And I had to admit, it *was* hard to feel much remorse for someone as unpleasant as Washington. Still, he must have been missed by *someone?* I thought of Justine Washington, with her sensual glamour and cool poise. I wondered if she missed her husband and grieved for his death. I knew that they were separated and she wasn't even living in the same country as him, but surely you must feel *some*thing for someone you had once been married to? Though they did seem to be truly estranged. After all, it seemed very odd for Washington to come all the way to England and not even bother to look up his wife...

I started to say something but a crooked finger tapped Devlin on the shoulder. He turned around to find himself facing Mabel Cooke, her arms folded, surrounded by the other three Old Biddies.

"Young man, I have some information for you," Mabel said.

"Yes, Mrs Cooke?"

"The victim's wife—Justine Washington—I met

her on Monday at a book club meeting."

"Yes?"

Mabel jutted her chin out. "She told us that she didn't know the American was in Oxford—that she only found out when the police went to question her after the murder."

"That's right."

Mabel jabbed him in the chest with her finger. "Well, she's lying, Inspector. I know for a fact that she met him on Saturday night at a bar in Oxford."

Devlin looked at her sharply. "How do you know this?"

Mabel sniffed. "I've got my sources."

I had to hide a smile as I saw the look of frustration on Devlin's face.

"Mrs Cooke, I'm afraid if you can't provide me with good reason of why you think Justine Washington had met the victim, I can't just take your word—"

"You tell that gormless sergeant of yours to go and ask the staff at Freud's," said Mabel. "Show them a photo of the American and his wife. I'm sure you'll get confirmation that they were there, late on Saturday night."

Devlin stared at her for a moment, then he gave a curt nod, muttered a goodbye to me, and left the tearoom.

I looked at Mabel. "Is it true? Are you sure?"

"Of course I'm sure."

So Justine *had* been lying. What else was she lying about? Her alibi? I thought back to Monday morning and that cool woman I'd met. Could I envisage her committing murder? *Oh yes.* Justine was the kind of woman who wouldn't let anything stand in her way. She would kill someone in cold blood—and not even soil her designer dress while at it.

But what about Geoffrey Hughes? I still couldn't shake off my gut feeling that the mystery of the murder was somehow connected to Oxford University. Hughes had behaved very oddly at High Table on Sunday night—I was convinced that he knew more than he was telling about Washington and the murder.

Whatever Devlin might say about Mike Bailey, I didn't think this murder was just due to a hot-headed argument which ended with an assault gone bad.

CHAPTER FOURTEEN

My parents were out that evening and I enjoyed a solitary early dinner without my mother's incessant commentary on my life. I had decided to go for a jacket potato: there's nothing like the simple, home-cooked aroma of a potato baking in the oven, and when it came out, the skin browned to a perfect crunch, I cut it open and covered the steaming, fluffy interior with a rich topping of butter, baked beans, and cheddar cheese grated on top. It was delicious.

Afterwards, I helped myself to a couple of Jaffa Cakes—something I'd missed terribly during my eight years in Australia—from the pantry, then retreated upstairs to my bedroom. While not as exciting as solving a murder, I had a few more mundane problems which posed a much more immediate threat to my well-being than a killer on the loose. Like the weeks' worth of dirty laundry which was sitting in a pile in the corner of my room. Normally, I would have just tossed the whole lot into the washing machine but my mother had an almost religious devotion to care labels and it would have been tantamount to sacrilege in her house. So I sighed and resigned myself to an evening of sorting out whites from colours, woollens from delicates.

But as I started tidying my room and making sure that I had nothing else to add to the laundry pile, I realised that my pashmina scarf was missing. Aside from the fact that it was a fairly expensive purchase, it had sentimental value for me—it was the special treat I had bought myself with my very first pay cheque. Alarmed, I searched in my handbag, the chest of drawers, the wardrobe, the chair beside my bed... but couldn't find it anywhere.

I sat down on my bed and thought of my movements over the weekend. I was sure I had been wearing it when I went to dinner at Gloucester College on Sunday night. In fact, I remembered draping it over my shoulder and looking at myself in the mirror before I left my room. And the next day? I frowned. I couldn't remember but I knew I wouldn't have worn it to the tearoom—I tended to dress much more casually there, especially as I had planned to do some cleaning and tidying up on Monday.

So I must have left it at Gloucester College on Sunday night. Feeling annoyed with myself, I got up and glanced at the clock. It wasn't late—I could pop down to Gloucester College and try to find it. Tossing a sweater around my shoulders, I grabbed my handbag and headed out of the house.

It was just past eight o'clock when I stepped through the main gate of Gloucester College and I could see several students walking across the quad, taking off their gowns as they went. They must have just finished Formal Hall. I ran lightly up the steps into the Porter's Lodge and went up to the old-fashioned wooden counter with sliding glass windows. A kindly-looking man in his sixties, wearing the traditional black suit of the college porters, gave me a smile and said, "Can I help you, luv?"

I explained about my pashmina and asked if anyone might have dropped it into their lost property box. He shook his head regretfully.

"There's been nothing of that description brought in. Where did you lose it?"

"I'm not sure," I said. "I was here last Sunday night for dinner at High Table and I think I might have lost it then."

"Have you looked in the Senior Common Room?"

"No... I thought someone would have brought it in here if they'd found it."

"If it was something in the S.C.R., the fellows might not have turned it in because they wouldn't consider it student property. They might just leave it in the Common Room thinking that one of the other fellows would retrieve it. Why don't you go along there and see?"

I thanked him for his help and made my way to the S.C.R., which was housed in the northwest tower of the main quadrangle. It was quieter in the college tonight, perhaps because it was a weekday and most students would be at various University clubs, society meetings, or parties, if not studying in their rooms (based on my own experiences, more likely the former than the latter).

My steps echoed hollowly as I climbed the wooden staircase up to the SCR and knocked on the heavy oak door. There was no answer. I pushed it open slowly. The room was empty, a fire burning down to the embers in the grate. I saw my pink pashmina almost instantly. It was draped across the back of one of the leather wingback chairs by the fireplace. I hurried across the room, grabbed it, and was out again in less than a minute. However, as I was about to make my way back down the staircase, I heard the sound of furtive whispering.

I paused and glanced up.

The staircase continued upwards into the tower, probably to various dons' private rooms where they would hold their tutorials. I wondered if perhaps a couple of students were huddled there, waiting to speak to their tutor. But the voices sounded too mature to be students. In fact, I realised, they sounded slightly familiar.

Curious, I turned around and mounted a few

steps of the next flight of stairs, peering upwards into the dimly lit stairwell. I saw four shapes huddled on the next landing, talking in loud whispers. They sounded like they were having an argument. My eyes widened in disbelief as I realised who they were. The Old Biddies, including Ethel who must have come back from Bath that afternoon.

I ran up to join them. "What are you doing here?" I hissed.

They froze and stared at me, like rabbits caught in headlights.

"Gemma!" said Mabel Cooke at last. "How lovely to see you, dear," she said, as if it was perfectly normal for her to be skulking about a college staircase every day.

"What are you doing here?" I repeated.

Mabel glanced at her friends and they all looked at me with equally guilty expressions. I had a sudden impression I was facing four naughty children, rather than four members of the senior generation.

"Well, you know... we just happened to see him... and we thought we'd tag behind..."

"Just a bit of curiosity..."

"Not that we were following him or anything..."

"No, no, of course not..."

"Following whom?" I said, confused.

Mabel threw a furtive look up the staircase to the next landing, then turned back to me and lowered her voice. "Detective Inspector O'Connor!"

"Devlin?"

"Shh!"

"You're stalking the inspector?"

"Not stalking," said Mabel indignantly. "We were just out in Oxford— it's Seniors Night at the Old Fire Station, you know—and we happened to see Inspector O'Connor... so we... uh... followed him for a bit and saw him walking into Gloucester College. Of course, we knew all about the murdered American having come here to meet one of the professors—"

"How did you know...?" I sighed. "Never mind."

"We were sure Inspector O'Connor must have come to interview this professor," said Florence eagerly.

Ethel nodded. "A suspect in the murder case!"

"Yes, so we hurried up right behind him and were just in time to hear him tell the porter at the gate that he had an appointment with Professor Hughes."

"But how did you get into the college? Don't tell me you managed to pass yourselves off as students," I said.

Glenda giggled. "Oh, well, the porter—Roger—is one of my beaus."

"Your... beau?" I didn't think people used that word anymore.

She nodded, giggling again like a schoolgirl. "Yes, I go dancing with Roger. Nimble on his feet, he is, for such a big man. And you know, it's true what they say about a man being as good in bed as he is on the dance floor..."

Ugh. I shut my eyes briefly. Okay, that definitely

fell into the category of Too Much Information. Whatever else I might have been curious about, I did not need to know about the active sex life of little old ladies.

"So Roger let you in," I said quickly.

"Yes, I promised him a private dance later as a thank you," said Glenda with a wink.

Double ugh. "And you followed Devlin here?"

Mabel nodded. "We saw him go up and heard him being received by someone. A man." She jerked her chin upwards towards the next landing. "He's just gone in." She turned to the others. "Come on."

"Wait—what are you going to do?" I put a hand on her arm.

She looked at me like I was stupid. "Eavesdrop on their conversation, of course!"

They began to creep up the staircase, clutching their linen handkerchiefs and lavender patent leather handbags. I stared at them, feeling like I was in a *Pink Panther* movie or something. Were they seriously going to eavesdrop on the interview?

I turned around and started to descend, but I hadn't gone two steps when I paused. I wanted badly to hear Devlin's conversation with Geoffrey Hughes. I looked back up the staircase. Was I going to be bested by four little old ladies, just because I was scared of doing the "wrong" thing? Yes, my mother had always hammered it into me that it was Terribly Rude To Eavesdrop—but so what? What had happened to my new determination to take risks and live a little dangerously?

I whirled and hurried up the staircase after the Old Biddies. I found them on the top landing, literally pressing their ears against the large oak door. It was such a ridiculous sight that I almost laughed out loud. Instead, I took my position next to them and pressed my own ear against the door too.

I heard nothing.

As was common with the fittings in most Oxford colleges, this door was a sturdy antique, carved of solid timber, and had probably withstood prying ears for centuries.

"It's no use—we can't hear anything through this door," I whispered to Mabel. "We might as well just give up."

She gave me a look of disdain and put her hand on the door handle.

"Mabel—!" I stared at her in disbelief.

Very, very slowly, she turned the handle. I was impressed someone of her age could have such steady hands. She managed to ease the door open a tiny crack—enough so that we could hear but not enough that anyone would have noticed that the door was open, unless they were specifically looking.

Thankfully, it seemed that Devlin was not specifically looking. I waited with bated breath but no one sprang up and came to see who had opened the door. Instead, we were suddenly able to hear the rumble of conversation inside. From the sound of it, Devlin had finished the preliminary background questions and was now asking Hughes about last Saturday afternoon.

"Yes, Brad Washington did come to see me. We used to be at Oxford together, many years ago. He had a new business venture that he was inviting me to invest in. We talked about it for a while, then he left at around five o'clock."

"And did you decide to invest in his new venture?"

There was a pause. "No, I decided that it wasn't for me."

"Any special reason?"

"N-no... You must understand, Inspector, that I am a world expert on this class of drugs and I'm constantly being asked to take part in research trials or get involved in some new product development. One can't take part in everything so one must pick and choose."

Devlin seemed to change tack. "So Brad Washington was an old friend—an academic colleague, I understand?"

"Yes, we both arrived at Gloucester College as graduates, to do a DPhil in Pharmacology. We worked together, actually, on the same research project. But we haven't seen each other in fifteen years."

"So why should he suddenly contact you now?"

"I already told you—to tell me about his new venture."

"Yes, but he must have had any number of new ventures in the past decade. Why only this one now?"

"I'm afraid you would have to ask him that."

"I can't do that. As you know very well, he's dead."

There was a pause.

"Yes, of course."

"And you never thought of contacting the police? You were probably one of the last people to see him alive."

"I... er... I didn't think our meeting would have any relevance. I heard a rumour that he had got into a fight with some local drunk and the man killed him later in retribution."

"Is that behaviour what you would expect of Washington? Getting into fights?"

There was a humourless laugh. "Yes, Washington had a big mouth and he wasn't afraid to use it. He was just the type to get into a fight with some local yob, especially if he started throwing money around."

"Had a lot of it, did he?"

"Well, when he left Oxford, he went back to the States with some of the findings of our research and—as the saying goes—made his fortune."

"So you were both here together, in the same field, and then he goes off and benefits enormously from the research you did together. Didn't you feel resentful?"

"No, why should I? He chose a life of commerce and I chose academia."

Devlin circled back. "So you had a discussion and then he left and you never saw Washington again?"

"I already told you. Yes, that was the last time I saw him."

"I still find it curious that you didn't come forward to the police. We made it very clear on the evening news that we were appealing to anyone with information on the victim."

"Yes, well..." Hughes's voice was uncomfortable. "Suppose I ought to have, but you know how it is... No one wants to get involved with the police, unless they have to."

"That's not been my experience at all," Devlin said dryly. "In my experience, the public love getting involved and are very keen to help with a murder enquiry. If anything, we usually have more hassle sorting through all the 'helpful' tips and phone calls we receive, full of unnecessary information. It tends to only be those with something to hide who don't want to speak to the police."

"Well, I have nothing to hide..." blustered Hughes.

"Good."

There was a tense silence. I couldn't see into the room but I didn't need to be in there to guess that Devlin was probably giving Hughes one of his famous steely-eyed looks.

"Your face is very swollen, Professor. Have you been in a fight?"

"No, I've got an allergy. I'm very sensitive to pet hairs and my neighbours just got a new puppy. They brought it over to show me on Sunday—it licked my face and I just started puffing up."

"I see. Isn't it a coincidence that this happened on Sunday—the same day that your friend, Washington, was murdered?"

"I don't know what you're getting at. I'm telling you, this swelling is due to an allergy. I can't go near pet hairs. I have to take prescription anti-histamines to control the reaction."

"And have you taken any this time?"

"I took some on Sunday night, once I realised... but it takes time for the symptoms to subside. Sometimes as much as forty-eight hours."

"Hmm... Well, Professor Hughes, that will be all for now. I may have some more questions to ask you but, for now, thank you for your time. Here's my card... If there's anything else you think of..."

There was a rustle from inside the room, the sound of people standing up, the floorboards creaking as weight shifted. Then footsteps approached the door, faster than we expected.

Mabel jerked back from the door. "He's coming out!"

CHAPTER FIFTEEN

I stumbled backwards in panic. There was no time to run down the staircase—Devlin would be sure to see us in the stairwell. We looked wildly around for a hiding place. This was the top landing in the tower and there was only one other door up here. Mabel ran across and flung it open. It was a broom cupboard, filled with cleaning equipment.

"Quick! In here!" she hissed at the other Old Biddies. They piled in, wedging themselves between the mops and brooms. I was amazed at how quickly four old ladies could squeeze themselves into such a tiny space, lavender handbags and all. The only problem was, it left no room for me.

"Sorry, Gemma, age before beauty," said Mabel ruthlessly and she yanked the door shut in my face.

I stared at the closed door in disbelief. *What? They're leaving me out here to deal with Devlin alone? I'm going to kill them, senior age or not!*

Whirling, I considered my options. I could hear the rumble of voices coming from Hughes's room—it looked like they had stopped to talk again just inside the door. It bought me a few more seconds reprieve. I glanced around. The only other thing I could see on the landing was a narrow Gothic window. I ran over and pulled the casement open. Instead of the sheer drop I'd expected, it led out onto a circular battlement which enclosed the tower. If I could climb out, I could crouch beneath the level of the parapet and hide from view until Devlin had gone down the stairs.

It was ludicrous and humiliating but not unsafe. I hooked a leg over the windowsill and started to push myself out through the narrow gap. It wasn't as easy as I'd thought. I was sitting astride the windowsill, half in, half out, trying to suck my stomach in—when I heard the dreaded voice.

"Gemma?"

Oh bugger. I froze, then slowly turned my head.

Devlin stood on the landing, looking at me in bewilderment. "What on earth are you doing?"

I thought of Mabel's trick and tried to act like climbing out of Oxford college windows was a perfectly normal mid-week activity for me. I gave a little trill of laughter. It was scary how much I sounded like my mother. "Ah, Devlin, ha-ha... Fancy seeing you here!"

It didn't seem to work. He came towards me, frowning. "What are you doing?"

"Um..." I wracked my brain for some excuse to explain my window-straddling position. I came up with nothing. "I... um... I was looking for my... pashmina! Yes, I've lost my pashmina, you see—and I thought I might have left it here when I came to High Table last Sunday night."

"And your pashmina managed to get by itself all the way up to the parapet outside Professor Hughes's room?" Devlin raised a sardonic eyebrow.

I flushed. "Yes... well... Funny how things end up in the strangest places."

"And I suppose you didn't know that I was interviewing Professor Hughes?"

"Oh, were you?" I opened my eyes wide, the picture of innocence. "What a funny coincidence!"

"Yes, isn't it?" Devlin said. "And I suppose it's also a funny coincidence that the door to his room was slightly open—when I knew I had definitely shut it firmly behind me when I arrived?"

"Oh... you know how draughty it can get in these old Oxford buildings..." I gave him a bright smile. "Probably the door didn't latch properly when you shut it and the wind pushed it open again."

"And naturally you didn't happen to overhear any part of my conversation with Professor Hughes..."

"Well... um... you know, the landing being so small... I did maybe overhear a bit of the conversation... not that I was really listening, of course..."

"Of course not," said Devlin blandly.

A muffled sneeze sounded next to us. Devlin turned sharply towards the broom cupboard. We could hear the sounds of shuffling coming from inside, accompanied by whispers of:

"Move over!"

"I can't! You move over!"

"There's no room!"

"It's your stupid handbag, Glenda! I told you not to buy that style."

"It's not my handbag, it's your bottom! You need to lose some weight, Florence."

"Rubbish!"

"Shh—they'll hear us!"

Devlin muttered under his breath, then stepped over and pulled the cupboard door open. It revealed four little old ladies clutching each other.

"Eeek!"

"Inspector O'Connor! What a surprise!" Mabel let go of the others and stepped out, recovering spectacularly.

Devlin gave a deep sigh. "Yes, another one. I don't think I can cope with any more surprises tonight. I suppose you were searching for Gemma's pashmina in the broom cupboard?"

Mabel darted a look at me. "Why, yes... of course! How clever of you to guess that! But of course, that's why you're such a brilliant detective... ha ha..."

They filed out, brushing themselves off and patting their helmet hair.

"Mrs Cooke..." Devlin sounded like he was making a huge effort to stay calm. "I appreciate your attempts to help the police but, as I have said before, I must ask you to leave the investigation to the professionals. You don't know what you are doing and you may get yourself—" he glanced at the others, "—and your friends hurt."

Maybe it was his tone or the hard look in his blue eyes, but for once, Mabel seemed to decide that it was better to hold her tongue and they shuffled, looking suitably chastened, back down the stairs. Devlin escorted us all back to the gate, and stood with his arms folded, watching as the Old Biddies trundled off together down the cobbled lane. I turned away to get my bicycle from the bike shed beside the Porters Lodge, but as I began to wheel it out of the college gates, Devlin came up to me and put a hand on my arm.

"Gemma, before you run off... fancy a drink?"

I looked at him in surprise. What was this? A social invitation? Or an excuse for further police interrogation? I hesitated, then gave a nod. "Okay."

He walked with me out of the college and down the lane. As we approached the corner of Broad Street, he jerked his head towards the King's Arms. "How about the K.A.?"

I hesitated again, then straightened my shoulders. If Devlin could go back to an old haunt without a flicker of feeling, then I could match his cool detachment. "Yes, fine."

I chained my bicycle to a post outside the building that housed the oldest pub in Oxford, then we went in. I caught my breath as I stepped over the threshold. It was as if I had stepped back in time. The long, wood-panelled bar was still there, with the lettered signs along the top casing advertising "Young's Stout" and "Addlestones Premium Cloudy Cider"; the dark, cosy rooms were filled with what looked like the same vintage leather sofas and sturdy wood chairs that I had once lounged on as a student; the familiar black-and-white photos, and old prints of Oxford hung on the walls. How many times had I stepped in here, just like this, with Devlin at my side, his hand on my elbow?

I shook off the memories and walked into the pub, deliberately taking a seat in the middle of the room, away from the cosy, intimate corners.

"What shall I get you—a shandy?"

I felt a silly rush of pleasure at him remembering my usual drink. "Yes, thanks."

He went off to the bar and I had ample time to compose myself by the time he came back with two glasses. I was also ready with some questions about the case, to save myself having to make awkward small talk.

"So... does Professor Hughes have an alibi for Sunday morning?"

Devlin took a swallow of his pint and regarded me

sardonically. "Has Mabel Cooke assigned you the task of pumping me for information?"

I grinned, relaxing slightly. "No, this is just my own nosiness."

He matched my grin with a boyish one of his own, looking suddenly a lot younger and making my heart give an unsteady flop.

"Yes, I had my sergeant check Hughes's alibi this morning—before I questioned him. The prof says he was in college, marking some essays in his room, and that seems to bear out. My sergeant spoke to a student, Tom Rawlings, who heard Hughes in his room, arguing with someone on the phone, at the time when Washington would have been murdered."

"So he's in the clear?" I said in disappointment.

"Well, I wouldn't say that. Hughes is definitely hiding something. But as far as his alibi goes, it certainly seems to check out." Devlin motioned to his phone. "I rang my sergeant before I left Hughes's room and asked him to check the story about the pet allergy and the anti-histamines."

"For what it's worth, Hughes's face did look slightly swollen when I saw him at dinner at High Table on Sunday night," I offered.

Devlin nodded. "I didn't think it looked like the kind of swelling you get from a fight injury—but of course, it never hurts to check. I'm not really expecting anything, though. If it had been Mike Bailey with a swollen face, that would have been a different story."

"Is he still your strongest suspect?"

"Yes."

"And..." I hesitated. "What about Justine?"

"What about her?" Devlin said, taking another mouthful of his ale.

"Did you check what Mabel said—about her meeting Washington on Saturday night in Oxford?"

"Yes." Devlin paused as if debating what to tell me, then he said, "Justine confessed that she did meet Washington. She hadn't wanted to mention it before because she knew that spouses were always one of the key suspects in a murder case, particularly when a spouse stands to gain by the victim's death."

I raised my eyebrows enquiringly.

"As his wife and without a will stating otherwise, Justine is the beneficiary of Washington's entire estate."

"Wow." I sat back in my chair. "That's enough motive for most people."

Devlin said nothing. I looked at him sharply.

"There's something else, isn't there? Another good reason for Justine to want Washington dead?"

Devlin inclined his head reluctantly. "She said that the reason she saw Washington on Saturday night was because he requested a meeting. He wanted a divorce. They were separated, but Justine had always balked at an actual divorce and Washington didn't seem to mind before. They've been living apart for the last couple of years, although he still supported her with a regular allowance."

A very generous allowance, I thought to myself, remembering Justine's designer clothes and expensive hair and make-up. And she obviously didn't work either. *I'll bet she wasn't happy to hear that Washington wanted a divorce.*

"I suppose those payments would have stopped once they were divorced?" I said.

"Yes. They had some kind of pre-nup agreement which stated that Justine wouldn't get any alimony payments unless they had children. They didn't. But it seemed that Washington was quite happy to keep the status quo until recently. We got some information back from Interpol," said Devlin. "It seems that Washington had a new girlfriend back in the States and she was putting pressure on him to get a divorce. Sounds like she was angling for his ring on her own finger."

"So Justine would have been left high and dry," I said. "Whereas now, instead, with Washington dead, she's a very rich widow."

Devlin drained his pint and sat back. "Yes. But at the end of the day, she has an alibi for Sunday morning. However much she might have wanted to kill Washington, the fact is, she couldn't have done it because she was somewhere else when the murder was committed." He shook his head. "In any case, I don't think it's her."

"How do you know?"

He shrugged. "Instinct. A hunch. Whatever you want to call it."

Lust, I thought sourly. I wondered if Devlin would have been so quick to insist that Justine was innocent if she didn't look like Jessica Rabbit come to life.

"Speaking of alibis..." Devlin said. "I thought you'd like to know that my sergeant managed to get hold of Ethel Webb at last and she confirms that she saw Fletcher leaving his house at 8:45 a.m.—which was after the murder was committed. So he's in the clear."

"Ohhh... he'll be so pleased to hear that," I said, smiling. "I'll tell him first thing tomorrow morning. It's been weighing on him, you know, especially with his cat going missing too."

"His cat?" Devlin raised an eyebrow

"Don't sneer," I said quickly. "His cat means a lot to him. Fletcher's very shy and he... he doesn't relate to people very well."

"I'm not sneering," said Devlin. "In fact, I've seen first-hand some cases where people are more upset to lose their pet than their spouse. And I've met many people who prefer the company of animals to humans. I have to say, though, I've always been more of a dog person, myself."

"Yeah, me too," I agreed. "In fact, until I met Muesli, I wouldn't have ever said I like cats... but... well, she sort of worms her way into your heart," I said with a laugh. "She's naughty and infuriating and mouthy and contrary... and generally drives me mad... but I can't help but like her."

"Sounds like someone I know."

I looked at him quickly but he had glanced away and was scanning the room, observing the other punters.

"So... you're still pegging Mike Bailey for the murder?" I said after an awkward pause. "It just seems so crude and simple—that Washington was killed as the result of some drunken brawl. It feels like it ought to be more complicated than that!"

"Real life often *is* crude and simple," said Devlin. "It's only in books and movies that they make it so romantic and complicated."

CHAPTER SIXTEEN

I got to the tearoom early the next morning. Fletcher was already there, making Chelsea buns. I joined him and we worked together in a companionable silence. Baking was definitely not a natural talent for me but Fletcher was a great teacher—patient, repetitive, his explanations simple—and since I'd started working with him, I found myself growing in confidence (and actually producing something edible) under his guidance.

Now as I kneaded the sticky dough and then spread it out and sprinkled the cinnamon, raisins, currants, and rich muscovado sugar across the surface before rolling it into a tight coil, I mulled over the mystery. It was partly to occupy my thoughts, otherwise I found them straying constantly to last night and the drink I had had with Devlin in the King's Arms—recalling each expression on his face, each gesture that he made, each nuance in his voice...

I pushed the memory away and dragged my mind back to the case. Mike Bailey. Justine Washington. Geoffrey Hughes. Each with a motive or an opportunity to kill Washington.

Mike Bailey was the obvious suspect, with his history of violent behaviour and his actual assault on the victim the night before. And he had no alibi for the morning of the murder. And yet, to me, he seemed the least likely candidate for the killer. It seemed too simplistic, too obvious—and it ignored all the other questions, such as Washington's enigmatic connection to Oxford University. But what if the answer really *was* that simple? I remembered Devlin's comment about how most crimes are just simple and crude—not the convoluted mysteries featured in books and movies. People killed each other all the time for the most mundane of reasons. Maybe I didn't want to accept it simply because I preferred the romantic idea of a complex murder mystery full of hidden secrets from the past.

What about Justine Washington? She *had* an alibi—but she also had a very good reason for wanting Washington dead. His demand for a divorce would have killed off the regular support payments and destroyed the cushy lifestyle she had become used to. Instead, she was now a very rich woman, the sole beneficiary of his entire estate. Yes, Washington's murder had worked out very well in Justine's favour. Devlin was vehement in his belief that the beautiful American wasn't guilty, but could his instincts be trusted where Justine was concerned?

And what about Professor Geoffrey Hughes? I had to admit that my personal impression of the man hadn't been a good one. That tight pursed mouth, those small, cold eyes behind the wire-rimmed spectacles... yes, I could imagine Hughes committing murder. And his connection to the victim's old college fit the mystery much better. On the face of it, he didn't seem to have a strong motive for wanting Washington dead, but who knew what the man was still hiding? I was certain that Hughes hadn't told Devlin everything about that "new venture" which Washington had been trying to get him to invest in. The murder must have been somehow connected with that—and with the University. It was just too much of a coincidence that Washington should come—furtively—to Oxford to speak to Hughes and then be killed by some random drunk he met in a pub...

But Hughes had an alibi, I reminded myself. Devlin said his sergeant had checked it earlier yesterday and a student—what was his name? Oh yes, Tom Rawlings—had confirmed that Hughes was in his college room during the time of the murder. The sergeant had also rung Devlin as we were leaving the King's Arms last night, confirming that he had verified Hughes's pet allergy story: the neighbours did indeed take their new Labrador puppy over to show Hughes on Sunday and the pharmacy confirmed that the Pharmacology professor had a standing prescription for a strong anti-histamine. So it looked like, so far, everything Hughes had told the police was the truth.

But still, I just couldn't trust him. He was hiding something—or lying about something... I paused suddenly in what I was doing. What if his alibi *was* somehow faked? After all, he had lied about meeting Washington on Saturday—who was to say he hadn't lied about his alibi as well? If we removed the assumption that he had a solid alibi for the murder, then all the other facts began to form a suggestive pattern...

I was still pondering this when Cassie arrived a few minutes later and we began preparing to open the tearoom for business. I'd been happily expecting a repeat of yesterday's flood of customers and was slightly taken aback when ten o'clock crept around and we still only had two people come in—one just for a cup of takeaway coffee at that.

"Bit slow today, isn't it?" commented Cassie from where she was perched on a stool behind the counter, drawing something on her sketchpad. I looked at the pile of completed sketches next to her, an indication of how quiet things were.

"That's the understatement of the year," I said

with a sigh. I frowned and looked out of the tearoom windows. "I don't understand it. Yesterday we were mobbed, and I would have thought that all that vulgar curiosity would have taken another few days to die down, at least..."

By lunchtime, I was becoming really concerned. I glanced at the clock: 1:15 p.m., usually the peak lunch hour. I looked around the room. Only one table was occupied. We had had our quiet days, of course, since we opened, and I had learned to cope with the ups and downs of a food business. But it had never been this bad. Today, the tearoom was dead.

As I was standing at the counter, staring at the empty room in front of me and trying not to worry, Cassie stormed in the front door, her face flushed and angry. She had popped down to the post office to pick up some stamps and I saw now that she was brandishing a tabloid newspaper in her fist.

"Absolute bloody tossers!" she snarled. "I'm going to kill whoever wrote this!"

"What, Cassie? What is it?" I cried, springing up in alarm.

She slammed the newspaper down on the counter in front of me. "Here! This is why we don't have any customers today!"

I looked down and recoiled in horror. On the front page of the newspaper was a picture of my tearoom accompanied by the lurid headline:

KILLER SCONES AT COTSWOLDS TEAROOM!

My eyes continued down the page, not wanting to read the words but unable to stop myself.

Death struck a quaint Cotswolds village last weekend when an American tourist was found murdered at the Little Stables Tearoom. But even more shocking was the discovery that the victim had choked on the very scones offered on the tearoom menu.

"I've eaten there several times—I had no idea that their scones were so dangerous," says one patron.

"The owner is new to the village and I heard that she's come back from overseas. Full of fancy foreign ideas and such. One wonders what she's putting into the food," says another village resident, who claims to have had a "dodgy tummy" after eating at the tearoom.

Other sources reported witnessing an altercation between the victim and one of the waitresses.

"I heard her threaten him," says a customer. "She was really angry and said she would choke him, in front of the whole tearoom!"

There is an atmosphere of fear and uncertainty in Meadowford-on-Smythe today and many are afraid to return to the tearoom.

"I don't want to be the next victim," declares a local resident. "That place is too dangerous! Why, they could add poison to your food if they decide that they don't like the look of you!"

Police are continuing with the investigation and appealing to anyone who might have information about the victim, an American tourist named Brad Washington (photo inset).

"They've just made up a load of rubbish!" Cassie fumed. "What are they going on about? I never threatened to choke anybody!"

I remembered something and looked at her with dismay. "Cass... I think it was when you said you hoped he'd choke on his scones. The whole tearoom heard you—remember?"

"Huh?" Cassie looked confused for a moment, then understanding dawned. "But they took my words totally out of context! I mean, it's just something you say when you're frustrated—and I had a good reason for feeling that way, after that creep copped a feel of my arse!"

"I know, I know..." I said. "But these papers specialise in taking things out of context. Otherwise, they'd have nothing to publish." I shut my eyes and rubbed my temples. "I saw a bunch of people being interviewed outside the front yesterday and I did wonder what they were saying..."

"Oh God, Gemma, I'm sorry," Cassie groaned. "I never thought my words would be misinterpreted like that—"

"It's not your fault," I said quickly. "If it hadn't been that, they would have dug up something else."

"Yeah, what's all this about poison?" said Cassie, looking back down at the article in disgust. "Now *that* is totally made up! It's no wonder people are afraid to come here! You should sue the paper for libel!"

I sighed. "The problem is, I'm sure they're used to avoiding legal action with the kind of articles they write. Look at all these phrases: 'sources report that...' and 'a patron claims...'—I'm sure you'd never be able to get them for anything if it came to court."

"Poxy liars," Cassie muttered, tossing the paper into the bin.

"Well, maybe it'll blow over," I said with false cheerfulness. "Maybe people will realise it's just a load of tabloid gossip and sensationalist rubbish."

I didn't want to show her how worried I really was. My little tearoom was only just getting on its feet. It wasn't established enough to weather this kind of bad press, nor did I have the kind of capital to sustain continuous losses. A week of no customers like today would be enough for the business to fold. My heart lurched uncomfortably in my chest as I thought of all my savings that had been poured into this place, not to mention all my hopes and dreams...

They needed to find the real murderer, I thought. That would put an end to all the speculation about my tearoom and the safety of its offerings. It would have helped if the police actually released more press statements about the case, to give the tabloids something else to latch on to, but Devlin was playing his cards very close to his chest. So far, the official position from Oxfordshire CID was that the investigation was "ongoing".

Fat lot of good that's doing me, I thought gloomily as I eyed the empty dining room again. They needed to make some progress on this case, solve the mystery behind Washington's death, and find the real person responsible.

I paused. No, wait.

Not *they* needed to make progress on this case and solve the mystery.

I did.

I needed to find the murderer. I couldn't just rely on waiting for the police—for Devlin and his smarmy sergeant—to make the connections and solve the case. My business could have been ruined by then.

No, I had to do something myself. I'd never been the kind of person to just sit back and wait for others to solve my problems. And this time, I knew I could make a difference. Like Mabel Cooke said, I was on the ground, I was local, I had a foot in the world of Oxford University, and I could find out things the police couldn't access... My visit to High Table at Gloucester College, for example, had provided valuable intel which the police would never have known...

My phone rang suddenly, startling me out of my thoughts. I groped in my pocket and glanced at the screen before I answered. It was my mother.

"Darling!" she trilled. "I'm just at Debenhams with Helen Green and we're trying to remember the name of the actress who played the ex-wife in the film *His Girl Friday...*"

"And...?" I said, bewildered. "I don't understand— what does that have to do with Debenhams?" *Or me?*

"Oh, we're in the kitchenware department and I thought the lady who's serving us looks just like her. But I can't remember her name."

I took the phone from my ear and stared at it to make sure I wasn't dreaming. I still didn't understand why my mother was calling me. I put the phone back to my ear.

"I'm sorry, Mother. I don't know who it is either. Um... do you have your iPad with you? Why don't you look it up online? I'm sure if you just search the internet for the details of the film, you'll find it."

"Oh, but that's exactly why I was ringing you, darling! You don't happen to remember my Apple ID password, do you? I thought it was 'gemmarose' but it's not working."

"*Mother*," I said, trying not to raise my voice. "I've told you a million times already. *You need to capitalise the first letter of the password.* Did you do that? If you didn't type a capital 'G', that's why it won't work."

"Oh..." There was the sound of rustling and my mother whispering bossily, *"Don't tap it like that, Helen! You have to keep your fingers upright"*—then she came back on the line. "Oh, it's worked, darling! How marvellous! Right, must dash. They're just bringing out the new Breville mixer and I must get to the front of the queue. Bye!"

I lowered the phone and stared at it again, feeling like I just had an out-of-body experience. Cassie was grinning next to me. Well, at least my mother's phone call had improved her mood.

"Maybe you should get it tattooed on her head or something," she suggested, chuckling. "What you need is to think up some jingle—or maybe a famous quote or something—you know, like a mnemonic, which would help her remember."

"Yeah, and then she'd be ringing me all the time, asking me what the quote was—" I broke off suddenly as I thought of something.

"What?" Cassie looked at me.

I stood up, a crazy idea stirring in my mind. "Listen, Cassie—can I leave you to look after things for a bit? I need to pop back into Oxford."

"Well, it doesn't look like I'm at any risk of being overwhelmed, does it?" said Cassie, casting a dark look around the empty room. She glanced back at me curiously. "What are you going to do?"

"I'll tell you when I get back. It's just an idea... it might not work."

I left Cassie starting a new sketch and wheeled my bicycle out of the courtyard. Before I got on it, however, I pulled out my phone and called Seth. He picked up on the first ring.

"Listen, Seth—would you know the students that Professor Hughes is tutoring at the moment?"

"You mean the First Years? Yes, I think I know

them... Why?"

"Apparently one of them confirmed Hughes's alibi for Sunday morning. His name is Tom Rawlings. I wanted to ask him a few questions. Do you know where I can find him?"

"Hmm... you could try the college library. I think I've seen him there in the afternoons—does a couple of hours of study before he goes off to the river at 5 p.m. Tom's on the college rowing team," Seth explained. "If you look in the library, you can't miss him. Big tall chap, with ginger hair and freckles."

"Great, thanks!"

I found Tom exactly as Seth had said, sitting in a quiet corner of Gloucester College library, hunched over an enormous biochemistry textbook. I went up to him and said in an undertone, "Tom Rawlings?"

"Yes?" He looked up in surprise.

I sat down next to him and spoke with as much authority as I could muster. "I understand you provided a statement confirming Professor Hughes's alibi for last Sunday morning? I just need to check a couple of details in your statement."

I held my breath, hoping that my bluff would work. I was counting on the fact that CID detectives didn't wear uniform and that, if I sounded natural and confident enough, he might just assume that I was a member of Devlin's team. Of course, if he asked to see my warrant, the game was up, but I was banking on my own memory of myself as a Fresher and hoping that he would be equally naïve and trusting.

My bluff worked. He nodded amiably. "Yeah, that's right. They wanted to know if the prof was in his room like he said."

"And he was?"

Tom nodded again. "Yeah, I went to see him to ask him a question about my essay that's due this Friday. I was going to knock on the door, but then I heard him inside, talking on the phone."

"Do you know with whom?"

"No idea. It sounded like they were having some kind of debate."

"About what?"

He shrugged. "I'm not sure. He was just going on about there being no absolutes. That's one of his pet peeves—that people are always thinking there is one 'correct' way to do things and he always insisted that there isn't, that there's a multitude of different ways to approach a problem."

"Can you remember his exact words?"

He looked at me in surprise. "I don't know. Is it important?"

"It could be," I hedged. "Could you try?"

"Well..." he furrowed his brow in concentration. "I think he was saying that he had his way and the other person had theirs and neither of them were correct... or something like that..."

I quoted slowly: "'You have your way. I have my way. As for the right way, the correct way, and the only way, it does not exist'—is that it?"

His mouth dropped open. "Yeah, yeah... that's exactly what I heard! How did you know?"

"I... er... I guess I'm used to Professor Hughes's way of speaking," I said lamely.

Thankfully, he didn't question me further and, after thanking him, I left the library, my thoughts whirling. There was a reason I knew the exact words Tom had overheard—it was because they were a quote from Friedrich Nietzsche. Suddenly I had an idea of how Hughes could have had a rock-solid alibi, but not actually been in his room at the time. I pulled out my phone and dialled a number, then asked to be put through to Professor Hughes's room. I listened for a moment, then ended the call and smiled to myself.

The pieces were starting to come together at last.

CHAPTER SEVENTEEN

I walked slowly through the cloisters back to the main quad, deep in thought over what I should do next. The logical thing was to contact Devlin and let him know. He would want to investigate Hughes further. *And he ought to give his sergeant a severe reprimand for not checking the alibi better*, I thought wryly. This new revelation completely changed things—especially Hughes's importance as a suspect...

Then I froze as I saw a tall, balding figure come out of the Porter's Lodge and head towards the staircase in the north western tower. *Geoffrey Hughes!*

I hesitated a second, then darted after him. I caught up with him just as he was climbing the first flight of stairs. He had a bunch of envelopes in his hand and had obviously just picked up his mail from the Porter's Lodge.

"Professor Hughes...!"

He turned around. I saw recognition flicker in his eyes.

"Ah... Miss Rose, isn't it? We met at High Table the other night."

I nodded, climbing the few steps until I reached his level. "Can I have a word with you? In private?"

He looked for a moment as if he would refuse, then he nodded and led the way up to his room. I hadn't thought of how I was going to tackle Hughes. I had acted on impulse and didn't really have a plan. Now, as I stepped into his room, I decided that the best plan of action was attack. Immediately. Before he got a chance to get on the defensive. So as soon as he had shut the door, before he could cross the room and put the hulking barrier of his big mahogany desk between us, I launched straight into it.

"You lied to me the other night at High Table, Professor Hughes."

He looked taken aback. "What do you mean?"

"You told me you didn't know Brad Washington when, in fact, you knew him very well. He was a friend and a fellow student here with you at Oxford—isn't that right?"

His face was expressionless. "Yes, I told this to the police. Washington and I were graduate students together, doing a DPhil in Pharmacology."

"And you saw him on Saturday afternoon, the day before he was murdered."

He gave a reluctant nod.

"So why did you lie?"

He looked down his long, narrow nose at me. "Not that it's really any of your business, but I just thought it would be easier."

"Easier?"

He made an impatient movement. "Yes, I saw the news of the murder on TV and I knew that things would probably get... 'messy' with the police. I didn't really want to be involved in a murder investigation and I certainly didn't want the rest of the S.C.R. gossiping about me. So I thought it was easier just to pretend that I didn't know him. After all, as I told Inspector O'Connor, my meeting with Washington had no relevance to the murder anyway."

I took a step forwards. "But that isn't the only thing you've lied about."

He pushed past me and went to his desk, putting it between us. "I don't know what you're talking about, young lady."

"I'm talking about your alibi for Sunday morning. You said you were here at the college, in this room, marking some essays..."

He dropped the envelopes on his desk, then made a great show of shuffling some papers, his long fingers rifling through the pages. "Yes, that's what I was doing. Look, I already went through all this yesterday, first with the detective sergeant and then

Inspector O'Connor in the evening. I really don't know why you're raking all this up again."

"Because you didn't tell Inspector O'Connor the truth," I said. "You weren't here at the college at all on Sunday morning. Your alibi was false."

He looked up angrily. "Now just a minute, Miss Rose! Who do you think you are, coming in here and throwing accusations around like that? I have a perfectly good alibi which the detective sergeant has already checked and verified. One of my students vouched for my being in this room."

"I know. I spoke to him just now."

He eyed me warily. "You did?"

"Yes, and he told me something very interesting. You see, unlike the sergeant, I asked Tom Rawlings to describe in detail what he had overheard. He said you were on the phone, arguing with someone— having a debate on your favourite topic: the ambiguity of absolute right and wrong. The thing is..." I moved forwards to lean across the desk. "What he overheard wasn't *you*, Professor. What he overheard was your *answering machine*."

"My what?"

I nodded. "I recognised the words Tom heard you say. It's a Nietzsche quote. And I remembered what the other dons had said about you at High Table— that you were obsessed with Nietzsche and his teachings. In fact, I remember one of them making fun of you and saying that you even had Nietzsche's quotes on your answering machine."

Hughes said nothing, although he had gone very pale.

"*'You have your way. I have my way. As for the right way, the correct way, and the only way, it does not exist'*," I quoted. "That's part of your answering message, isn't it?" I glanced at the answering machine next to the phone on the corner of his desk and I saw his eyes travel in the same direction. "When the police asked for your alibi, you bluffed and made up something about being here at the college. It was pure luck that Tom happened to come up to your door just at the time that someone called you and your answering machine switched on. It really was one of those rare lucky coincidences which let you off the hook. And when you heard, you must have been delighted. All you had to do was keep quiet and let everyone assume that Tom's account was the truth."

"I don't know what you're talking about," he blustered. "This is all nonsense! Utter fabrication! You can't prove anything!" His eyes slid again to the answering machine on the corner of his desk and I knew what he was thinking.

"Oh, no, don't think you can erase the message as soon as I'm gone," I said. "I rang the college and asked to be put through to your office, just before I saw you. I have the recorded message—in your voice—and I'm sure if Tom Rawlings is asked again, he would be happy to confirm that that is exactly what he heard. It's right here—recorded in my phone." I held up my mobile. "And I'd be happy to pass it on to the police."

Hughes looked as if he was going to argue again, then he seemed to deflate like a balloon, right in front of my eyes.

"What do you want?" he asked dully.

"I want the truth. Where were you on Sunday morning? Why did you lie about your alibi?"

He sank into his chair, his expression defeated. "All right. I wasn't here in college that morning. I was in Meadowford-on-Smythe." He grimaced as he saw my expression. "Yes, I was at your tearoom. Or rather, I was supposed to meet Brad there. We had a meeting on Saturday afternoon, just as I told the police, and Brad wanted to meet up again, to... to discuss things further. He suggested your tearoom because he had enjoyed the food there and it was close to his hotel. It suited me as I didn't really want to be seen with him at some café in Oxford. We were supposed to meet at 8:15 a.m. and I got there around ten minutes late. When I walked into the courtyard, he was already dead." He shook his head. "I panicked. It was such a shock, seeing him like that. Then I saw that folder on the table. I... I don't think I was thinking very clearly. I just had some vague idea of not wanting to be connected to him in any way. So I grabbed the folder and ran." He shrugged. "That's all."

"But if that's all, why didn't you tell this to the police?"

"Are you joking? There's no way they would have believed me! I didn't want to get involved in a murder investigation! I knew I wasn't the one who had killed him—he was already dead when I arrived—so I knew I didn't have anything to do with it. I thought the easiest thing would be if I removed the folder and pretended our meeting never existed."

"But... it makes no sense," I said. "If you didn't kill him, why would you be scared of the police knowing that you were supposed to meet him?"

He made an impatient sound. "Oh, for God's sake, haven't you ever watched any of those crime dramas on TV? The fact that I was supposed to meet him at the same time that he got murdered would have made me a prime suspect already, never mind me discovering his body! It was simpler all round if I just... 'erased' my presence. If the police knew that I was supposed to meet Brad, it would just confuse matters and push the case in the wrong direction. They would waste a lot of time investigating me when they should be after the real culprit."

I frowned. In a way, what he said made sense, although I couldn't get over the feeling that I was missing something.

Hughes ran a hand over his face and rubbed it tiredly. "To be honest with you, mainly I just panicked. You don't really behave logically when you're panicking, do you? It's not exactly every day that I come across a dead body. One just reacts without thinking. I was halfway back to Oxford with the folder in my possession before I realised what I'd done."

"And what did you do with the folder?"

He looked at me evenly. "I burnt it."

He had an answer for everything. I had to give him that. Something about his smooth delivery annoyed me, but there was nothing else I could do. He had a very plausible story.

"You'll tell this to the police?" I said.

"I don't have much choice now, do I?" He gave me an irritated look. "Yes, all right, I'll call Inspector O'Connor later and tell him the truth about my alibi. Now, if you'll excuse me... I'm very busy..."

Before I could think of something else to say, he hustled me out of his office and slammed the door behind me. I stood for a moment facing the shut door, then slowly, I descended the wooden staircase and stepped out into the autumn sunshine of the main college quadrangle.

CHAPTER EIGHTEEN

My earlier impulse to speak to Devlin was even stronger now. This wasn't just Hughes providing a false alibi—this was Hughes actually admitting that he had been at the crime scene on the day of the murder! It changed everything. No matter what he said, it made him a strong suspect. Besides, I still had the feeling that he was hiding something, that he hadn't told me the full truth. Maybe Devlin would have better luck getting it out of him.

As soon as I left Gloucester College, I pulled out my phone to call him, then remembered that I didn't have his number. Devlin had blocked his caller ID so that his number never showed on phones. I hesitated, then rang Oxfordshire police, asking to be put through to Detective Inspector O'Connor. I was informed that he was out of his office, investigating a case, and to leave my information with the General

Enquiries line.

"But I really need to speak to him. I have some information which could be pertinent to the case. Can't you give me his mobile number or let me know where I might be able to find him? I'm in Oxford at the moment."

"Well, we can't just give out his number to any Tom, Dick, or Harry. It would waste too much of his time to keep fielding calls from everyone."

"You don't understand," I said impatiently. "I am not just some random member of the public. I'm involved in the case that he's currently investigating. It's the murder at the Little Stables Tearoom in Meadowford-on-Smythe and I'm the owner of that tearoom."

There was a pause at the other end of the line, then the woman said, "I'll tell you what—I'll put you through to his sergeant."

A moment later, the familiar cocky voice of Devlin's sergeant came on the line. I hadn't liked him when I met him on the weekend and it seemed that his manner hadn't improved. I took the wind out of his sails, however, when I revealed the gaping hole in Hughes's alibi.

"Shi—" He bit off the curse and muttered, "The inspector's going to give me a right bollocking for this."

"Where is he at the moment—do you know? I need to speak to him urgently."

"He's interviewing someone about the case. You

can to talk to me instead," he said importantly.

"No, I think I'd prefer to pass the information to Inspector O'Connor directly," I said crisply. "I'd rather not risk any more cock-ups."

I could feel the wince across the line.

"Look, if I tell you where he is, will you... uh... put a good word in for me? Make it so that it wasn't really my fault that I missed the alibi...?"

"All right," I said with a grin. He sounded so young and anxious—and I suppose it wasn't really his fault that he didn't know about the connection to Nietzsche.

"The inspector's at the Randolph Hotel. You should be able to find him in the Morse Bar—he's meeting someone there."

I thanked him and hung up, then hurried down Broad Street and right, along Magdalen Street, until I reached the Randolph on the corner. Housed in a 150-year-old Victorian Gothic building, the Randolph claimed pride of place as Oxford's largest luxury hotel. Not that it was one of those five-star chain monstrosities. No, the Randolph was a boutique hotel, full of historic charm and elegant grandeur, with sumptuous wood-panelled interiors, Gothic arches, and a sweeping carved staircase, which dominated the front reception. And the Morse Bar was probably its most famous attraction.

I saw Devlin as soon as I entered the bar. He was sitting in one of the secluded corners, legs crossed, suit jacket off, his blue eyes trained keenly on the person next to him. And sitting beside him, her body draped sensuously in her chair, was Justine Washington.

I stopped in my tracks. They hadn't seen me yet—the layout of the bar was such that I was partially hidden by the bar counter. Without conscious thought, I drew back and pressed myself against the wall so that I was completely hidden from view. There were a few other patrons in the bar—mostly tourists by the look of things—but they didn't pay me much notice. All *my* attention was focused on Devlin and the woman next to him.

There was something in the cosy intimacy of the scene that made my heart beat uncomfortably in my chest. As I watched, Justine reached out and languidly brushed her fingers along Devlin's arm. She was saying something, her eyes wide and appealing on her face. I couldn't hear what they were saying but there was no mistaking the suggestive look she gave him.

I couldn't see Devlin's face properly from this angle but I saw him nod, then lean forwards and incline his head towards her. I pulled back, feeling slightly sick. A feeling of betrayal washed over me and I whirled and ran from the bar. I stumbled out of the main hotel entrance and retrieved my bicycle.

Somehow I climbed aboard and made my way out of Oxford, cycling blindly and negotiating the roads without really being aware of them. All I kept seeing in my mind was that image of Justine Washington smiling as she reached out to stroke Devlin's arm and then his head inclining towards her... Okay, so I didn't actually see him kiss her, but somehow I doubted that he was just leaning forwards to tell her that she had dirt on her nose.

I looked up and realised to my surprise that I was entering Meadowford village high street. I had no recollection of how I had got here. I alighted from my bicycle in front of the tearoom and wheeled it into the courtyard, securing it by the back door. Then I went in. I found Cassie still at the counter, still sketching—and the room still empty.

"Well?" She looked up at me eagerly.

I waved towards the empty room. "Any...?"

She shook her head. "Sorry. I'm thinking we might as well close early."

I winced but, looking around again, I decided that she was right. I doubted there was going to be any change this late in the day and sitting here was just depressing.

"If we close early, we can help Fletcher put some posters up," added Cassie.

I looked at her questioningly. She held up the paper she was working on and I saw that it was a sketch of Muesli, sitting the way she often did with her tail curled around her front paws and her cheeky little face looking up expectantly. It was a fantastic likeness, drawn from memory. I'd known Cassie almost all her life and still I was continually surprised and awed by her talent.

"That's brilliant, Cass. It looks just like her."

She nodded and quickly added a border around the drawing, then in big letters across the top: "HAVE YOU SEEN THIS CAT?" followed by a request to call and Fletcher's phone number.

"Yeah, I'm hoping that if we make several copies of this and stick it up around the village and maybe a bit farther out too, someone might ring up and say they've seen her. Anyway, it would be good just to do something. It would help to cheer Fletcher up a bit."

"So he's still not had any sign of her?"

Cassie shook her head. "He's really upset about it. I told him after we put these posters up, 'I'd go back with him and help search the woods by his house."

"I'll come too," I said.

I hoped Muesli was okay. Not just for Fletcher's sake. I didn't want to admit it but I had grown very fond of the little feline and the thought that something might have happened to her made me feel ill. I sighed. This was turning out to be a nightmare week. Ever since Brad Washington appeared on the scene, it had been one bad thing after another.

Cassie looked at me curiously. "So where did you go?"

Quickly, I told her about my encounter with Tom Rawlings, the Nietzsche quote on the answering machine, and my confrontation with Hughes.

"That was bloody clever, Gemma, the way you worked out his false alibi." She looked at me admiringly.

I waved her praise away. "Get this: Hughes was actually here on Sunday morning to meet Washington," I said excitedly.

"Here?"

I nodded. "He found the body when he arrived so he panicked and ran away."

"Wow." Cassie digested this for a moment. "This totally changes things. You realise, he could easily have been the one to kill Washington. He just has to lie and *say* he found the body. It's the best double bluff in the world. Admit that he was here—which he can't hide anymore—but say that he didn't do it."

I frowned. "The only thing is—I can't think of a motive for him to want to kill Washington."

"He and Washington used to be mates here at Oxford, right?"

"Yeah, they were graduate research students here together."

"Well, maybe something happened back then— something Washington did to Hughes, perhaps. That Washington was a creep—and a bully. I wouldn't put it past him to take advantage of the weaker man. So... maybe Hughes has been nursing a grudge all these years and then on Sunday, he decided to get revenge..."

I shook my head impatiently. "But why wait till now? It's been fifteen years since they matriculated. If it was something that happened when they were young and Hughes was still mad about it, wouldn't he have wanted revenge long before now? Why wait until fifteen years later to murder him?"

"I guess that's the police's responsibility to find out." She looked at me sharply. "You *have* told Devlin, haven't you?"

"I... I left a message," I said.

Cassie narrowed her eyes. I tried to keep my face expressionless. My best friend knew me too well and the last thing I needed was for her to start asking awkward questions about things I didn't even want to face myself.

"So what happened last night with Devlin? You never told me."

"Nothing happened," I said lightly.

"Gemma." She looked at me with mock severity. "You can't fob me off that easily. You had drinks with the only man you ever loved and you're telling me nothing happened?"

"He's not the only man I ever loved," I muttered. "I *have* dated other guys."

"You mean like that accountant in Sydney? Or the guy who gave you surfing lessons?" she scoffed. "Gemma, this is Devlin! Devlin O'Connor! I was there, remember? I know how much you loved him. Bloody hell, you were thinking of marrying him!"

"Well I didn't," I said shortly, turning away. I thought of that scene in the Randolph Hotel again. "And anything that was between us is over."

Cassie started to say something else but I cut her off.

"Anyway, getting back to the case—I think the

answer lies in what happened between Hughes and Washington fifteen years ago. If I can find out more about that, maybe I can find out why Hughes would have had a reason to want Washington dead."

"Have you tried the Oxford City Library?"

I looked at Cassie in puzzlement. "Why would that help?"

"Duh... detectives in movies are always going to libraries and looking up microfiches or something..."

"I don't think they have microfiches anymore these days," I said, laughing. "But you know, maybe that's not a bad idea..."

I thought of the outrageous tabloid article about my tearoom. Technology and fashions might have changed but the tabloid papers and the thirst for gossip would have been the same fifteen years ago. Picking up my phone, I put a call through to Oxford City Library and got a very helpful librarian on the line. I explained my search for any articles mentioning students at Gloucester College, in particular with the names "Brad Washington" or "Geoffrey Hughes"—or any reference to some kind of trouble or scandal at the college.

"I can put in the request to search the archives for you," said the librarian. "It might take a while—but I can probably let you know by tomorrow morning."

"Thank you, that sounds great."

I gave her my details, then hung up. Now all I could do was wait and hope that my hunch was correct.

CHAPTER NINETEEN

I went into the kitchen to tell Fletcher about closing early. I found him busy washing up some baking trays.

"Hey Fletcher, how's it going? Listen, we're going to close early today. Why don't I help you wash up here?"

He nodded and we worked in a companionable silence for a while. As we stood by the sink, I said, "I'm sorry to hear that Muesli is still missing."

He nodded gravely. "It's been four days now."

I grimaced. With each day that passed, the chances of the little cat turning up unharmed were getting slimmer and slimmer. But I didn't want to worry him further. Instead, I cast my mind around for something to distract him. There seemed to be nothing in the past few days that didn't involve the murder... then I remembered the book club meeting at my parents' house and began telling him about that.

"Have you ever been in a book club, Fletcher?" I said as I finished.

He shook his head shyly.

"Do you think you'd like to join one? It might be a nice way for you to meet people."

He shrugged. "Don't read much."

"Well, I don't think the people in my mother's book club read much either," I said with a chuckle. "It seems to be more of a social gathering than anything else. You know, a way to make friends..."

He said nothing and I was about to try another topic when he asked, "What are they reading in the book club?"

"A book by Jane Austen. It's called *Persuasion*. Have you heard of it?"

He shook his head. "I've heard of *Pride and Prejudice*."

I laughed. "Yes, everyone's heard of *Pride and Prejudice*. It's the more famous one. But I think *Persuasion* is actually my favourite Austen novel."

"Why?"

I gazed out of the kitchen window. "I guess... because it's about second chances and starting again. It's about a girl who gave up a man she loved when she was very young because her family told her that he wasn't right for her and then they meet again eight years later and he's now very successful and very rich and she realises that she never stopped loving him..." I trailed off, suddenly uncomfortable as I became aware of what I was saying.

Fletcher looked at me curiously. "Do you believe in second chances, Gemma? Do you think people can start again—even when they've made a mistake?"

I thought of Justine and her cynical remarks to me that morning at the book club meeting. Did they mean anything? Was there something in Justine's past—or was she referring to something Brad Washington had done?

I came out of my thoughts and smiled at Fletcher. "Yeah, I believe they can. I think if you want something badly enough—and you really want to change—then yes, you can start again."

Fletcher looked at me searchingly, and I had to resist the urge to squirm. Sometimes he could be like a child in his directness. Nobody likes to be thought to be transparent, but it didn't take a genius to work out that this tearoom and everything it represented was my "second chance", my bid to start again.

Slowly Fletcher smiled and nodded. "Yes," he said encouragingly. "Yes."

Cassie stuck her head in through the kitchen doorway. "Are you guys almost done? I want to get to the post office before it shuts, so I can make some photocopies of this poster."

Half an hour later, we were making our way to Fletcher's place, having stuck up several posters of

Muesli all over the village. We walked down the row of neat terraces until we reached the end, passing Ethel pruning roses in her garden. She waved as we walked past and I waved back. We followed Fletcher into his obsessively neat little cottage and out the back door to the large woods which surrounded one side of the house. It extended for several miles and my heart sank slightly at the thought of trying to find one small cat in all this wilderness.

Nevertheless, we began searching methodically, calling Muesli's name and peering through the undergrowth. We hadn't gone very far, though, when my phone rang, the shrill sound piercing in the quiet of the woods. I dug it out of my pocket and stared at the screen. The number was withheld. I suddenly remembered the last time I had had a similar call—when Devlin had rung me on Monday. I hesitated, then tossed the phone to Cassie.

"Can you do me a favour? Answer that for me and if it's Devlin, tell him I'm not available."

She gave me a look but obediently answered the phone. "Hello? Gemma's phone." She listened, her eyes flicking to mine for a moment. "Oh hi, Devlin. No, she's busy right now. Can I take a message?" She paused. "Yeah, I'll get her to give you a ring as soon as she's free. Cheers."

She ended the call and tossed the phone back to me. "Okay, now what was that all about?"

I thought of fobbing her off again, then I saw the look in her eyes and knew that I wouldn't get away with it this time. I glanced at Fletcher. He was searching behind some bushes a few feet away and seemed to be lost in his own world. I lowered my voice.

"I... um... I just don't feel like talking to Devlin right now."

"Why?"

"I saw him earlier today." I paused. "At the Randolph. In the Morse Bar. With Justine Washington."

Cassie raised an eyebrow.

I flushed at her look. "I just... well, they didn't look very... uh... professional."

"Professional?" Cassie choked back a laugh. "Why don't you just admit that you're jealous?"

I scowled at her. "I'm not jealous! He's a free agent after all. But you should have seen them—she was practically in his lap! He was supposed to be interviewing her but it looked to me a lot friendlier than a police interview."

"Well, maybe that's his method," said Cassie. "He might just be softening her up or something..."

I made a rude noise.

"Okay, well, whatever..." Cassie threw up her hands. "Look, I don't know what's going on between you and Devlin, but you've got to speak to him. You've got important information about the case and you have to pass it on. You're just being childish, not talking to him."

I hated to admit it but Cassie was right. Still, I

couldn't face the thought of speaking to Devlin tonight. Besides, there was nothing that was really urgent. "I'll speak to him tomorrow morning."

Cassie sighed. "Fine."

We continued searching but the light was fading rapidly now and it was soon hard to see anything. We were forced to abandon the search. Gently, we urged Fletcher back to his house, promising to return and search with him again tomorrow. The phone was ringing as we trooped back in and my heart leapt with hope. Perhaps it was someone who had seen the posters and was ringing with news of Muesli. But Fletcher listened without saying much and hung up after a moment. He met our looks and shook his head despondently.

"Never mind," said Cassie. "I still believe that she'll turn up, just when you're least expecting it, looking completely unbothered that she's put us to so much worry. Typical cat." She glanced at her watch. "Yikes—I'd better go. I promised my mother I'd be there for a family dinner tonight."

I suddenly remembered that I'd made a similar promise to my own mother. She had been very insistent that I be home for dinner and I'd given my word to be on time. I bade goodbye to Fletcher and Cassie, and raced back to Oxford, arriving just in time to find my mother laying the table.

"Gemma, darling, you're not going to have dinner dressed like that, are you?" she said, looking at me in dismay.

I glanced down at my jeans and faded sweater. "Yeah, I was—why?"

"Oh, darling—how uncivilised! There's still time. Why don't you run upstairs and put on a nice dress?"

I looked at her in puzzlement. "Mother, I never change for dinner—"

"Nonsense, dear. You used to get changed for dinner every night when you were in college."

"Yes, but that was different. I was going to Formal Hall every night and that was one of those Oxford etiquette things. But I'm not at college anymore."

"Well, you could *pretend* that you are," said my mother brightly. "Wouldn't you like to look more... er... presentable, for a change?"

I eyed her in sudden suspicion. "Mother, why is it so important for me to look presentable tonight? Is someone coming to dinner?"

She tossed her head and said airily, "Oh, didn't I say? I invited Lincoln Green over to join us."

"*Mother!*" I said in exasperation. "I *told* you! I don't want to be set up with Lincoln Green!"

"Whoever said anything about setting you up? I just thought the poor boy would enjoy some home cooking. He's all alone in that huge house of his and he must be at loose ends in the evenings. And his mother is my oldest friend. Why, it would be rude of me not to invite him when he only lives around the corner."

Argh! For a moment, I considered making a run for it. I could have bolted out the door and been halfway to central Oxford before my mother could stop me. But then what would I do? Wander aimlessly around the streets of the city, waiting for Lincoln Green to finish eating and leave? It seemed ridiculous to be skulking around in the night just because you didn't want to meet a man in your own home. Besides, my mother would never forgive me and you don't know what "passive-aggressive" really means until you've seen my mother in action.

I sighed. It would be easier just to grit my teeth and get it over with. It was only one night. Besides, it would make my mother happy. I felt a faint stab of guilt. I'd been a pretty disappointing daughter in so many ways recently—what would it cost me to put on a dress, sit at a table, and smile nicely for a couple of hours?

I gave another deep sigh. "Fine."

"Wonderful!" my mother trilled. "Make sure you wear something pink, darling—it's your best colour. And put on some make-up and jewellery. There's not much you can do with your hair..." She eyed my pixie crop with distaste. "I can never understand why you want to chop off your hair when you've got such lovely thick waves to play with."

I ruffled my short 'do. "I like my hair. It's practical and convenient." I didn't add that, in my private moments, I liked to think it gave me a shot at Audrey Hepburn's elfin charm.

My mother sniffed. "No man likes a woman with short hair, darling. It's so unfeminine!"

"I'm not trying to impress a man," I muttered.

"Maybe you could put a hairband in it," my mother suggested suddenly. "One of those cute Alice-in-Wonderland styles with a bow on the side."

"What?" I recoiled in horror. "No, no, I don't want—"

"I know! I'll come and help you get dressed."

"No, Mother, no..." My protests fell on deaf ears as I found myself being hustled upstairs to my fashion doom.

CHAPTER TWENTY

The doorbell rang punctually on the dot of eight and I made my reluctant way downstairs. I nearly screamed when I caught sight of myself in the hall mirror. I looked like a cross between a Laura Ashley bedspread and a vintage lampshade. I might not have been interested in Lincoln Green but I had enough pride not to want him to be repulsed by me.

Lincoln looked like an older, taller, slightly heavier version of the boy I used to know. He had the same serious expression and the same neat side parting in his brown hair. He was dressed in a navy blazer and beige designer chinos, and looked every inch the successful young doctor as he stepped over our threshold and politely handed my mother an enormous bouquet of flowers.

"Oh, how lovely!" my mother gushed. "Such a well-brought-up young man you are, Lincoln. And of course, you remember Gemma?" She stepped aside and shoved me forwards.

Lincoln offered his hand. "Yes, of course I remember. How are you, Gemma? Nice to see you again."

"Now, now, no need to be so formal," my mother said, giving Lincoln an arch look. "Shaking hands? This isn't a business meeting! Doesn't everyone kiss each other nowadays?"

"*Mother!*" I hissed out of the side of my mouth.

Lincoln stepped forwards and gave me a dutiful peck on the cheek. I knew my face was red. I hoped Lincoln would realise that it was a sign of angry humiliation and not romantic bashfulness. Thankfully my father came into the foyer at that moment and diverted the attention. He was delighted to discover that Lincoln was a cricket fan—cricket being one of the few things in the "real world" that's powerful enough to take my father's nose out of his textbooks—and he monopolised Lincoln for the next five minutes, discussing the result of the test match between England and Pakistan. By the time my mother managed to shepherd us into the dining room, I was relieved to find that the awkward atmosphere had eased a bit.

We filed dutifully towards the dining table, which was covered in a snowy white linen tablecloth and gleaming with even more crockery and wine glasses than usual. Lincoln pulled out my mother's chair with an old-fashioned gallantry that had her beaming. She threw me a proud look, like someone showing off a well-trained puppy, and I had to resist the urge to roll my eyes. I have to admit, I took a wicked pleasure in managing the monumental task of pulling out my own chair and seating myself at the table before Lincoln came around to me, leaving him looking a bit nonplussed. My mother frowned at me but I pretended not to see.

"So, Lincoln…" my mother said brightly as we started on the first course of honeydew melon wrapped in paper-thin slices of *prosciutto* ham. "How are you settling back in Oxford?"

"Very well," said Lincoln. "It's nice to be back and I'm enjoying the work."

"Do you have many friends here still? Does it get lonely sometimes?"

"No, actually, the hospital is a pretty sociable place. There's a good entertainment committee that organises events for the medical staff. Pub crawls and karaoke nights and that sort of thing."

"Oh, well, if you ever need a partner for anything, I'm sure Gemma would love to oblige," my mother said gaily. "She doesn't go out much and she's always free in the evenings."

I glared at her. Okay, so it was true that I didn't have much of a social life, but there was no need to make me sound like some kind of pariah. Besides, I stayed in by choice. Since opening the tearoom, I had found that I was too exhausted most evenings to contemplate the thought of a night on the town.

"I did wonder..." my mother continued, giving Lincoln another coy sideways glance. "...if you were coming alone tonight."

Lincoln looked a bit confused. "Yes, I have come alone."

"Oh... because I did say in my invite to include a friend, if you like?"

I squirmed in my seat. Lincoln looked even more confused.

My mother continued blithely, "Well, you being such a handsome young man... one expects you wouldn't be alone. I thought you might have someone special you wanted to bring along?"

I cringed. I wondered why she didn't just come out and say: *"Lincoln, are you shagging anyone at the moment, dear? Because if not, my daughter is available."*

Lincoln—to his credit—seemed to take things in his stride. "No, it's just me," he said with a smile.

"Just you in that huge house? Don't you feel a bit lonely rattling around in there by yourself?"

"I'm all right. To be honest, I'm not home most of the time. It's long hours at the hospital and I'm often on-call."

"Oh, well, of course it's different if you had *someone* to come home to," said my mother meaningfully and flicked her eyes towards me.

I squirmed and wished that there was a

convenient hole I could dive into. Lincoln gave an awkward laugh and made a great show of cutting up his melon, portioning it into bite-sized pieces with surgical precision. Suddenly I felt a twinge of sympathy for him. For all I knew, he had been press-ganged into coming to dinner tonight by his mother as well and was dreading it as much as I was.

I looked at Lincoln with slightly more charitable eyes. He was quite good-looking, I admitted grudgingly. His nose was straight, his mouth firm, and his brown eyes humorous in an open, pleasant face. The kind of face you wanted on your doctor. Respectable, professional, trustworthy.

Lincoln looked up and made a desperate bid to change the subject. "I'm sorry to hear about the bit of unpleasantness with your tearoom, Gemma."

How like an Englishman to make an understatement about everything. A brutal murder was reduced to "the bit of unpleasantness". I suppose the British newspapers reported the sinking of the *Titanic* as "a regrettable excursion". Still, I was grateful for the chance to get away from my mother's heavy hints of our future nuptials and jumped at the cue he offered.

"Yes, it's been a bit of a week," I said with a wry smile. "It's not every day that you have someone murdered in your tearoom."

My mother gave a little scream. "Gemma, darling! Is this really a subject for the dinner table?"

"Oh, I'm sure Lincoln won't mind. Being a doctor,

I'm sure he's used to all sorts of gory topics at the dinner table," I said, giving him a grin.

"There's certainly very little you can say that would disgust or offend me," said Lincoln, returning my smile. "And a murder mystery is always fascinating. Have the police made any progress on the case? Are they close to finding the killer?"

I shrugged. "I wish I knew. They have a few suspects, but I don't think they're about to make an arrest any time soon."

"There was a piece about the murder in the papers today," said Lincoln. "I was reading it at the hospital this morning. The victim was an American named Brad Washington?"

I nodded.

"I've heard of Washington," said Lincoln. "He's head of a pharmaceutical company in the States. Very bright guy. Not the nicest man, from what I've heard, but very shrewd, especially in business. His company specialises in drugs which treat lumbar spondylosis and arthritis. There was a lot of talk about them in the medical field earlier this year—a lot of excitement about a new drug they're developing."

"A new drug?" I looked at him with interest.

"Well, it's actually not completely new. It's a drug they've got already, called Lassitomab, which works to treat arthritis. But they've discovered that it could help those suffering from Chronic Fatigue Syndrome as well," Lincoln explained. "It seems to ease the symptoms so that sufferers are able to return to work and lead a normal life again. It's a bit similar to another drug called Rituximab, which was used in cancer treatments and also thought to have benefits for those with CFS—but Washington's drug promises to deliver even better results. It's very exciting."

"Is it on the market already?"

"Not for this particular use, no. It *has* been approved for arthritis use but it hasn't gained FDA approval yet for treatment of CFS. I believe it's going through the final stages of the process now but it will need to pass a special committee first. If approved, this drug could be one of the biggest advances in medicine in recent years and really make a difference to the quality of life of many sufferers. And of course, make Washington a fortune. Or rather would have made him a fortune if he was still alive," added Lincoln soberly.

Yes, I mused. Washington's death seemed to have been very convenient—or inconvenient, depending on how you looked at it—for a number of people. Justine Washington benefited hugely from it. And Geoffrey Hughes? Did Washington's old academic colleague benefit from his murder? I thought back to my conversation with Cassie about Hughes's lack of motive. The Oxford don had admitted that Washington had come to see him about investing in a new venture. I was sure now that it was the development of this drug. It was just too much of a coincidence that the American should return to

Oxford to see Hughes just before the launch of his revolutionary new drug. And Hughes was a professor in Pharmacology... What had really happened at their meeting on Saturday afternoon? After all, you didn't kill someone just because you didn't want to invest in their business venture. No, there was something Hughes wasn't telling.

I had a feeling that I was on the brink of a big discovery. Seth would be able to help me dig up more information, I thought. I wanted to run upstairs and call him immediately. I could barely sit still through the rest of the dinner. My mother frowned at me as I fidgeted in my chair. She dragged out the meal for as long as she could, but even the delicious rhubarb crumble we had for dessert couldn't quite make up for the strained atmosphere. My heart sank when we'd settled in the living room for the customary after-dinner tea, coffee, and chocolates, and she suggested a trip down Memory Lane via some family photo albums.

"I'm sure you and Gemma would love to see some pictures of when you were children together," she said with a coy laugh. "You were such a handsome little boy, Lincoln—so proper and polite—and Gemma used to adore you and follow you around everywhere!"

I choked on my tea. That was an utter lie. To my great relief, Lincoln politely but firmly said that he had to leave as he had an early start at the hospital the next morning.

"Oh, what a shame! But we must do this again soon—it's been so lovely to catch up with you, Lincoln. I hope you won't mind if Gemma sees you out?" My mother gestured to the TV screen which my father was watching. "Such a riveting programme—I simply can't miss a moment of it!"

Since the only thing showing on the screen was a five-day cricket match between India and Bangladesh, which was only marginally more exciting than watching paint dry, her lie was embarrassingly obvious. I flushed and gritted my teeth as I turned and stalked back out to the foyer with Lincoln at my heels.

However, as I turned around to face him by the front door, I felt slightly guilty. It wasn't his fault that my mother was behaving the way she was. If anything, he had been remarkably good-humoured about everything and had done his best to deflect her ploys. Looking up at him in the light of the front hall, I had to admit again that he was not bad looking at all. In fact, if we weren't being hounded by my mother's matchmaking machinations, I might have actually enjoyed spending time with him.

As if reading my thoughts, he cleared his throat and said, "Well, that could probably go down in history as the most awkward dinner of all time."

"I'm sorry about my mother..." I said, shame-faced.

"It's all right. I have the same at home." He paused, then gave me a hesitant smile. "But mothers aside, I *would* really like to see you again, Gemma. Perhaps we could have dinner sometime? Alone," he added hastily.

I stared up at him. This man would never make my heart race or leave me speechless and furious, like Devlin did. But perhaps that was a good thing. I'd been burned once by a wild passionate love affair. Now that I was older and wiser, maybe it was time I sought a different romantic ideal. Lincoln was a nice guy—and very pleasant company. I realised that I *would* actually enjoy getting to know him better.

"Thanks, I'd like that," I said with a smile. "But on one condition."

"What's that?"

"That you don't breathe a word of it to your mother and I won't say anything to mine. Otherwise they'll probably sit at the next table, orchestrating our every move and eavesdropping on our conversation."

He chuckled. "You're on. Shall I give you a call sometime next week?"

I agreed and gave him my number, then stood on the threshold and watched as he walked down the street. As soon as he had disappeared around the corner, I shut the door and hurried up to my bedroom to call Seth.

Romance was all very well but I had bigger things on my mind. I had a murderer to catch.

CHAPTER TWENTY-ONE

I paced up and down my room, listening to Seth's phone ring. I hoped that he wasn't out at some University society event. He answered finally, sounding slightly flustered.

I launched in without preamble. "Seth, listen—I was just speaking to a doctor who told me that Washington's company is trying to get FDA approval for a drug called Lassitomab to be used to treat Chronic Fatigue Syndrome. Do you know anything about this?"

Seth was silent for a moment. "Well, I'm no pharmacologist, but since organic chemistry does cross over in some ways, I do have some knowledge in this area. I've got access to MIMS online—that's the database of pharmaceutical drugs—which might give me some information. If you hold on, I can do a quick search for you. It does sound vaguely familiar..."

I waited, listening to the sound of his keyboard clacking in the background. After what seemed like ages, he came back on the line.

"Found it. I had to search a few other databases and research archives to find out about the new application but, yes, Lassitomab is being hailed as the next big thing in the treatment of CFS. There's been a preliminary trial with over two hundred patients." He sounded quite excited. "They're not quite sure how it works but they believe it's by targeting the autoantibodies to the adrenergic receptors found on endothelial cells—which are present in postural orthostatic tachycardia syndrome—and helping in the elimination of EBV or CMV, which is the principal mechanism for—"

"Er... Seth? In English, please."

Seth took a breath. "Basically, the drug works by destroying the white blood cells that make the autoantibodies that are responsible for the symptoms of CFS. But what's exciting about it is that it not only targets the cells making those autoantibodies but also binds to the autoantibodies themselves. So instead of the usual several months' time lag after treatment, people start to respond within days."

"Sounds great. So why isn't it on the market already?"

"Well, these things need a lot of large-scale trials and studies to determine their safety, you know, just in case there are side effects."

"Does this drug have side effects then?"

"All drugs have side effects," said Seth. "It's just a matter of whether the positives outweigh the negatives. In this case, there are a lot of positives. I'm actually quite surprised it hasn't been brought to market yet... there must be something..." His voice trailed off and there was more clacking on the keyboard. I tried to wait patiently. Finally, he came back again.

"Hmm... it seems that it was almost approved a few months ago but was blocked by a member of the approval committee. A world expert in pharmacology maintained that the research wasn't adequate to license the drug for safe use."

I felt my heartbeat quicken. "Can you find his name?"

"How do you know it's a 'he'? It's an equal opportunity world these days," said Seth.

"Huh. Not when I last looked. Women are still earning less in the same jobs and being excluded from the 'old boys' club'," I retorted. "But I'm not here to debate women's rights with you. Can you find a name?"

"I'm looking... I'm looking... hold your horses, Gemma..."

I waited again, trying to contain my impatience.

"Ah yes... here... Professor Geoffrey Hu... Hughes! Bloody hell, it's Prof Hughes here in my college!"

"I knew it! Seth, that's the missing piece of the

puzzle! I found out this morning that Hughes gave the police a fake alibi." Quickly, I recounted my confrontation with the Oxford don. "He told me that he just panicked and ran away. But I had a feeling that he was hiding something. I think this is it! He lied—or at least, he was economical with the truth—about his meeting with Washington. They must have discussed Lassitomab and I'll bet you anything that the real reason Washington came to Oxford was to persuade Hughes to retract his objection. Hughes was the only thing that stood between Washington and mass marketing this drug."

"But wait, Gemma, it doesn't make sense..." said Seth. "Why should that give Hughes a motive to murder Washington? If he didn't want the drug to go to market, all he had to do was block its approval, like he's done once already. No one can get him to change his professional opinion."

"Yes, but what if Washington was trying to *force* him to change it?"

"How can he do that?"

"Well..." I thought furiously. "What if Washington had some kind of hold over Hughes?"

"You mean like blackmail?"

"Yes... I've been thinking..." I mused. "I'm sure this is all somehow connected to something that happened at Oxford fifteen years ago when Washington and Hughes were here as students."

"What happened fifteen years ago?"

"I don't know. I think that's something for the

police to dig up," I said reluctantly, realising that I had yet another reason to speak to Devlin now.

"Well, if you think it might help, you can always come back and speak to some members of the S.C.R. here in Gloucester College," Seth offered. "Some of the older dons have been here for yonks and might remember something relevant from fifteen years ago. Hey, why don't you come to dinner on High Table again?"

"Thanks, but once a term is more than enough for me," I said dryly. "But thank you for the invitation. Why don't you ask Cassie?"

"Oh... um..." Seth stammered. "I don't know... I'm not sure if she would..."

"I'm sure she'd enjoy it. Just ask her, Seth."

He mumbled something and I could practically feel him blushing across the line. I decided to let the subject drop. We bade each other good night and I hung up. Going back downstairs, I joined my mother in clearing the table and washing up. She was brimming with excitement over Lincoln's visit and wanted to pump me for details of our "good bye". I answered her distractedly, for once not minding her prying. My mind was elsewhere.

I knew who the murderer was now. I just had to find a way to prove it. And the answer lay in finding out what had happened in Oxford fifteen years ago.

The next morning brought me answers quicker than I expected. My phone rang as I was about to leave for work. It was Seth.

"Gemma," he said excitedly. "I ran into Prof Wilkins this morning in the quad and we had a chat. You remember I said some of the old dons here might remember something relevant?"

His excitement was infectious and I felt my pulse speeding up in response. "Yes?"

"Listen to this: he told me that he remembered Washington. He saw a picture of the American in the local papers and it triggered his memory. He said that when Washington was here as a graduate student, there had been some scandal associated with him—some kind of cheating scandal."

"Cheating scandal?"

"Yeah. It seemed that Washington was part of a group of students who managed to plagiarise their exam papers."

I frowned. "Cheating can get you sent down, can't it?"

"Yes, or if it's discovered later, then your degree would be stripped from you."

"Is that what happened? Washington was expelled from Oxford?"

"No. Somehow Washington got away with it. They weren't able to prove that he cheated. But listen to this—" Seth sounded even more excited. "It wasn't just him in on this cheating scheme, right? It was a whole group of students. And guess who was one of the other students also implicated? *Geoffrey Hughes!*"

I drew a sharp breath in. "Hughes! So... you think

Washington might have had some hold over his old friend because of this scandal?"

"Yes! Hughes obviously got away with it too. But if Washington had some kind of proof... and if it came out now that Hughes had plagiarised his thesis or some other research... he'd be done for."

"But wait—how can Hughes be employed as a tutor and be a respected member of the S.C.R. if people thought he had cheated?"

"I told you, there was no proof. He obviously managed to hush it up. Prof Wilkins did say to me that there was a lot of talk in the S.C.R. when Hughes was first given a position in college—behind the man's back, as it were. Even now, I would say Hughes isn't particularly liked and I get the feeling that a lot of the other fellows have doubts about his academic integrity. I guess mud sticks. Maybe that's why he's so sensitive about things. You know, it's a bit of a joke among the students how much he insists on citing sources and stuff like that in his tutorials. I mean, that's obviously good academic practice, particularly in the sciences, but he takes it to the extreme. I think he's trying to make up for his past reputation."

I thought for a moment. "What if Washington came and threatened Hughes with exposing his part in the cheating scandal? He could have used it as leverage against Hughes, to force the latter to agree to approve Lassitomab for the market."

"Yeah, it would certainly be some leverage,"

agreed Seth. "I mean, aside from his personal pride, if the truth came out that he cheated, Hughes would be stripped of his professorship and lose all his academic standing. In effect, it would kill his whole career."

I felt a surge of excitement. "That would be more than enough to drive a man to murder."

***

I stared at the phone in my hand, then looked up out of my bedroom window. I had to speak to Devlin—there was no way of delaying it any longer. It wasn't just a case of reporting Hughes's false alibi; now that I knew that he had a motive as well for killing Washington, I had to share the information.

I sighed and looked back down at the phone. This was stupid. *I should just call him and get it over with.* I pressed the number and was put through to Oxfordshire police. Once again, I asked to speak to Devlin and once again, I was thwarted.

"Inspector O'Connor is unavailable at the moment. He's out on a murder investigation."

"I know," I said. "But this is important. It's *about* that murder investigation."

"Well, I'll take a message and ask him to—"

"I really need to speak to him. It's urgent. Can't you give me his number?"

"I'm afraid that's not possible, Miss. As I said, I'll pass on your message and ask him to call you back when he can."

I swallowed a sigh of frustration. "All right." I gave my number and hung up. But I had barely put the phone down when my phone rang.

"Hello?"

"Gemma? Devlin here. They said you needed to speak to me."

I was slightly taken aback at his brusque tone. I had been intending to treat him with cool indifference but, faced now with his curtness, I didn't quite know how to begin.

"Gemma?" Devlin's voice rose in impatience.

"Yeah, I'm here," I said hastily. "I... um... I have something to tell you."

"Look, Gemma I can't speak right now. I'm in the middle of something. Can it wait? We can talk later tonight."

"No, I don't think it can. I think this information will help you find the murderer."

Devlin went silent for a moment, then he said cautiously, "Yes?"

"I think I know who killed Brad Washington." I took a breath, then said in a rush, "It's Geoffrey Hughes, the Professor of Pharmacology at Gloucester College."

There was a pause, then Devlin said, "What makes you say that?"

"Because he lied about his alibi for Sunday morning. He wasn't in college at all—he was actually at the tearoom; he had gone to meet Washington there." I told Devlin about the talk with Tom Rawlings, the answering machine, Nietzsche's quote, and my confrontation with Hughes.

Devlin cursed under his breath. "I'm going to have to have serious words with my sergeant about being thorough," he said savagely.

"Well, I suppose it wasn't really his fault—anyone could have been fooled if Tom simply said he heard Hughes talking on the phone in the room. It was only because I was at High Table that night and found out about Hughes's Nietzsche obsession that I was able to make the connection. But listen, it wasn't just that..."

Quickly, I told him about Washington's new drug and Hughes's obstruction of its approval, and then what I had learnt from Seth about the two men's chequered history at Oxford.

"I'm sure that Washington came to Oxford to persuade Hughes to retract his objections about the drug and he used the threat of the cheating scandal to try and force this from Hughes. This must be what they were discussing when they met on Saturday afternoon. And maybe Hughes panicked at the thought of losing his whole career so he killed Washington to silence him," I finished triumphantly.

"It's a nice theory but it won't wash," Devlin said.

"Why?"

"Because Geoffrey Hughes was murdered last night."

CHAPTER TWENTY-TWO

"*What?* Hughes was murdered?"

"His body has just been discovered. I'm at the crime scene now."

"But... are you sure it was murder?"

"Well, if it was suicide, then Hughes must have been the most dextrous man in history to be able to bash himself in the back of the head with enough force to smash in half his skull."

I shuddered. The image was not a pleasant one. "Hughes is dead...?" I whispered, sinking slowly down on my bed. "I was so sure that he was Washington's killer..."

"Oh, I have no doubt that his death is related," said Devlin grimly. "Two murders in the space of a week is too much of a coincidence, especially with the connections between them. I'm willing to bet that the person who murdered Hughes is also the person who murdered Washington. Which means that—nice as your theory is—it couldn't have been Hughes who killed Washington on Sunday."

Devlin's voice hardened. "And it also means that this murderer is dangerous, Gemma. I know you've been doing some investigating on your own. I appreciate your efforts to help and I know that with your knowledge of Oxford and the University, you have an insider's advantage. But I'm telling you to leave it well alone now. In spite of what Mabel Cooke thinks, this isn't some Agatha Christie novel where everything will be nicely explained in the library— this is the real deal. And this killer has just shown that he's not afraid to kill again. You could be in serious danger, Gemma. The next person the killer decides to silence could be you."

In spite of myself, Devlin's words sent a shiver up my spine. Even though I had been the one to find Washington's body, it had all felt slightly surreal. It was only now that I felt the breath of menace on my neck for the first time and realised that this wasn't some TV crime drama... this was the real thing. And I was caught in the thick of it.

I cleared my throat, not wanting to show Devlin that his words had scared me. I was pleased my voice sounded quite calm and steady as I asked, "Do the other suspects on the case have alibis for last night?"

"I've spoken to Mike Bailey and no, he hasn't got

an alibi. He claims that he was at home watching TV—not something that's easy to prove or disprove."

"What about Justine Washington?"

There was silence at the other end of the line. "Justine doesn't have an alibi either, although I wouldn't class her as a strong suspect in this case."

"Well, of course you would say that."

"What's that supposed to mean?"

"Nothing," I said. Then I burst out, "Why are you so reluctant to consider Justine as a suspect? You know as well as I do that she has a perfectly good motive to kill Washington. *And* she lied about not knowing that he was in Oxford... and about meeting him on Saturday night... She *should* be one of the prime suspects and probably would be if it weren't for you tiptoeing around her dainty stilettos."

"Jealousy doesn't become you, Gemma."

"I'm not jealous!" I snapped. "But I know a suspect when I see one, which is more than I can say for some people!"

I ended the call and slammed the phone down. Seething, I finished dressing and left the house. I was an hour late, I realised. The call with Seth and then the conversation with Devlin had delayed me. But I knew that Fletcher and Cassie would be at the tearoom already—hopefully they could hold the fort until I arrived. If there was any fort to hold, I thought dourly.

My spirits didn't improve when I arrived in Meadowford-on-Smythe. I pulled up in front of the tearoom and could see at a glance through the windows that the dining room was empty. I sighed. It didn't look like today's business was going to be any better than yesterday's. I felt fear clench my stomach again. If this case didn't get solved soon, my little tearoom was doomed.

Cassie looked up as I walked in and said, "So Hughes is dead."

My mouth dropped open. "How did you know? I only just heard from Devlin myself and he can't have even spoken to the press yet."

She grimaced. "Fletcher found the body."

"What?"

"Yeah. He was out searching for Muesli again this morning—just near where we were last night—and he found it, dumped behind some bushes. He was the one who notified the police." She sighed. "He's really upset about it, as you can imagine. He called to let me know what happened and I told him to take the day off. I didn't think he'd be much good here anyway."

"Oh my God... do you think we should go and see him?"

She shook her head. "I'm not sure he'd appreciate it at the moment. He sounded like he just wanted to hole up in his house and be left alone. I think I can understand that—especially with the police crawling all over the woods next to his house. I think he just wants some peace and security, in an environment he can control." She gave a wry smile. "I told him that maybe there'll be a silver lining—that with the police combing the area, they might find Muesli. I think that cheered him up a bit. He said he was going to speak to one of the officers and ask them to keep an eye out for a grey tabby cat."

I thought of our search in the woods last night and wondered if the body had been there already. We might even have walked right past it. I shuddered.

Cassie looked at me curiously. "So you spoke to Devlin at last?"

In a terse voice, I repeated the conversation I had had with him. "I can't believe he said I was jealous of Justine!" I fumed.

"Well, aren't you?" said Cassie with a teasing smile.

I glared at her. "Not you too! Why does everyone think that I must be motivated by jealousy where Devlin is concerned? I couldn't care less if he wants to sleep with every woman in Oxford!"

"I'm not going to comment on what a blatant lie that is," said Cassie. "But you have to admit, Gemma, that you took against Justine from the beginning. I mean, you were immediately convinced that Devlin must be biased towards her because he's attracted to her. Isn't that jumping to conclusions?"

"I'm not jumping to anything. I saw them together," I muttered. "Anyway, my point is—Justine is just as strong a suspect as Mike Bailey but no one is focusing on her! We've all been chasing after Hughes—or Mike—when actually, she could be the murderer and getting away with it! Oh, she's clever... She's so smooth and she has an answer for everything. She even fooled me," I said, shaking my head. "She played her part so well that, like everyone else, I didn't take her seriously as a suspect. Instead, I got so distracted investigating Hughes that I never even considered her part in the affair..."

I paced up and down next to the counter, thinking furiously. Suddenly, I stopped. "I'm not going to accept it. I don't care what Devlin says—I'm sure Justine is involved. In fact, if Hughes's alibi for Sunday morning turned out to be false, why not Justine's as well? She *says* she was at a yoga class, but if Devlin's sergeant did such a poor job of checking Hughes's alibi, he could have missed something with Justine's too."

Cassie rolled her eyes at me. "So what are you going to do—check it yourself?"

I smiled slowly at her. "You know, that's not a bad idea."

"Gemma, I was joking," she groaned.

I ignored her, thinking out loud to myself, "We need to go to the dance studio and find some way of checking that Justine did attend her class last Sunday morning."

"That's easy," said Cassie. "I'm sure this is what the sergeant did. All members of the studio have a concession card which gets stamped each time they come for a class. The stamp has the date and time on it. So just checking her card will tell you whether she was at that class."

"Oh..." I said in disappointment. "That won't work then. How am I going to find a way to see her card?"

"Well, actually, the members don't keep their cards on them. We developed the system because people kept forgetting their cards, and nowadays everyone has so many cards, they hate having to carry another one in their wallet. So what we do is we keep the cards at the studio. It's a pretty old-fashioned system: they're basically like index cards, kept in those catalogue drawers, like from an old-fashioned library. Each drawer covers surnames starting with certain letters of the alphabet—you know, like one for A/B, one for C/D, then E/F... all the way up to Y/Z. Yeah..." She nodded ruefully at my expression. "This isn't anything like modern gyms with their digital readers and barcodes and things... hey, this is Oxford. What worked for the Tudors is good enough for us." She grinned.

"So members just ask for their cards when they come in and get them stamped for their classes?"

"Pretty much."

"But—isn't that easy to scam? I mean, anyone could come in and pretend to be someone else and scrounge a free class."

"Well, in theory, yes," Cassie admitted. "But in reality, you'd have to know the full name of the person you're pretending to be, pick a class that that person has signed up for... and besides, it's a small place. The receptionist pretty much knows all our members. You couldn't walk in there and pretend that you're Nicky Wilcox. Aside from the fact that they'd recognise you look different immediately, they'd ask you where your baby was, whether you had blonde highlights done last week, how your husband's promotion was coming along, and whether you liked the cake recipe Mrs Doyle gave you." Cassie grinned. "You won't believe how much gossip and idle curiosity there is in small villages. It's probably harder to fake your way past the locals than to get into the Pentagon with a false identity."

"Okay... so basically what you're saying is if we can get access to that drawer catalogue behind the reception desk, we'd be able to check Justine's card and see if it was stamped for Sunday morning."

"Yes, but I don't know what you're trying to achieve. I'm sure the sergeant would have already done that."

"I can't explain it, Cass—I'd just like to see it for myself."

She threw her hands up. "Fine. I'll tell you what—why don't we go over this afternoon, then, after we close here? I could distract Barb, the studio receptionist, while you sneak behind the counter and have a look."

I looked around the empty dining room. "I don't know why we don't just go now," I said despondently. "I might as well close for the day."

"Hey, you never know—things might pick up around lunchtime," said Cassie.

She turned out to be right—but only marginally. We had a tenth of our usual business at lunch and a little dribble for the rest of the day, but I was grateful to have *any* customer at all. At least it was better than yesterday when the tearoom had sat empty all day. But it still wasn't enough to save me from closure. I needed faith restored in my tearoom and business to return to what it had been—and the only way I could see that happening was if the mystery of the murder—*double* murder now—was solved.

CHAPTER TWENTY-THREE

I'm not sure what I expected when we headed down to the dance studio late that afternoon. Okay, so maybe I had a vision of Cassie and me in skin-tight black bodysuits, ducking expertly around corners and skilfully picking locks to secret drawers while a creepy soundtrack played in the background...

The reality was far more banal than my *Charlie's Angels* fantasy. We arrived at the studio to find the reception fairly empty and a class obviously in progress from the sound of mystical music coming from Studio 2. The only person we could see was Barb behind the reception. She looked up at the jingling of the bells attached to the studio door and smiled as we came in.

"Hiya, Cass—I didn't think you were teaching any classes tonight?"

"I'm not," said Cassie. "I just came in to... uh... take a look at some of those new dance shoes we ordered recently."

Barb's eyes lit up. "Ooh, they're beautiful. I've been thinking of getting a pair myself, even though I don't do ballroom dancing. Shame they've got soft suede soles—they'd get ruined if I had to wear them out and about, especially in the rain. Otherwise, I really fancied a pair."

"Which was your favourite?"

"Here, I'll show you. There's one in gold satin with a T-bar that's just gorgeous!" She came out from behind the counter and led Cassie into Studio 1, where a shoe rack stood in the corner, displaying several pairs of dancing shoes. Cassie gave me a wink and followed her into the room. They disappeared from sight around the corner of the doorway but I could see their reflection in the mirrors that lined the studio walls.

I kept my eyes on that reflection. As soon as I was certain that they were safely in the corner with the shoe rack, I darted behind the reception counter and went up to the chest of miniature catalogue drawers sitting against the back wall. I found the drawer marked "W/X" and searched hurriedly. *Walsh... Webster... Wilcox... Willeton... Woodley... Wright...* No Washington.

Dismayed, I rifled through the cards again. No,

definitely no Washington.

Then I had a thought. Quickly, I shut the drawer and opened the one marked "S/T" and looked through the cards there.

Bingo.

I pulled out the card labelled: "Justine Smith". Of course! Justine had mentioned at the book club meeting that she mostly used her maiden name these days. I flipped it over and looked at the grid on the back. There it was, clearly stamped, the date and time for her Sunday morning yoga class. My hopes sank. Looked like she had been here after all.

The jingling of the bells alerted me one second before the studio front door opened. I managed to shove the card back and slam the drawer shut before I whirled around to face who had just come in.

"Gemma!" Glenda Bailey and Ethel Webb regarded me with delight. "What are you doing here?"

I slid casually out from behind the reception counter. "Oh, I'm just waiting for Cassie. She wanted to check out some dancing shoes."

At that moment, Barb and Cassie re-joined us in the foyer. Glenda looked at the receptionist eagerly and pointed in the direction of the music.

"Oh, Barb—is that the Seniors Yoga class? Have they started already?"

"That's the Yoga for Expectant Mums."

Glenda frowned. "But... isn't the Seniors Yoga on at 6:30 p.m.?"

"Yes, but it's only just gone half past five," Barb

said, nodding at the small clock on the reception counter. "The Seniors Yoga class isn't on for another hour—I'm afraid you have a bit of a wait."

"Dearie me, it's all my fault," said Ethel. "If only I'd remembered about changing the clocks. It's no wonder I've been arriving early to everything this week." She made a sound of distress. "Oh dear... does this mean we have to wait around here for another hour?"

"Oh, let's not wait," said Glenda. "You can always come with me to try the Sunday morning class instead."

I looked at Glenda with interest. "You do the yoga class on Sunday mornings? Were you there last weekend?"

Glenda beamed. "Yes, I've been doing that class for three months now. Oh, you must try it, Gemma. Yoga is ever so good for you! I was reading an article in *Cosmo* which said that yoga is how all the celebrities manage to look so young and stay so—and it does wonders for your sex life!"

I wondered why on earth Glenda was reading *Cosmo*, whilst Cassie muttered under her breath, "Too much information..."

I tried to bring the conversation back on subject. "Is the class on Sunday normally quite busy?"

"Oh yes, it's very popular. I think half of Oxfordshire must be here." Glenda laughed. "The teacher is marvellous so I know several ladies who come from miles away to attend the class."

"I suppose... you know a lot of the regulars?" I didn't know where I was going with this line of questioning but I was just following an instinct.

Glenda nodded. "It's mostly the same people who come every week."

"There's an American woman called Justine who's in that class too, I think?"

"Oh, Mabel was telling me all about Justine," Ethel piped up. "She's in Mabel's book club too. She's very attractive, isn't she? Mabel says she's a real man-eater."

"Ooh, I'd better take some lessons from her!" Glenda giggled.

Cassie rolled her eyes. I stifled the urge to laugh.

"And apparently she's the wife of the man who was murdered in your tearoom," added Ethel. "Fancy that! It's a small world, isn't it?"

I could see Barb listening with wide-eyed fascination and realised suddenly that all of this would be on the village grapevine by tomorrow morning. I gave Cassie a look and she took the hint, turning and dragging Barb behind the reception counter on some pretext. I put a gentle hand under Glenda's elbow and steered the little old lady away from the counter, so that we were out of earshot.

"So, this Justine... was she at your class last Sunday?" I asked casually.

Any hopes I might have had that the stamp on the card was wrong were dashed when Glenda said, "Oh yes, she was right next to me. We usually have the same spots, you see, every week. I'm normally in the front right corner and Justine's right behind me."

"So she was *definitely* at the class last Sunday," I said desperately. I knew I was grasping at straws but something egged me on.

Glenda nodded. "She was there already when I arrived." Then she paused and added, "But she hardly stayed for the class! She left so early. We were doing the Three-Legged Down Dog and she suddenly got up from her mat and left."

"What time was this?" I asked sharply.

Glenda frowned. "I think it was about ten to fifteen minutes after the start of class."

Which would have made it around 8:15 a.m. at the latest. Washington had been killed sometime between 7:45 a.m. and 8:40 a.m., when I had discovered him. Geoffrey Hughes had arrived late for his meeting with Washington—probably around 8:25 a.m.—and the American was already dead by then. It was tight but there would have been time for Justine to nip down the road from the studio and do the deed.

"Gemma, dear—are you all right?"

I came back to myself with a start. "Yes, sorry, Glenda." I smiled warmly at her and gave her hand a squeeze. "Thank you so much! You don't realise how much you've helped me!"

"Well, I'm always glad to help if I can, dear," she said, looking slightly bemused.

Leaving Glenda and Ethel to chat with Barb, I dragged Cassie back out into the street. Quickly, I recounted what Glenda had told me.

"You realise what this means? It means that Justine lied about everything! First she claimed that she didn't even know Washington was in Oxford—when she actually met him on Saturday night—and now we find that she lied about her alibi too. Why didn't she tell the police that she left the yoga class early? She must be hiding something."

"Hey, you've convinced me," said Cassie with a shrug. "The thing is, I'm not the person who needs to be convinced—Devlin is."

I compressed my lips. "Well, he's going to have to listen to my suspicions about Justine now. He can't ignore this and he can't protect her anymore."

**

Twilight was falling by the time I started cycling for home. Not that that bothered me. I'd cycled in the dark before and my bike headlights lit the road well in front of me. It was crisp and cold, my breath coming out in clouds of steam in front of my face and the wind stinging my cheeks as the bicycle picked up speed. I pumped the pedals hard, partly to warm up and partly to give myself something to do as my mind churned with doubts and questions.

I knew I had to speak to Devlin again. I had to tell him about Justine's fake alibi for Sunday morning. But a part of me was dreading the discussion. Okay, so maybe I *was* a little bit jealous of her. Who wouldn't be? She was the kind of woman that would make anyone feel insecure. And the thought of listening to Devlin defending her made me squirm.

Why did it bother me so much? I leaned slightly into the curve of the road as the bicycle negotiated the bend. Was it the thought that Devlin might care for her? But she was a suspect in the case.... He couldn't seriously be contemplating getting involved with her? Surely, there must have been police rules against this sort of thing... conflict of interest... abuse of power... biased investigations...

Then I remembered the gossip at the book club, how my mother's friends had been talking about Devlin's "scandal" up north where he had been accused of becoming romantically involved with an attractive female suspect on his last case. Maybe Devlin didn't care about breaking the rules.

I frowned. There had always been a wild, rebellious streak about him—especially back when we were students together—but somehow I always felt certain of a core of integrity in him. I just couldn't imagine him jeopardising a case for his own personal pleasures. At the heart of it, I knew he was a good detective and cared passionately about seeing justice served. Would he really let his feelings, and a passing physical attraction, cloud his judgement so much?

But what, I reminded myself bitterly, did I *really* know about Devlin O'Connor? It had been eight years since I last saw him—and people can change a lot in eight years. I had certainly never expected him to become a detective! I didn't know what I expected him to be when I met him again—perhaps the leader of a rock band at the Glastonbury Music Festival. I laughed wryly to myself at the image.

I leaned back on my seat and let the bicycle coast for a bit as my thoughts drifted back into the past. I wondered if Devlin still played his guitar. He used to play the most hauntingly beautiful melodies, strumming them softly as we sat together on summer evenings in the college gardens, the air soft and balmy around us and the sky painted with streaks of sunset pink and orange... the long, carefree days of student life... I could still remember the way he had looked, that dark lock of hair falling over his eyes as he bent over the strings, concentrating on the chords... and then he would look up and lean across, lowering his head to mine...

I shook my head sharply, dispelling the memory. I had to stop doing this! Whatever we had was in the past now and I had to put it behind me—which meant accepting the fact that Devlin was now a different man and could easily let his feelings for another woman cloud his judgement on a case...

Suddenly, I became aware of a noise behind me. It had been growing faintly but I had been so lost in my thoughts that I had barely noticed it until now. I looked over my shoulder and saw a shape looming out of the darkness. It was a car. Big, powerful, and gaining on me.

I pedalled a bit faster as I felt suddenly uneasy.

Devlin's words from that morning came back to me.

"You could be in serious danger, Gemma. The next person the killer decides to silence could be you."

CHAPTER TWENTY-FOUR

I threw a look over my shoulder again. The glare from the car's headlights blinded me and made it impossible to see who was behind the wheel. I faced front and pedalled harder. The expanse of tarmac stretched out in front of me—there were still at least a couple of miles before the suburbs of North Oxford. Suddenly I realised how very quiet and empty a country road could be.

I tried to pedal faster, panting as I leaned over the handlebars. My legs were beginning to ache. I could hear the car coming behind me now, faster and faster. I pumped my legs harder, my breath coming in quick, short gasps. I threw another look behind me. I knew I shouldn't have kept looking—it only slowed me down—but the need was almost compulsive. I still couldn't make out what kind of car it was or the face of the man at the wheel.

Or woman, I thought suddenly. I tried to remember what kind of car Justine drove. It was black, I remembered my mother saying. *Just like this one...*

I turned back to the front and looked desperately ahead. The road was entering the outskirts of the suburbs now but I couldn't see anyone else on the streets—no pedestrians, no other cars or cyclists. The muscles in my thighs were screaming in agony and my hands were sweaty where they were clenched on the handlebars, but I didn't dare slow down.

Then I spotted a section of pavement up ahead where the edge sloped down gradually to meet the road rather than ending in a sharp curb. It must have been designed for wheelchair access. It would also enable me to gain the pavement with my bicycle. The car wouldn't be able to follow me. I'd be able to cycle between the houses and maybe down one of the back lanes and escape it.

Hope surged through me, giving me new energy. I yanked my handlebars to the left and headed for the incline, pumping my legs furiously, my aching muscles forgotten. But just as I was about to reach the pavement, the car suddenly gunned its engines and shot past me, pulling over with a screech directly in front of me. I swerved and narrowly avoided hitting my front wheel on its bumper. My bike tipped sideways and I lost my balance, screaming as I fell over and hit the ground.

The driver's door swung open and a figure stepped

out.

"Gemma! Are you all right?"

"Devlin?" I gasped, squinting up at him. All I could see was a black silhouette outlined against the blinding headlights, which hadn't been switched off.

He dropped down next to me and put a gentle hand on my arm, helping me to my feet.

"What the blazes is going on, Gemma? You were cycling like a lunatic! You could have had an accident!"

"I thought... I thought..." I could barely speak as I tried to catch my breath. Then suddenly, I began to laugh uncontrollably. Devlin looked at me like I had lost my mind.

"I'm sorry," I said, wiping tears from my eyes. "It was just that... Oh, I was so stupid... But you gave me a scare..." I put a hand on my chest, trying to regain my composure. "I thought you were someone coming after me... You know, after what you said to me this morning—"

"Well, I'm glad to hear that *something* I say gets through to you," said Devlin dryly.

I took a long shuddering breath. "It was just because it was dark and I couldn't see you behind the wheel—all I could see were these two headlights bearing down on me like creepy monster eyes and the car sounded really ominous. What kind of car is it anyway? You've got an engine on it like a sabre-tooth tiger."

"It's a Jaguar XK." Devlin sounded amused. "And

I wasn't gunning the engine or anything. In fact, I was driving in quite a leisurely fashion and following you sedately, until you started cycling like a maniac from the Tour de France. Then I was just trying to catch up with you to ask what the matter was."

"Why were you following me anyway?"

"I was coming down to North Oxford to speak to you and happened to see you ahead of me on the road." He paused. "I wanted to give you an update on the case and what we'd found out about Hughes."

I was surprised. "Oh... thanks. That's really nice of you. Did you find any leads to his killer?"

"No, nothing. We searched the whole area where his body was found—nothing. We also searched his room in college. The only thing we turned up of note was an open envelope on his desk, addressed to him with no return address. The letter inside was missing. But what was interesting was that the envelope had a postmark showing that it was posted on Tuesday, from Meadowford-on-Smythe."

"From Meadowford?"

"Yes, and given that that's where his body was found... I think there's a connection. Of course, it would help if we could find the letter but although we searched his office twice—and his house too—we couldn't find it."

"Maybe he destroyed it."

Devlin inclined his head. "Very probably. There *were* some ashes in his fireplace, which could be the remnants of the burnt letter. I guess we'll never know."

"So you can't take a guess at what was in the letter?"

"At a push, I'd say an invitation from someone in Meadowford, enticing Hughes to go out there."

"Or—it could be someone who purposefully posted the letter from Meadowford-on-Smythe, to divert suspicion. People come here all the time from other places—to the antique shops and market stalls on the weekends, to my tearoom, to the pub, to the dance studio..."

"True," Devlin acknowledged. "And Oxford is only ten—fifteen minutes away by car. My sergeant will be going to the Meadowford post office tomorrow and making some enquiries, to see if anyone remembers anything from Tuesday."

"I hope he does a better job than what he did with the alibis," I muttered under my breath.

Devlin's gaze sharpened. "What do you mean?"

"I've got new evidence against Justine Washington," I said, raising my chin slightly. "I double-checked her alibi for Sunday morning. She said she was at a yoga class at the dance studio in the village."

"Yes, I know."

"Well, she may have arrived for class, but she certainly didn't stay for it. She left after ten minutes."

"Yes, I know," said Devlin again.

"You knew?" I stared at him. "So you knew that she was lying about her alibi all along?"

He looked exasperated. "Gemma, do you think I don't know how to do my job? I didn't trust my sergeant's report so I spoke to Justine again myself and she admitted to me that she hadn't told the full truth."

"I'm surprised you even doubted her."

He narrowed his eyes. "I'm beginning to get tired of your snide comments where Justine is concerned. If you have something to say, just come out and say it."

"Fine! I think you're completely biased towards her and giving her preferential treatment. She's a suspect in this murder case but you deliberately ignore evidence against her."

"Are you questioning my professionalism?" Devlin said in a silky voice.

I hesitated. There was nothing overtly threatening in his tone or words, but somehow I had a feeling that I didn't want to push him.

"I just think that... maybe you don't want to admit it, but you're prejudiced towards Justine. You're letting your emotions affect your judgement. You *have* been known to let things get too... er... personal in the past, with suspects in murder investigations."

His expression hardened. "I suppose Mabel Cooke and her friends have been gossiping about me?"

I shrugged. "It was in the papers. I'm sure it's common knowledge. And besides, you should know by now that no secret is sacred in a small village."

"It wasn't a secret. There was nothing between me

and the suspect in that case up in Leeds," he said curtly. "I simply felt sorry for her. I knew she wasn't guilty. In any case, I would never let my personal feelings interfere with an investigation."

"Well, of course you would say that—but what if you're not aware of it?" I said. "I mean, you say you knew that Justine lied about her alibi but you're not doing anything about it. Why aren't you taking it more seriously?'

"Because when you've been doing this a while, Gemma, you begin to realise that people lie for all sorts of reasons—but not always to do with murder."

"I don't understand."

He sighed. "I don't expect you to. Just... trust me, okay? I'm telling you that Justine is not the murderer. I... I have an instinct about it."

"That's a pretty handy instinct," I sneered.

"Why don't you be honest and say what this is really about?" he snapped. "You're just jealous of Justine."

"Me?" My voice was shrill. "I'm not jealous!"

"You could have fooled me."

"How dare you!" I found that I was trembling with anger. "Don't try to twist things around and make this about me, Devlin! Just because I felt something for you once doesn't mean that I'd be so weak again."

He stepped closer to me, his blue eyes blazing. "I'm not the one who's been disappointed that things between us aren't what they once were. Yes, don't deny it—I can see it in your eyes every time you look at me. Bloody hell, Gemma! This isn't some novel! Did you really think we were going to see each other again after all this time and everything would fall back into place? Is that what you were hoping for? That I would send you some fervent letter telling you that *'I am half agony, half hope'*?"

I flinched. I didn't think those beautiful words, which I had always loved, could hurt so much coming out of his lips.

"I don't expect anything from you, Devlin O'Connor!" I said furiously.

"Oh, really? Because every time we've been together, I see that look in your eyes—"

"What look?"

"The look wanting me to..." He leaned suddenly towards me.

My heart hammered in my chest. I realised that he was going to kiss me—and I didn't know if I wanted him to or not. All I could think was that no one made me feel as angry and defensive and indignant and frustrated—and gloriously alive as this man did. I stood there, staring up at him, trembling as he paused inches from my face.

Then slowly, Devlin raised his head and eased himself back. I felt a stab of disappointment. He sighed and ran a hand through his hair, causing a lock to fall forwards over his eyes. My fingers twitched and I had to fight the urge to reach up and brush it back across his forehead.

"I'm sorry," he said in a more controlled voice. "I

don't normally lose my temper like that. You just seem to..." He broke off and gave a humourless laugh. "I'm sorry," he said again. "I behaved unprofessionally just now and I apologise."

I swallowed. "It's fine," I said in a small voice. I couldn't quite meet his eyes.

There was a long, strained silence, then Devlin gave another sigh and said, "Look, Gemma... we're both living in the same city now. It's inevitable that we would run into each other—even if we weren't involved in a murder investigation together. We're both adults. Don't you think we could just bury the past and have some sort of civil relationship? Find a way to get along with each other?"

I hesitated, then said, "Yes, you're right. I'm sorry—I...I think I let my emotions get the better of me sometimes."

He smiled slightly. "Okay, so... Friends?"

I stared at him wordlessly for a moment, then gave a brief nod. "Friends."

He stepped back from me. "And I need you to trust me, Gemma, and trust that I'm doing everything needed in this investigation. I do take every piece of evidence into consideration, whatever my personal feelings might be—"

"What about Justine?"

The shutters came down over his eyes. "I promise you, I'm not giving her any special treatment."

With that, I had to be satisfied.

CHAPTER TWENTY-FIVE

I woke up before my alarm the next morning and lay in bed, staring up at the ceiling. I'm not usually a morning person—I need a hot shower and a strong cup of tea before I can speak in anything more than monosyllables—but this morning, I found myself surprisingly awake and clear-headed. I lay in bed, my mind buzzing with the events of yesterday: the news of Hughes's death, the cheating scandal at Gloucester College, the conversation with Ethel and Glenda in the dance studio, Justine's fake alibi, and then the frightening bike ride and finally the scene with Devlin... I shied away from the last one. Instead, I focused back on the dance studio. Something about that was bothering me—something in my conversation with Ethel and Glenda when they were talking about being early for the yoga class... But I couldn't put my finger on it.

I lay in bed thinking about it for another ten minutes, then gave up. I rose, showered, dressed, and headed for Meadowford-on-Smythe. Maybe it would be nice to get to the tearoom super early for once, before the whole village was up—as long as I didn't find another dead body this time.

The Little Stables Tearoom was blessedly quiet—and dead-body free—when I got there. I had a full hour to myself, before Cassie and Fletcher would probably arrive, and I set to work in the kitchen. Fletcher had been attempting to teach me how to make his famous scones and I went through the steps now: sifting the flour into the bowl, adding a pinch of salt, mixing in the caster sugar, and then a teaspoon of baking powder, just to make the mixture even lighter and fluffier. Then I added the fresh butter and used my fingers to rub it into the mixture.

I remembered Fletcher's instructions and tried to incorporate as much air into the mixture as I could, getting my fingers nice and floury, until it resembled very fine bread crumbs. Then I cracked two eggs and beat them into the dry mixture, followed by a dash of milk, which I poured in very slowly and carefully. Not too much milk, I reminded myself—recalling Fletcher's instructions—otherwise the mixture would get too wet and the scones would "drop" and lose their shape. I mixed it all slowly with a wooden spoon.

Finally, I tipped the dough mixture out of the bowl and onto the floured board, then lightly began to knead it. Here was the real skill of making great scones. The mixture had to be kneaded but not "handled" too much, otherwise the scones would come out horrible and hard. So it was a delicate balance, carefully rolling the dough, taking it from the outside and pushing it gently towards the middle. Fletcher actually advised leaving the dough to rise in the fridge before working it too much, even leaving it overnight—but I was disobeying him this morning as I was too impatient. So I worked at the mixture until it looked smooth, then I scattered a bit more flour across the board and picked up the rolling pin.

Now came the other secret to really good scones. I had to make sure that I didn't roll the mixture out too thinly. I pressed the rolling pin across the dough, turning it with one hand as I rolled with the other one, until the dough had been flattened into a sort of circular slab about an inch and half thick. Feeling pleased with myself, I picked up the cutter and carefully pressed out the scone shapes, transferring them to a baking tray. Then I brushed the top with an egg wash—so that they would come out of the oven with a lovely golden sheen—and finally popped the whole tray in the pre-heated oven.

The rhythm of baking was so soothing that I was in a serene mood by the time Cassie and Fletcher arrived to start the day. The wonderful smell of baking scones was already permeating the kitchen and Cassie sniffed appreciatively as she came in.

"My God, Gemma—don't tell me you've been baking? And it actually smells edible!"

I laughed. After the stressful week, it was nice to finally have a bit of light-hearted banter. "You know, I've discovered that baking isn't that hard—if you follow the recipe instructions and measure the ingredients."

Cassie snorted. "Really? So you have to actually follow the recipe, instead of thinking you're Jamie Oliver and tossing things in at random, huh? I would never have guessed."

I laughed again and threw a tea towel at her.

"Well, I really have Fletcher to thank for being such a good, patient teacher..." I glanced at Fletcher, who had come in after Cassie. My high spirits disappeared as I remembered what had happened yesterday.

"Fletcher, I'm sorry. I heard that you found the body of Professor Hughes. That must have been horrible," I said quietly.

He nodded silently.

"And... did the police find any sign of Muesli?"

He shook his head. I bit my lip and glanced at Cassie, who gave a helpless shrug.

"Would you like us to come and help you search again after work today?" I asked.

He shook his head again. "It's no use anymore." There was despair in every line of his body.

I went over to him, patting his shoulder

awkwardly. "Aw, Fletcher, don't talk like that! I've known people whose cats disappeared for a month or something and then suddenly returned, completely fine. You mustn't give up hope, okay?"

He nodded and looked slightly cheered. He walked over to the oven and opened it to peer at my scones. I awaited his verdict with bated breath.

He sniffed and nodded approvingly. "They look good, Gemma."

"Wait till you taste them before you decide," said Cassie darkly, with the bitter experience of someone who has suffered my attempts at baking in the past.

I was about to retort when my phone rang. It was a local Oxford number I didn't recognise. I went back out into the quiet of the dining room to take the call.

"Hello? Gemma Rose speaking."

"Miss Rose? This is Cheryl White from the Oxford City Library. You put in a request for some information from the newspaper archives?"

"Oh yes, that's right." I had completely forgotten about this.

"Well, we've retrieved a couple of articles which might be of interest to you. Sorry for the delay—it took us longer than usual as they were held in the older archives and we had to put in a special request."

With Hughes dead now, it seemed pointless looking through the articles. I'd originally requested them when I was searching for a motive for Hughes to murder Washington but now that I knew about the cheating scandal via Seth and his chat with the old don, Professor Wilkins, I already had that information. And in any case, it was irrelevant since Hughes wasn't the killer after all. I was about to thank her and apologise, when she added:

"We're trialling a new system—we're digitising our archives so that we can now email members a link to access digital copies of articles held in the library database. Saves you having to come physically to the library. All you have to do is subscribe to the library archive service."

I considered. To be honest, I felt a bit bad—after she had obviously gone to so much trouble—to tell her that I didn't need the information anymore. It seemed easier just to accept the links.

"That sounds great," I said. "Thank you."

"You're welcome. We're very excited about this new service and it would be wonderful if you could answer a survey afterwards on how user-friendly the system is. It would be very helpful to us."

"Sure, of course."

"The link to the survey will be in the email, along with links to the files. You'll need your library card and membership number to set up the subscription."

A minute later, my phone beeped with the email. I opened it absentmindedly and went through the motions of subscribing to the archive system, then clicked on the links she had sent me. The first was a copy of a page in an internal University publication. There was a short, succinct paragraph mentioning the cheating scheme and saying that disciplinary measures were being brought on the students involved, with no extra details. Well, I didn't imagine that Gloucester College would want to dwell much on such an incident.

The second piece was from one of the tabloid papers and had much more detail, though I wondered how much of it was gossip and speculation. Having been the victim of such an article myself now, I was much more cynical about anything published. It was filled with the usual disclaimers such papers use: "It is rumoured that...", "A source claims...", "Apparently..."—but very little actual fact. They did mention the names of the students involved, however. I recognised Washington and Hughes from the list immediately: "M. Smith, **D. Washington**, **G.C. Hughes**, S. Greer, N.F. Wilson, T. O'Keefe, M. Williams, and D.E. Owens".

I was surprised to see the large number of names—it had obviously been a syndicate of some kind—but it seemed a very brazen attempt to fool the college officials. According to the article, only two students had been found guilty and were "sent down"—the Oxford University euphemism for "expelled". The rest had been cautioned but essentially let off due to lack of evidence.

My gaze sharpened on the first name on the list: "M. Smith". I remembered that Justine's maiden name was Smith. Could there have been a connection? Smith was an awfully common surname though—common enough that two people having that same surname wouldn't mean much. Or was it too much of a coincidence?

***

It was another depressingly quiet day. I kept telling myself not to panic—to give it time. Today was Friday and maybe things would get back to normal again by next week. After all, everything blew over after a while, and next week the tabloids would be filled with some new scandal and everyone would have forgotten about the murder in my tearoom. Next week, the tourists would be back in hordes, I told myself.

But deep inside, I knew that if this case wasn't solved soon, my little tearoom would be joining Washington and Hughes as casualties.

I was almost glad when Cassie suggested again that we shut early. This time I agreed. I let her and Fletcher go first, hanging on for another half an hour in vain hope. But when four o'clock rolled around without a single customer in sight, I sighed and walked over to the front door and flipped the "OPEN" sign over to "CLOSED". Then I switched off all the lights and gathered my things, trying to shake off the feeling of depression that weighed on my shoulders.

As I was locking the front door, my phone rang. I answered it absentmindedly, tucking the phone between my right ear and shoulder as I continued to wrestle with the stiff old lock.

"Hello?"

"Gemma? This is Justine Smith."

I stopped what I was doing and slowly moved the phone to my hand.

"Justine... How nice to hear from you," I said.

"I hope I haven't caught you at a bad time?"

"No, not at all... I'm just shutting up the tearoom, actually."

"You're in Meadowford?"

"Yes, but I'm just about to head back to North Oxford, if you—"

"No, actually, I'm near Meadowford myself." She hesitated, then said, "I was wondering if I might speak to you, Gemma—privately."

"Oh... er... of course, go ahead."

"No, not over the phone. I'd prefer to meet in person. Are you free at the moment?"

"Um... I... I suppose I am," I said, caught off guard.

"Great. How about if we meet at the old village smithy in half an hour? I've got my car and I can give you a lift back to your parents' place afterwards if you like."

"Oh, um... sure."

"Great. I'll see you then."

I ended the call and stared at my phone. Why did Justine want to meet me alone? Had she found out that I was asking questions about her yesterday at the dance studio? I thought back to the article from the library archives and that student name on the list: "M. Smith".

I had to speak to Devlin. He had finally given me his direct number before we parted last night, to save me having to beg the Oxfordshire police operator for access again. I rang it now. It went straight to voice mail. I left a terse message asking him to call me back. After a moment's deliberation, I tried Cassie. Her phone went to a messaging service too. Frustrated, I ended the call. Then, on an impulse, I put a call through to Lincoln Green.

A brisk woman's voice answered. "Dr Green's phone."

"Can I speak to Lincoln—I mean, Dr Green, please?"

"Dr Green is in a consult right now. Is it something urgent?"

I hesitated. What could I say? *Yes, sort of—I think this woman might be a murderer and she wants me to go and meet her alone and I was hoping Dr Green might accompany me...?* It sounded totally stupid, even to my own ears. Besides, if Lincoln was consulting, he could hardly abandon his patients and come to meet me—and the hospital was at least half an hour's drive away, anyway.

"No, it's all right. I'll... I'll try him again later."

I hung up and chewed my lip. *What should I do now?* I still didn't like the idea of going to meet Justine alone—without "back up", as it were. *Should I send Justine a text, telling her that I couldn't meet her after all...?*

I frowned. Something in me balked at that. It seemed a bit pathetic. And what if Justine was able to tell me something valuable about the case? It wasn't like I was going to meet a known terrorist or criminal gang leader, for heaven's sake.

Besides, what was the worst that could happen? The old village smithy was a bit far from the centre of the village but it wasn't completely isolated. It was a local historic site, kept for the tourists really, and there were a couple of stone benches outside the building, which were popular with locals and visitors as a place to have their lunch whilst enjoying the view of the surrounding Cotswolds countryside. If anything happened, surely I could scream for help and somebody from the village would hear me?

I looked back down at the half-composed text, then deliberately deleted it. I would go meet Justine and see what she had to say.

CHAPTER TWENTY-SIX

I started walking down the village high street, heading towards the old smithy. The days were getting shorter now and darkness was already closing in, despite it being barely past four in the afternoon. The temperature was falling rapidly too—winter was really in the air—and there were few people out braving the chill weather. A couple of old ladies walked past me on the other side of the street, warmly wrapped up in coats and scarves. They made me think of the Old Biddies. Perhaps I could ask them to accompany me? I cringed slightly at the thought. No. Whatever Justine said to me would be broadcast across the whole of Oxfordshire if they came along. Besides which, I didn't think she would talk to me if they were there.

A man came towards me on my side of the street—a thickset young man with a short crew cut and a pugnacious expression. I realised belatedly that it was Mike Bailey.

"What are you staring at?" he snarled as he came near.

"N-nothing," I stammered quickly, giving him a wide berth.

He grunted, then continued down the street. I hurried on, throwing a couple of glances backwards a few times to make sure he wasn't coming back after me or anything. *Shame I'm not friendly with Mike*, I thought wryly. A big, belligerent man would have been the perfect escort for my meeting with Justine.

Then I thought of Fletcher. OK, so he was anything but belligerent, but he *was* big—and his house was on the way. I could ask him. If Justine had some nefarious plan for me, she would think twice if I was accompanied by a man—of course, Fletcher was more the type to run away than fight, but she didn't have to know that.

Quickly, I made my way across the village to the little row of terraced houses. Fletcher's was at the very end and I was pleased to see smoke coming from his chimney. I knocked and he opened the door after a moment, holding a tea towel in one hand.

"Hello, Gemma." He looked surprised to see me.

"Fletcher—are you busy? Can you do me a favour and come with me to see someone?"

"Who?" he said curiously.

"It's a… a lady I know. Don't worry, you don't have to speak to her or anything. In fact, you could just wait for me nearby while I have a quick chat with her. Would you mind?"

He nodded. "Okay. But I just boiled the kettle. To make a cup of tea."

I could hear the sounds of an old-fashioned kettle whistling in the background.

"Oh… well, can you have that tea when we get back? I'll have one with you."

He nodded amiably and opened the door wider to allow me in. "I will take the kettle off the stove," he said, leading the way through the front hall.

I paused as I walked into his cosy, neat living room. "Actually, Fletcher—can I use your loo before we leave?"

He pointed to a doorway on the other side of the living room, leading to a rear hallway. "It's the second door."

I found the toilet—practically no bigger than a broom cupboard—and noted appreciatively that Fletcher's compulsive neatness had extended here too. In fact, I marvelled at how he had managed to fit all the usual toilet knick-knacks so tidily in such a small space, including a cat litter tray in the corner. I was about to undo my jeans when I noticed that the toilet roll was empty. Annoyed, I searched around for a replacement. It seemed that even Fletcher was a typical bachelor. Why couldn't men remember to replace the toilet paper?

There was a cupboard underneath the sink and I crouched down to open it. Then my eyes caught sight of something on the floor. It was wedged between the waste bin and the side of the cupboard—obviously someone had meant to throw it in the bin and had missed, and it had fallen unnoticed into that corner. It looked like a small, flat, cardboard box—the kind that you get from the pharmacy, containing a packet of pills. I picked it up. It was empty but there was a prescription label stuck on the side of the box. I stared at it in puzzlement.

G. Hughes (14/08/1973)
Chlorphenamine: one 4mg tab by mouth
every 4 ~ 6 hours with food

A prescription medication of some kind... for... Professor Hughes? I remembered suddenly about Hughes's pet allergy and his need for special anti-histamines. But why was this here?

My phone beeped suddenly, startling me. I pulled it out of my pocket. It was a message from my mother:

Sorry to bother you, darling, but what's my Apple ID password again? I can't seem to get into my iPad. I was sure it was gemmarose but I've tried that 3 times now and it won't work. Is it gemmarose29 maybe?

Aaargh! How many times did I have to tell her that the Apple ID password required a capital first letter? Honestly, I hoped I didn't become this forgetful when I got older because—

I froze.

My mind whirled as something that had been bothering me fell into place. Being forgetful... forgetful old ladies... Ethel Webb... being early for yoga class... saying she had been early for things all week because she had forgotten to change the clocks... the clocks had changed last weekend...

And Ethel had been the one to confirm Fletcher's alibi.

She said she had seen him leaving his house at 8:45 a.m., *after* the murder had been committed and I had met him arriving at the tearoom myself, just before 9 a.m. He had been breathless and flustered, I remembered, as if he had been running and he said he had overslept.

But if Ethel had forgotten to change her clocks, then she hadn't actually seen Fletcher leave his house at 8:45 a.m. Her clock would have been telling the wrong time because she had forgotten to move it an hour back.

So, in fact, she had actually seen Fletcher leave his house at 7:45 a.m.—one hour earlier.

So where had Fletcher been for that one hour? Why had he let everyone believe that he had overslept and only left his house very late that morning? What had he been doing that had made him so agitated?

I felt slightly sick. My mind recoiled violently from the idea that was forming inside my head. No, no, it couldn't be. There was no connection between Fletcher and the American... or was there? I thought back to last Saturday—when Fletcher had first come out of the kitchen and seen Washington. He had been shocked. I could still remember the look of horror on his face as he stared at Washington. At the time, I'd assumed it was because the American had kicked Muesli. But what if it wasn't because of that? What if it was because Fletcher had *recognised* Washington? They were about the same age. Could it be...?

On a sudden hunch, I flipped to the photo gallery on my phone and brought up the picture of the Matriculation photo again. I zoomed in and stared at the faces of the students sitting next to Washington. There was Hughes on his right... then my eyes widened as I suddenly recognised the tall, lanky student on Washington's left. He was a lot thinner and had a lot more hair then. He was also squinting at the camera, screwing his face up slightly, which was probably why I hadn't recognised him immediately. But now that I was looking, I could see it without doubt.

It was Fletcher.

Fletcher had been a student at Oxford University—in fact, he had matriculated the same year that Washington and Hughes had joined Gloucester College. *Why hadn't he ever told me?*

I flipped to the next image in my gallery—the one of the back of the Matriculation photo with all the student names. I moved along the row until I came to the name next to Washington's: "N.F. Wilson".

Oh my God. I scrabbled to open my email account on my phone and brought up that article from the Oxford City Library archives again. I stared at the list of student names: "M. Smith, B. Washington, G.C. Hughes, S. Greer, N.F. Wilson, T. O'Keefe, M. Williams, and D.E. Owens".

This time, one name from the list jumped out at me: "*N.F. Wilson*".

Fletcher Wilson.

I didn't know if Fletcher went by his middle name but it wouldn't have surprised me. After all, lots of people used their middle names if they didn't like their given first names. You didn't have much say, did you, in what your parents chose for you. I was lucky that I actually liked my name but I suppose if my parents were '60s hippies and had given me the first name of Rainbow or Leaf, I'd be...

I was rambling, I knew. My mind was just trying to prevaricate, to wriggle away, to evade and deny— anything rather than face the sudden, horrible truth that was staring at me:

Fletcher was the murderer.

CHAPTER TWENTY-SEVEN

A sudden knocking sounded at the door. "Gemma? Are you okay?"

I jumped at the sound of Fletcher's voice. The phone slipped from my hands and fell with a resounding *plop!* into the toilet bowel.

"Aaarrggh!" I stared in dismay.

"Gemma?"

"Uh... yeah, I'm fine, Fletcher. I'll be out in a minute," I called as I knelt down next to the toilet bowel and reached my arm in. I grimaced as my fingers dipped into the cold water, then they found the edges of the phone and I fished it out. I grabbed a towel from the rail and rubbed it dry, then pressed the power button, praying silently.

The screen remained black. It was dead.

"*Damn!*" I whispered.

Slowly, I stood up again and took a deep breath. Maybe I was wrong, I thought desperately. It could all be coincidence, right? So Fletcher had lied about his alibi for last Sunday morning—so what? Devlin himself had said that "people lie for all sorts of reasons—but not always to do with murder". And yes, okay, so Fletcher had hidden the fact that he used to be at Oxford. That didn't make him a criminal. Maybe he didn't want to talk about it, maybe he was embarrassed...

...*especially if he had been expelled from the University as part of a cheating scandal*, I thought suddenly. The library article hadn't confirmed it but I was willing to bet that Fletcher was one of the two students who had been sent down following that fiasco.

Now, years later, Washington re-appeared out of the blue and Fate had caused the two of them to meet again in my tearoom. Maybe Fletcher had realised that it was all Washington's fault... maybe the American had taunted Fletcher about it... or they had argued... something had caused him to totally flip and lose it. And he had killed the American on Sunday morning.

And Hughes...? Hughes had been involved in the cheating scandal too. Perhaps Fletcher had invited the Pharmacology professor out to Meadowford-on-Smythe... *that envelope the police had found, postmarked from Meadowford on Tuesday!* Yes, and I remembered now the phone call that Fletcher had taken when we had come back in to his house after searching for Muesli. That had been Wednesday night and had probably been Hughes answering Fletcher's letter and arranging to come to Meadowford that evening.

So Hughes had come... and the cat hairs everywhere had triggered his allergy again—perhaps he had taken some anti-histamines when he used the toilet—and then... Fletcher had killed him too. And dragged the body into the woods outside his house. Then called the police on Thursday morning and pretended to have found the body while out searching for Muesli...

There were still several unanswered questions but everything else fit. And besides, *I knew*. In the pit of my stomach, I knew. I understood now what Devlin had meant about having an instinct for something.

I felt nauseous.

What was Fletcher doing now? Did he suspect that I knew? I strained my ears for sounds from the rest of the house. There was the faint creak of floorboards, then the muffled sounds of banging—it sounded like it was coming from the living room. *What was he doing?*

I looked desperately around the tiny toilet. I couldn't stay here forever. Even if I wanted to, the toilet door didn't have a lock and there was nothing in here that I could wedge against the door to prevent it opening.

I would have to take my chances outside. If I could just act calm and natural, and casually tell Fletcher that I'd changed my mind—that I didn't need him to accompany me after all—then I could simply say goodbye, open his front door, and walk sedately away from his house...

Taking another deep breath, I turned the doorknob and opened the door, stepping into the hallway. Slowly, I walked back to the living room. Fletcher looked up as I came in. He was standing by the living room windows, which had the drapes drawn back, showing the black darkness of the garden and surrounding woods outside.

I froze, staring at the hammer he held in his hands.

"Uh... um, Fletcher..." I licked dry lips. "I've changed my mind, actually. I don't think I need you to come with me after all."

"It's okay," he said, coming towards me. "I will come with you."

"Uh... well, there's really no need," I stammered, edging away from him. "And... um... it's such a horrible, cold night... Wouldn't you rather stay here in the warm, enjoying your nice cup of tea?"

"No, I can have tea afterwards, like you said." He raised the hammer and I flinched.

"Why... why do you have a hammer, Fletcher?"

He looked at his hand in surprise, as if he had forgotten that he was holding it. "Oh, to fix the window." He gestured to the living room windows, which were slightly open. One of the handles was hanging loose. A cold draught wafted in, bringing in the chill of the night air outside. I shivered.

"Ah... right..." I said, trying to calm my racing heart.

I stole a glance around the room. Fletcher was standing between me and the doorway to the front hall. I could try to make a run for it but I didn't think I'd get to the front door before he caught me. My eyes slid past the doorway and continued around the room. Then I spotted it, on the side table just a few feet away from me. An old-fashioned, landline telephone.

If I couldn't get out, maybe I could call for help. All I had to do was find a way to creep over and dial 999 before Fletcher realised what I was doing. I had to find a way to distract him—send him out of the room somehow...

I looked down at his feet. "Fletcher—why don't you change your shoes? I think where we're going might be muddy. Do you have a pair of wellies?"

"Yes," he said. "Okay, I will change into them."

He turned around and went through the doorway on the other side of the room, disappearing into the front hall. I heard him fumbling by the front door. I knew I wouldn't have much time.

I flew across the room to the telephone and dialled rapidly.

"Emergency—which service do you require? Fire, Police, or Ambulance?"

"Police!" I hissed in a whisper. I gave Fletcher's address and continued breathlessly, "I'm in danger. I'm with Fletcher Wilson. He's the killer in the recent murders of—"

"Gemma?"

I whirled around, dropping the handset. Fletcher was standing behind me, the hammer still held in his hand, his feet now encased in wellington boots. But it was his face I focused on. His brows were lowered in a frown.

"Why are you calling me a killer?"

I shifted my weight. "Because... because you are, Fletcher. You murdered Brad Washington—"

"NO!" he yelled, his face puckering. "I didn't mean it! I didn't mean it! He was saying nasty things, horrible things—I wanted him to stop! He was calling me names! Saying I was *STUPID*! Laughing at me! He said I deserved to be kicked out of Oxford even though I didn't cheat in my exams, because I was *STUPID*!"

He waved the hammer as he spoke, his face red, his eyes wild. I stared at him in horror. I had never seen him like this before. He came towards me, speaking earnestly:

"I went to the tearoom early. It was nice and quiet. Then I saw Brad. He was loud and rude. He said nasty things. He sat outside and laughed at me. He told me that *he* was the one who had cheated many years ago—but he made the college think that it was *me*! He made them kick me out!" Fletcher's face flushed even redder. "It wasn't fair! *He* was the one who was wicked, not me! And then... and then he took out a scone from his paper bag and laughed at me. He said I was too *stupid* for Oxford anyway—that I was only good enough to make scones in a tearoom..."

Fletcher's face twitched spasmodically. "I wanted him to stop—to stop talking! I told him to stop! I begged him to stop! And when he wouldn't, I pushed the scone into his mouth, to... to shut him up!"

"And you killed him by accident," I said with sudden realisation. "Because of his dysphagia. He choked."

Fletcher looked at me, his eyes blank. "I just wanted him to stop calling me *stupid*."

"Yes," I said, as soothingly as I could manage. I wondered how long it would take the police to get here. I just had to keep Fletcher talking until then. "I'm sure you didn't mean it."

"I wanted a second chance," said Fletcher brokenly. "Remember, you told me about that book—*Persuasion*? About the girl who gets a second chance—and the man she loves who comes back like a different person. Remember?"

"Yes... yes, I remember," I said nervously.

"I want to come back like a different person. And you told me that people can have second chances and start again, if they want it badly enough. *I* want it badly enough. I want another chance. I wrote a letter to Gloucester College and asked if I could go back. They said no, because I cheated. EXCEPT I DIDN'T!" he yelled suddenly, smashing the hammer down on the coffee table.

I cringed as the wooden surface splintered. I remembered Devlin telling me that Hughes's head had been bashed in by a heavy, blunt instrument. My eyes were riveted on the hammer. Was that what Fletcher had used to kill Hughes?

As if reading my mind, Fletcher said, "I thought Geoffrey would help me. Brad told me that Geoffrey had known about the cheating too. So I sent him a letter and asked him to come and see me. I was very polite, you see. I asked very nicely. I asked him to tell the college the truth—that it wasn't me. That he and Brad did it and blamed it on me. But he wouldn't!"

"Oh... er... that wasn't very nice of him," I said. I couldn't believe I said that, but I didn't know how to respond. I didn't want to get Fletcher riled up any more but I also didn't want him to think I was being unsympathetic either, in case that angered him too.

Fletcher's hand clenched convulsively around the hammer and I took another step back.

"He wouldn't do it for me! And he said I'm not allowed to talk about the cheating ever again. He said if I told anyone about the cheating, then he would tell everybody that I killed Brad!"

He shook his head vehemently. "But I didn't mean to kill Brad! I just wanted him to stop laughing at me! And then... and then Geoffrey started calling me STUPID too! So I made him shut up..." Fletcher raised the hammer menacingly.

"Ah... well, I'm not calling you stupid," I said hastily. "In fact, I think you're very clever, Fletcher. An absolute genius!"

He looked at me, tilting his head like a puzzled dog. "I am not a genius. Why do you call me that, Gemma?"

"Oh... er..." I stumbled backwards, feeling my way blindly. The living room windows were behind me and I remembered that they were open. If I could reach them, maybe I could somehow dive through them, out into the garden...

Okay, it was a silly idea but it's hard to think clearly when you're facing a maniac wielding a hammer. It was obvious to me now that Fletcher's hold on reality was very tenuous. I didn't know what might set him off.

I took another step back, feeling the edge of the windowsill press suddenly against my hip. A wave of relief washed over me. At least I'd got here. Now if I could just—

A black shape erupted out of the darkness outside and landed on the open window. I jumped back and screamed.

Then I saw what was sitting on the windowsill.

"Oh my God, Muesli! You stupid cat, you scared me half to death!" I gasped.

Then I froze as I realised what I had just said.

"DID YOU CALL MUESLI STUPID?" shrieked Fletcher, swinging the hammer above his head. He lunged at me, his eyes bulging.

I screamed and dived to the side. There was a yowl and I saw a blur of tabby fur shoot past me, darting between Fletcher's legs. He tripped, gave a cry, and pitched forwards, smashing his head against the side of the windowsill as he went down.

Then all was silent.

Slowly, I stood up, my heart still pounding in my chest. In the distance, I could hear the faint wail of sirens. Police—coming to my rescue. But there was no need anymore.

I looked at the man in front of me, out cold on the floor. Then I looked at the nonchalant creature sitting a few feet away, placidly washing her face. I never thought that one day a little tabby cat would save my life.

CHAPTER TWENTY-EIGHT

"I can't believe it. I still can't believe it." Cassie shook her head as she stood next to me at the tearoom counter.

"How do you think I felt?" I said wryly. "Standing there, facing my sweet, lovely, gentle chef who had suddenly turned into a hammer-wielding psycho!"

Cassie squeezed my hand. "That must have been horrible."

I sighed. "Actually, do you know what was more horrible? When he came round and they handcuffed him and were leading him out... he was perfectly normal again. It was like he had flipped a switch or something." I shuddered. "That was... I don't know. Just awful and heart-breaking and scary and sad all at the same time." I shook my head. "I couldn't sleep when I finally got home on Friday night after they'd finished questioning me at the police station—I just kept thinking about that."

Cassie gave me a sideways look. "I have to say, Gemma—you're taking it all pretty well. I would be... well, I feel sick enough already and I wasn't the one who had to face him."

"I do feel sick about it," I admitted. "But at the same time, I feel like... well, it wasn't really him, you know? I don't know how to explain it. That wasn't the Fletcher I knew—the Fletcher who was my friend, who had taught me so patiently to bake and who was that sweet, gentle guy. It was like he was..." I shook my head, sighing. "I don't know... possessed or something. Like he was a different person."

"They'll take that into account, won't they?" said Cassie. "I mean, you could argue that Fletcher wasn't in his right mind and wasn't really aware of what he was doing..."

"Yes, Devlin said he would make sure that Fletcher got a good solicitor—someone who had experience in such cases."

"And I hate to sound callous but... what are we going to do here?" Cassie waved a hand around the tearoom. "We've lost our chef."

I grimaced. "I know. I've been thinking about that. I'm a lot better at baking than I was and I think I've mastered a couple of Fletcher's recipes, but I wouldn't say I'm ready to take on the whole menu. Besides, even if you and I could make everything

perfectly, who would serve the customers out here?"
I sighed. "No, we need someone full-time in the
kitchen."

"Well, I suppose you could go back to your original
plan of hiring someone from London..."

"There was one other idea..." I said reluctantly.

"Yeah?"

"My mother has volunteered to help out—just to
tide us over until we can find someone suitable. I
wouldn't have said yes except that she's really very
good—her baking is absolutely divine—and she'd be
working for free."

"Your mother!" Cassie bit back a laugh. "Bloody
hell, Gemma, if she comes to work in the kitchen
here, there'll be another murder soon—and they
won't have to look very far for the culprit!"

"Shut up," I said, good-humouredly. "So, okay, my
mother is a bit trying, but I'm an adult now. I'm sure
I can manage a professional, working relationship
with her."

"Yeah, right..." Cassie grinned. "I'm going to enjoy
watching this from the sidelines."

I ignored her and walked over to flip the sign on
the tearoom door to "OPEN", thinking that I probably
shouldn't even bother. The tearoom had been
completely closed yesterday, Saturday, while the
police wrapped up the case and I lay prostrate on my
mother's sofa. Okay, that might be a slight
exaggeration, but the whole experience *had* taken it
out of me. To be honest, all I had wanted to do today

was remain on my mother's sofa, hiding from the world. But I had forced myself to come in. I felt that I owed it to myself—to my new self, anyway—to face my troubles and not run away from them (can you tell that I was brought up on repeats of *The Sound of Music*?).

So I got here this morning at the same time as always and was grateful for the moral support when Cassie showed up soon afterwards. It felt strange and sad not having Fletcher arrive as well—he had become so much a part of my daily routine. *Well, anyway, at least it won't matter that we're missing a chef today*, I thought. It wasn't as if we were going to have enough business to need it.

But to my surprise, I was proven wrong. Ten minutes after we'd opened, we had several customers sitting at various tables and more coming through the door. Cassie and I exchanged wide-eyed looks as we rushed to serve them. Devlin had given a press conference yesterday and had made a point to stress that Fletcher had acted completely independently and that the murdered victims were not connected to the tearoom in any way. It looked like our reputation was slowly being repaired.

If anything, the ghoulish curiosity and gawkers' mentality had returned with a vengeance and, by lunchtime, we were run off our feet. Thank goodness I had finally mastered Fletcher's scone recipe and made a fresh batch that morning, because our "Warm Scones with Jam & Clotted Cream" was the most popular item on the menu and several customers even asked eagerly if it was the same kind that was "used to murder the American tourist".

I felt a warm glow as I stood at the counter at lunchtime and looked out across the dining room, which hummed with laughter and conversation again. It seemed like my little tearoom might have a chance after all.

"Is Seth free this evening?" I asked Cassie. "We must see if he can come and meet us for drinks at the Blue Boar. I haven't had a chance to speak to him properly since the arrest and he must be dying for the details."

"Well, actually, he's invited me to High Table this evening," said Cassie.

I turned to look at her in surprise. "He has?"

Good old Seth—so he finally got up the courage to ask her. I smiled to myself.

She returned my smile, not realising what it was for. "Yeah. It's going to be weird returning to that world again. I might even go the whole hog and dig out my old gown."

"Well, you can tell Seth everything, then. And please thank him for me—if it hadn't been for his help, I would never have figured out half the things in this mystery."

My phone rang and I was surprised to hear Lincoln's voice on the line.

"I missed the news last night and only just heard from my mother," he said. "It's unbelievable. I hope you're okay, Gemma?"

I was touched by his concern. "Yes, fine. He didn't touch me. It was really more of a shock than anything else."

"Well... if you need someone to... uh... talk to... about anything," he said awkwardly.

"Thanks, Lincoln—that's very sweet of you."

"Um... I was also wondering... well, maybe we could meet up sometime next week, when things have settled down a bit?"

"That sounds nice."

"Great." I could feel his smile across the line. "I'll give you a ring with the details. Take care of yourself, Gemma."

I ended the call, aware that Cassie had been listening with avid interest.

"Ooh, sounds very cosy..." she said with a teasing smile. "Is that the dishy doctor asking you out on a date? I wonder what a certain handsome detective might have to say about that. And speaking of the devil... or the Devlin, in this case..."

She nodded towards the windows where we could see a tall, dark-haired man step out of a black Jaguar XK parked at the curb. Reporters swarmed around him—yes, the press were back in force and camped outside the tearoom again—but he brushed them away like flies as he headed for our front door. A moment later, he came into the dining room.

"I'll leave you two to your *tête-a-tête*." Cassie smirked as she turned and headed into the kitchen.

I straightened to my full height as Devlin approached me. I hadn't seen him since Friday night when he had rushed in, white-faced, through Fletcher's door. He had run up to me and, for one crazy moment, I had thought that he was going to pull me into his arms. Then—as his sergeant and other officers swarmed into the room—he had stepped back and asked rather formally if I was unharmed. Now, there was no sign of that tense man. Devlin was back to his usual laconic self, his blue eyes cool and guarded.

"I see that business is back to normal," he said, indicating the full dining room.

"Yes, it's a great relief," I said, hiding a smile as I saw four pairs of geriatric ears turn in our direction. The Old Biddies weren't at their usual table by the window but at one next to the counter, and I could see that they were delighted with this circumstance. They all leaned sideways, no doubt hoping to eavesdrop on my conversation with Devlin. He caught my eyes and his blue ones twinkled, letting me know that he was well aware of our listeners.

"Have you... er... tied up all the loose ends on the case?" I asked.

"Pretty much. There wasn't really much beyond what you'd discovered. Fletcher *was* one of the students implicated in the cheating scandal fifteen years ago and it turns out that he was used as a scapegoat by Washington. He was the 'fall guy', so to speak, and took the blame and punishment for the others' crimes. He had a really tough time when he was sent down from Oxford—he went into a depression for six months and never managed to enrol at another university. After that, he just ended up drifting between various dead-end jobs. Effectively, the whole thing ruined his life."

"Poor sod," I said with a sigh. "It really was unfair, what happened to him. I know murder is wrong but... well, you can't help feeling that Washington—and Hughes—got what they deserved. And that Fletcher was almost driven to it."

Devlin looked at me curiously. "That's an unusual attitude from someone who was almost a victim. Most people in your situation would be feeling betrayed and bitter—"

"No." I shook my head vehemently. "I don't know how to explain it but I don't hate Fletcher or fear him. I feel... sorry for him, really. Oh, don't get me wrong— I was terrified on Friday night and it was a horrible experience. In a way, I still feel sick when I think about it. But it was also like... well, I was trying to explain this to Cassie earlier—it was like it wasn't *him*, you know? It was like I was facing a different person."

"That is the approach the defence lawyers are going to take," said Devlin. "Manslaughter on the grounds of diminished responsibility. He will probably go to a special facility, rather than prison."

I nodded, looking out of the tearoom windows. "I knew Fletcher—I *understood* him, I think. His mind was... well, he related to things differently from the rest of us. He had a very simplistic view of the world. And I don't think he meant to hurt me that night—it wasn't like it was premeditated or anything. He was just reacting. I think it was when I said the trigger word 'stupid', he flipped and totally forgot who I was. Like an animal backed into a corner lashing out. You can't be bitter about a horse who kicks you because it's scared, can you? It doesn't understand what it's doing and doesn't do it with intention."

Devlin regarded me for a moment, then said, "I'm glad to hear you say that because I have a message for you from him."

"From Fletcher?"

He nodded. "He's obviously not allowed to have any contact with you—but he asked if I could pass a message on to you. Normally I wouldn't allow it, but in this case... well, I guess I share your feelings. Anyway, he wanted me to give you this."

He handed me a crumpled piece of paper. I unfolded it slowly and read the childlike scrawl:

I am very sorry, Gemma. I did bad things. I did not mean to hurt you. I hope you can forgive me one day.
Fletcher.

I swallowed past the sudden lump in my throat. "Please tell him... I've... I've forgiven him already."

Devlin inclined his head. "And he also asked if you could do one thing for him."

"What's that?"

"Look after his cat. Make sure she goes to a good home."

I swallowed again. "Tell him I will."

I folded the piece of paper and tucked it into my pocket. Then, in an attempt to lighten the mood, I cleared my throat and said, "So my theory about the drug, Lassitomab, was completely wrong?"

"Oh no, I think you were on the right track there. Washington did come to Oxford to persuade Hughes to approve the drug—and I think he *was* using the threat of exposure to force his old colleague's hand. It just wasn't the reason he was murdered. It was one of those rare coincidences—or maybe you could call it karma—that he happened to come to your tearoom, bump into Fletcher, and set everything in motion. Of course, he had his own personality to blame too. If he hadn't been such a nasty bully, he might never have provoked Fletcher and would still be alive."

"And Justine?" I asked stiffly. "She *did* lie about her alibi on Sunday morning. Was that also nothing to do with Washington?"

"No, it wasn't." Devlin glanced over his shoulder to where the Old Biddies were still straining their ears. He turned his back to them and lowered his voice, so that I had to lean close to hear him. "Justine lied about her alibi, yes, because she didn't want to admit where she had really gone that morning: to meet a respected member of Oxford City Council.

She's having an affair with him," Devlin said baldly at my confused look. "But he's married—and he's hoping to run in the local elections next year—so it's crucial that their liaison isn't discovered by the public. Justine admitted everything to me and asked me to be discreet for her lover's sake. I agreed. We often come across such situations in the course of CID investigations and we always try our best to respect the privacy of individuals if it doesn't impact on the case."

"An affair with a council member..." I murmured.

"That was the reason she rang you and asked to meet. She heard that you were asking questions about her alibi at the dance studio and she was worried that you would dig out the truth and spill it to everyone—so she was hoping to speak to you privately to ask for discretion."

I shook my head ruefully. "And here I thought she was luring me to my doom or something!" Something else occurred to me. "Oh, of course! My mother was wondering how Justine got the permit to park directly in front of her house so easily..."

"Yes, I imagine her liaison comes with certain perks," said Devlin with a wry smile. He paused, then added, "I hope you'll believe me now when I say I wasn't prejudiced towards Justine. I suppose you could say I *was* giving her special treatment of sorts—but only because I knew she wasn't really a suspect in the case. Her lover verified her alibi—she was with him the whole time."

"Oh..." I looked down, embarrassed and ashamed of my past accusations now. "I... well... yes, I'm sorry if I doubted you. I realise now you were telling me the truth."

"Not quite," said Devlin. He hesitated, then said, "I did lie to you, Gemma, about one thing."

I looked at him in surprise. "About what?"

"I said that I would never let my personal feelings interfere with an investigation..." He met my eyes, his own very blue. "It was a good thing *you* weren't a suspect in this murder, because I would have broken my own rule."

I stared at him, my heart thudding in my chest. He smiled slightly and reached out, brushing his fingers along my cheek—a feather-light caress which sent goose bumps across my skin. I was conscious of the Old Biddies watching us, goggle-eyed, from the nearby table.

"I'll see you around, Gemma." Devlin winked at me, turned, and left.

I stood staring at the door for a long time after he had gone.

***

The next morning, I arrived bright and early at the tearoom. As I walked about the dining room, drawing back the curtains, switching on the lights, arranging the tables and chairs, I couldn't believe that it had been a little over a week since I had gone about these same rituals, preparing for the day, never knowing that, in a few hours, I would be meeting a man who would be murdered in my tearoom. So many things had happened in the past week!

"Morning!" Cassie sailed in through the front door, a smile on her face. She was clutching a tabloid newspaper in her hands. "We're becoming a fixture on the front page..." Her smile widened and she gestured towards the outside of the windows. "But this time, they can talk about us as much as they like! It's great for business!"

I glanced out of the windows and saw that she was right. Already, there was a small crowd forming in the street outside, waiting for the tearoom to open. I felt my own face light up.

"What are we going to do about the food, though?" asked Cassie worriedly. "I mean, with so many customers—and no proper chef yet—"

I turned to her. "Well, actually, Cassie, speaking of a chef..."

As if on cue, the tearoom door opened and my mother stepped in, looking resplendent in a vintage gingham dress with an enormous frilly apron and a white chef's hat perched atop her perfect coiffure. I gaped at her.

"Mother, why are you dressed like that?"

"What do you mean, darling? Helen Green has been helping me with my outfit and she assures me that this is the latest thing in cuisine wear."

"Yeah, if it's 1940," I muttered, trying to ignore

Cassie grinning in the corner.

"It's vital to look the part, you know, now that I'm a 'working woman'," said my mother importantly. "Now, where is the kitchen, darling? Oh yes, through here... no, don't worry, I can sort myself out..."

Her voice faded away as she went through the swinging door, only to get louder again a moment later as she called out: "Oh, by the way, darling, Helen was telling me about this exciting thing called Twitcher. She says I simply must get onto it and then I can twitch all the time! And people will follow me and I'll be able to tell them all about what I'm baking in the kitchen—*as it's happening!* Isn't that just marvellous? But I'll need you to show me how to do it. Apparently, I can do it right from my phone..."

I groaned and covered my face with my hands, while Cassie fell about in uncontrollable laughter. Taking a deep breath, I removed my hands from my face. It was okay. I could do it. I had faced a maniacal murderer. Dealing with my mother should be a piece of cake...

EPILOGUE

The low brick building rose in front of me and I paused, setting the cat carrier down on the ground next to me. I could see a young couple coming out of the sliding doors, their faces wreathed in smiles as they looked down at the fluffy puppy in their arms. Passing them in the other direction, heading into the building, was a family with a child who pointed eagerly to the poster on the wall, showing a kitten with the words: "Adopt a cat today and take home your new friend!"

I looked back down at the cat carrier by my feet. Muesli's little face showed through the bars. She was eyeing her surroundings curiously, her ears pricked and her whiskers quivering as she took in the sights and sounds.

"*Meorrw?*" she said, looking up at me.

She'll find a good home here, I told myself. Oxford Animal Shelter had one of the best reputations in the country and the shortest times for rehoming. Muesli wouldn't have to stay in a cage for long... and she'd make friends with the other cats... and have the chance to find a family who'd be able to lavish her with love and attention...

There was no other option really. No one else could look after her and I didn't even have my own place—there was no way she could live at my parents' house, where she would probably shred their cream silk upholstery and dig in my mother's prize flowerbeds... Besides, I was busy at the tearoom all day and didn't have the time for a pet...

No, no, this was definitely the best option for her and I knew I was doing the right thing.

So why did I feel so awful?

I took a deep breath, picked up the carrier, and walked into the shelter building. There were several people ahead of me and I had to wait my turn at the reception. Finally, a woman behind the counter smiled and asked if she could help. I explained my mission.

"You'll have to fill out some information about the cat—the more you can tell us, the more it'll help us place her in a suitable home," she said, handing me a clipboard with a form attached.

I heaved the cat carrier up onto the counter next to me, then picked up the pen and began filling in the spaces.

Name: *Muesli*
Age: *1+ year?*
Breed: *Moggie*
Colour: *Grey tabby with white chest and paws*
Sex: *F*
Vaccinated: *Yes*
Spayed: *Yes*
Microchipped: *Yes*
Personality & quirks: *very sociable and inquisitive, talkative, bit of an escape artist, likes to hide under rugs and ambush your ankles when you walk past, enjoys belly rubs for 2.5 seconds then freaks out, hides in boxes, will come when called...*

I stopped and stared at what I'd written. Next to me, Muesli stuck a little paw through the bars of her carrier and batted my hand playfully, trying to catch the pen tip.

"*Meorrw!*" she said.

"All finished?" The woman came back and smiled at me. She reached out to take the form. "You can hand her over to us now and we'll get her settled—"

"Actually..." I held on to the clipboard, pulling it back from her. "I... I've changed my mind."

She looked at me in surprise. I pulled the form off the clipboard and crumpled it up.

"I'd like to buy some cat supplies—I thought I could get them from the shelter store and have the money go to a good cause..."

"Oh, that's very kind." The woman smiled at me warmly. "What would you like to buy, dear?"

"Um..." I couldn't believe I was doing this. "A cat litter tray and a couple of bowls... and a cat bed, I guess?"

"You'll need a scratching post as well," said the woman with a grin. "And some food. And maybe some toys. We've got some gorgeous new feather mice, which have been very popular. And some kitty treats would be nice too—to reward good behaviour."

"Do cats even know the meaning of those two words?" I asked dryly.

She laughed out loud. "Sounds like you're all set to be a cat owner." She poked a gentle finger at the cat carrier next to us. "She's gorgeous! I love her little pink nose and those beautiful green eyes with that black eye liner... what's her name?"

I looked at the little tabby and felt an unexpected flash of pride. "Muesli," I said. "Her name is Muesli. Like the cereal."

"Muesli! What an adorable name!" She laughed as Muesli put out a playful paw again and batted her finger. "I can see that you're going to have a lot of fun with her."

Yeah, a lot of fun, I thought sourly as I found myself back outside the shelter building, staggering under the weight of a ton of feline paraphernalia. *I must be mad,* I told myself. *What am I doing adopting a cat?*

"*Meorrw?*" said Muesli from the carrier next to me.

I glanced down at the little tabby face and scowled. "And don't think you're coming on my bed."

"*Meorrw,*" said Muesli complacently.

As I was beginning to learn, cats always got the last word.

FINIS

For other books by H.Y. Hanna,
please visit her website:
www.hyhanna.com

AUTHOR'S NOTE

This book follows British English spelling and
usage. For a glossary of British slang and
expressions used in the story, as well as special
terms used in Oxford University, please visit:
www.hyhanna.com/british-slang-other-terms

TRADITIONAL ENGLISH SCONE RECIPE

Scones have a long history, originating in Scotland in the 16th Century, and are said to have taken their name from the Stone of Destiny where Scottish kings were once crowned. They are a "quick bread", a bit similar to Southern "biscuits" in the United States. The original version was triangular-shaped, made with oats and griddle-baked rather than baked in the oven. They have since become one of the highlights of British baking—no traditional English afternoon tea would be complete without warm scones with jam and clotted cream!

A great debate rages in the United Kingdom over the correct way to pronounce "scone"—those in the North say it should rhyme with "cone" whilst those in the South insist that it should rhyme with "gone".

Meanwhile, people have come to blows over whether you should put the cream on first and then jam... or the jam on first and then the cream!

There is now a huge variety of scones, both sweet and savoury, made with dried fruit, nuts, vegetables, cheese, chocolate chips—and even a recipe with lemonade! This is a recipe for a traditional English plain scone, but it can be modified with the addition of your favourite treats.

INGREDIENTS:

- 500g of plain flour *(US: 4 cups)*
- 4 teaspoons of **double-acting** baking powder *
- ½ cup of caster sugar
- 125g of butter, at room temperature *(US: 1 stick)*
- 150ml of full fat milk *(US: 2/3 cup - may need slightly more if dough is too dry)*
- 2 eggs beaten lightly
- egg & milk for the "egg wash" to glaze the scones

* "double-acting" baking powder contains both cream of tartar and baking soda and causes the dough to rise only *after* heat is applied. If you use single-acting baking powder (which rises immediately), then you must not leave the dough to "rest" but must cut the scones and bake them immediately.

A SCONE TO DIE FOR

INSTRUCTIONS:

1)   Pre-heat the oven to 205C / 400F.

2)   Sieve the flour and baking powder into a large mixing bowl (this is important to add more "air" to the mixture).

3)   Rub the butter into the flour mixture with your fingers – it is important to coat the flour with butter as much as possible. Keep doing this until the mixture has a consistency of fine breadcrumbs.

4)   Add the sugar to the mixture and mix well with your fingers.

(This is the stage when you can add in extra ingredients such as raisins and currants, if you wish.)

5)   Add the egg and some of the milk—do not add all the milk at once; go slow and check that the dough does not become too wet otherwise the scones will "drop".

6)   Mix well with your fingers until the dough forms a ball.

7)   Tip the dough out onto a floured board, scatter some more flour on top, and then knead lightly. Very important not to over-work the dough otherwise the scones will become very hard.

8)   When the dough looks smooth, gently pat it out (or use a rolling pin) into a thick slab, about 1 – 1.5 inches thick. This is one of the secrets to great scones—not rolling the dough out too thinly.

(The dough should now be rested for at least 30 minutes—unless you are using a single-acting baking powder. Some chefs say that resting the dough for hours, even overnight, is the secret to getting really light, fluffy scones.)

9)   Using a cutter of your choice, stamp out the scones from the dough. Be careful not to twist the cutter as you are pressing it down—only twist it gently at the very bottom to free it. Roll up the leftover dough and spread it out again—keep cutting out scones until you have used up all the mixture.

10)   Place the cut rounds onto the greased baking tray or baking paper.

11)   Brush the tops with the egg & milk wash—this will give them a lovely golden glaze.

12)   Bake in the hot oven for about 12 – 15 minutes.

13)   Cool the scones on a wire rack.

14)   Serve warm with some jam and butter or clotted cream!

Enjoy!

ABOUT THE AUTHOR

USA Today bestselling author H.Y. Hanna writes fun mysteries filled with suspense, humour, and unexpected twists, as well as quirky characters and cats with big personalities! She is known for bringing wonderful settings to life, whether it's the historic city of Oxford, the beautiful English Cotswolds or other exciting places around the world.

After graduating from Oxford University, Hsin-Yi tried her hand at a variety of jobs, including advertising, modelling, teaching English and dog training... before returning to her first love: writing. She worked as a freelance writer for several years and has won awards for her poetry, short stories and journalism.

Hsin-Yi was born in Taiwan and has been a globe-trotter all her life, living in a variety of cultures from the UK to the Middle East, the USA to New Zealand... but is now happily settled in Perth, Western Australia, with her husband and a rescue kitty named Muesli. You can learn more about her and her books at: **www.hyhanna.com**

Sign up to her newsletter to get updates on new releases, exclusive giveaways and other book news!

https://www.hyhanna.com/newsletter

ACKNOWLEDGMENTS

A huge thank you to my beta readers: Basma Alwesh, Rebecca Wilkinson, Jenn Roseton and Melanie G. Howe for their invaluable feedback. I am also grateful to Winnie Lim for her help with the manuscript, as well as to my editor and proofreader and the rest of my publishing team. Special thanks goes to retired West Yorkshire Police Inspector, Kevin Robinson, who shared his wealth of knowledge with me and helped me check the police procedural details in the story with so much patience.

And as always, I am so grateful for the support and encouragement from my amazing husband—who not only does everything he can to give me more time to write, but also patiently endures endless discussions on plot holes and character motivations, as well as weathering the ups and downs of writer's block, "sagging middles" and creative terrors!